HONEYMOONS CAN
BE HAZARDOUS

Also in the Amish Candy Shop Mystery series by
Amanda Flower

Assaulted Caramel

Lethal Licorice

Premeditated Peppermint

Criminally Cocoa (ebook novella)

Toxic Toffee

Botched Butterscotch (ebook novella)

Marshmallow Malice

Candy Cane Crime (ebook novella)

Lemon Drop Dead

Peanut Butter Panic

And in the Amish Matchmaker Mystery series

Matchmaking Can Be Murder

Courting Can Be Killer

Marriage Can Be Mischief

Amanda Flower

HONEYMOONS CAN BE HAZARDOUS

Kensington Publishing Corp.
www.kensingtonbooks.com

KENSINGTON BOOKS are published by

Kensington Publishing Corp.
119 West 40th Street
New York, NY 10018

All Kensington titles, imprints, and distributed lines are available at special quantity discounts for bulk purchases for sales promotion, premiums, fund-raising, educational, or institutional use.

Special book excerpts or customized printings can also be created to fit specific needs. For details, write or phone the office of the Kensington Sales Manager: Attn.: Sales Department. Kensington Publishing Corp., 119 West 40th Street, New York, NY 10018. Phone: 1-800-221-2647.

The K and Teapot logo is a trademark of Kensington Publishing Corp.

First Printing: January 2023
ISBN: 978-1-4967-3746-5

ISBN: 978-1-4967-3747-2 (ebook)

10 9 8 7 6 5 4 3 2 1

Printed in the United States of America

For Dan, Melissa, and Jonah

Acknowledgments

Thank you to my readers, who are willing to travel back to Harvest again and again, both in the *Amish Matchmaker Mysteries* and the *Amish Candy Shop Mysteries*. These series would not still be going without your support. Millie, Bailey, and I could never thank you enough. That goes for Jethro and the goats, too.

Thank you always to my super-agent Nicole Resciniti, who is my friend and advocate, and my editor Alicia, who is so kind and supportive of my work.

Thanks to reader Kimra Bell for catching things I might miss while writing.

Love for my husband David Seymour.

Finally, gratitude to my Heavenly Father, who gave me the ability to write these stories.

It's our greed to extract more from good
that turns it into evil.
　　　—Amish Proverb

Chapter One

"Can you smell the love in the air, Millie?" my dearest friend, Lois Henry, asked as she walked across the Harvest Square and inhaled deeply. "It's positively magical."

I didn't know anything about the air being magical. It wasn't something Amish women thought or spoke about. Then again, I was Amish, but Lois most certainly was not. She wore a bright red beret over her short purple-red hair. Pink plastic hearts hung from her earlobes, and she had completed the outfit with a neon pink winter ski coat over light blue jeans.

I glanced down at my black boots, long navy skirt, and black wool coat, and then touched the wide brim of the black bonnet that covered most of my head. We could not have been more different.

"I just smell snow," I said. The ice crust covering

the snow that blanketed the square crackled with every step we took across the lawn.

Lois held her arms in the air and took in a long breath. Her arms fell at her sides. "Oh, Millie, your literal Amishness can get old at times." However, she said all this with a smile to prove she was teasing me. "On a side note, what does snow smell like? It's just water, right? How can it smell like anything at all?"

"I think it has a scent, or maybe not the snow exactly. The air does. Clean and crisp, I suppose."

Lois cocked her head as she considered this, and the bright red beret slid to one side. She caught it before it fell off completely. "This silly thing. It won't stay in place." She stopped in the middle of the frozen square, opened the giant purse that was always at her side, stuck her hand inside, and came out with a fistful of bobby pins.

It was amazing to watch. There was no limit to the items Lois could pull out of that bag, and she always seemed to know the exact location of each and every thing she sought. It was like pulling a rabbit out of a hat. Which proved I knew a little bit about magic, or at least the traveling kind that comes to the Holmes County Fair every year.

She adjusted the beret on her head and jabbed half a dozen bobby pins into it. "There. This sucker isn't going anywhere now!"

"Isn't it the purpose of a winter hat to sit down over your ears to protect them from the cold?" I asked.

"If I wore it that way, no one would see my earrings." She tapped the back of her left ear, and the chain of pink and red hearts swung back and forth from her earlobe. "What would be the point of my outfit without the earrings?"

It wasn't a question I could answer. I had essentially been wearing one form or other of the same dress since I was a toddler. Even with my own plain background, I could recognize that her ensemble was something noteworthy. She stood head to toe in red, white, and pink. No one could get into the holiday spirit quite like Lois, and it didn't even have to be a major holiday like Christmas or Thanksgiving. Lois dressed up for all holidays. It didn't matter how small. She donned a top hat on Lincoln's birthday, for example.

A flyer posted on the gazebo flapped in the winter breeze.

"Oh," Lois said. "That's going to fly off, and then won't Margot pitch a fit?"

Margot Rawlings was the village's community organizer. I honestly didn't know what her real title was, but I knew she was responsible for spearheading all the events that occurred on the square, and thanks to Margot, there were a lot. Her goal was to make Harvest as much a tourist destination as the better-known villages in Ohio's Amish Country, such as Sugarcreek and Berlin.

The flyer was for the Valentine's Day spaghetti dinner, and it was happening that evening at the church on the square. The event was to be hosted by the village of Harvest, the church, and several Amish communities to raise money for a drug counseling center in the village. The church would donate the space for the counseling center, and the fundraiser was to hire trained drug counselors for those seeking help. Over the last decade, drug use in rural Ohio had skyrocketed, and the Amish weren't immune to it, either, although it was only whispered about in the community. Lois and I both had tickets to the dinner.

Lois reached into her purse, came out with a staple gun, and stapled the flyer back to the gazebo post. I didn't even blink at the staple gun. It was par for the course with her.

She tucked the staple gun back into her purse and patted her hat one final time. "We had better pick up the pace. I promised Darcy I would be back by now. She usually doesn't mind my running a little late, but tonight she has a date. She wants to go home and get ready," Lois said in a loud whisper. "On Valentine's Day weekend. Isn't that wonderful? Who wants to be alone on Valentine's Day?"

"Is the date with Bryan?" I asked.

Bryan Shell was a writer working on his first novel, or so he had told us. He wrote at the café every day. However, he spent more time watching Darcy than typing into his computer. It seemed that finally, he'd got up the courage to ask Darcy on a date after months of pining for her.

"Bryan Shell?" She shook her head. "Oh no. Darcy said that she wasn't interested in him, and I haven't seen him in the café for over a month. He fled. We haven't seen him since."

Now that she mentioned it, I realized I hadn't seen Bryan in the last several weeks when I'd popped into the café to visit Lois and have some of Darcy's blueberry pie. That came as a relief to me. I was a matchmaker and had a sense when two people should or shouldn't be together. It was a gift from *Gott*, but one I only used if asked.

I didn't charge money for my matchmaking services—I didn't feel that it was right to make money off someone else's happiness. It was just something I did because I cared about my community and wanted to see as many people happy in life and as happy in love as my late husband Kip and I were for our full twenty years of marriage.

Darcy never asked me if she thought Bryan was right for her, so I never shared my opinion with her. I was glad to hear that she'd come to the correct conclusion on her own. However, I was just as curious as her grandmother about this mystery man she was going out with.

"You won't be alone. We are going to the spaghetti dinner tonight. Half the village will be there. It seems to be the way many villagers are spending their Valentine's Day." We left the gazebo and walked side by side across the snow-covered square. I was grateful for my sturdy boots, which kept me from slipping in the snow.

"Half the village, but not my better half, because I don't have one." She sighed. "I'm starting to get the itch, Millie."

A gust of wind blew a chilly draft into my bonnet, and I tied its ribbons more tightly under my chin. "The itch?"

"Yes, to get married again. I know, I know what you're thinking. That's how I ended up married to Rocksino-Guy, which by any account was a disaster. He was a weasel through and through."

"You pushed him into a swimming pool," I said. A small part of me wished I had been there to see it. Lois did everything with a flourish. That farewell was sure to have made a big splash, both literally and figuratively.

"He deserved it," she said with an uncharacteristic scowl on her face. Just as quickly, the scowl changed into her more common beaming smile. "And I have to say it was memorable. It's the best way I could have imagined to tell a man I wanted a divorce. I would know, too, since it wasn't my first time around the block."

It certainly wasn't. Lois had had a string of marriages since her twenties. Four, to be exact. She'd divorced three of those husbands, while her second husband had died. By her account, her second husband was the only man she'd ever truly loved. She'd married the two after him just searching for that spark again. So far, she hadn't found it.

"Are you sure that you want to marry again?" I asked. "It hasn't been easy." I thought, as her closest friend, it was my place to talk some sense into her.

"Nothing worthwhile is easy, Millie. You know that better than most people." She sighed. "I don't ever want to give up on love. When I do, well, that would be the end of me."

I envied Lois for being a hopeless romantic. I was far from it, and had been for a long time. I had my own sad stories speckling the past. The most notable was losing the love of my life, Kip Fisher, after twenty years of marriage and not even having a child to hold onto after that loss. The Lord did not bless us in that way.

After Kip died, I poured my energy into caring for my extended family. I realize now that I lost a bit of myself in that time. However, in truth, I didn't mind. Helping others had distracted me from my own pain, and I felt fulfilled by caring for my family. I gave up on romantic love. Why should I expect to love again when I'd already been so happy with Kip? A year ago, I thought that I might have had another chance with an old childhood friend, Uriah Schrock, but it was not to be. He left Holmes County six months ago to live closer to his children in Indiana. I hadn't heard from him since he'd left, and I did not expect him to return. My chances for love had come and gone. I hoped the same wasn't true for Lois. I didn't want her to give up on love, either. One of us needed to hold onto that dream.

I walked beside Lois as we crossed Church Street on our way to the Sunbeam Café.

The Sunbeam Café was a relatively recent addition to the businesses around the Harvest Square. It sat just on the other side of the cemetery and playground. By the cemetery, there was a large white church, where the spaghetti dinner would be held that night. Lois attended that church on occasion. Whether or not a person in Harvest was a member of the congregation, the building was familiar to all. Most of the village activities were held on the square, and the *Englisch* church, which had a committed and active congregation, often participated.

No one was more committed to the church than the pastor's wife, Juliet Brook. Since marrying Reverend Brook two years ago, she had taken on the role of preacher's wife with aplomb. There was nothing she wouldn't do for the congregation, and nothing she wouldn't do for her husband . . . except maybe give up her pet pig, Jethro. Not that Reverend Brook would ever ask her to. It would have been a scandal of sorts in the village. Jethro, for better or worse, had become the mascot of Harvest.

It had started with the success of *Bailey's Amish Sweets*, a candy-making television show starring Bailey King, the local candy shop owner from Swissmen Sweets. Bailey wasn't Amish, but her grandmother, Clara King, who owned the store with her, was. They still made candies using the traditional Amish methods, but I think Bailey snuck in a few ideas of her own from her days as a chocolatier in New York City. There were rumors in the village that big changes were coming to Swissmen Sweets, but I had learned not to believe rumors. It was always better to gather news from the source. Neither Bailey nor Clara had said anything to me about changes to the shop. Perhaps that wasn't true. I wasn't one to pry when no one was in danger. I had poked my nose into a murder or two in the village, but only to protect others.

I had seen snippets of the candy-making show on Lois's phone. She'd asked me to watch bits she found particularly funny. I tried not to watch too much; it was not the Amish way to do such a thing. However, I think even the Good Lord could find the humor in a little pig from Ohio becoming a national television star.

If Juliet, who was decidedly biased when it came to Jethro's acting talents, could be believed, the network powers-that-be were thinking of giving him his own show.

I was thinking about Juliet and Reverend Brook and their second-chance love story when Lois opened the glass door to the café. I expected her to waltz right in as she always did, so I kept walking and kept thinking until I ran into her. I bounced back. "Lois, why'd you stop?"

I had never heard of the café being so crowded that a person couldn't step inside. Maybe that was true during one of the many festivals on the square, but not in the middle of a winter afternoon. Well, I supposed it *was* Valentine's Day, but it seemed early yet for any big crowds to gather at the café.

"Lois?" I asked when she didn't answer.

"*You!*" Lois said in the most threatening voice I had ever heard her use.

"Me?" I squeaked.

Lois didn't respond to my comment, and I stood on my tiptoes to look over her shoulder. At the cash register, Lois's granddaughter, Darcy, was ringing up a sale for a couple at the coffee counter. The woman, who I would guess was close to forty, stood next to a much older man, who could have been her father. However, they were standing close together and holding hands, so I guessed I was way off in thinking they were parent and child.

"Who's that?" I asked.

"Rocksino-Guy!" Lois yelped.

My eyes went wide. *This* was Lois's fourth husband?

Chapter Two

I couldn't help staring at the couple where they stood at the cash register across from Darcy as the man paid their bill. When he turned around, I noted he was shorter than the woman. He had gold rings on his fingers, and his hair was cut short, except for the comb-over that he'd used, unsuccessfully, to cover the bald spot on the top of his head.

The woman, meanwhile, was tall and broad-shouldered, and had a bright smile. Her hair was blond and shoulder-length.

"This is Rocksino-Guy?" I asked. It was hard for me to believe. All of Lois's husbands—at least the ones I had known—had been handsome men. Lois called them tens all the way. This man was pleasant-enough-looking, but I couldn't imagine what she had seen in him. Then again, they had been divorced for several years now. Maybe he had changed. Time wasn't always kind.

She called him by that name because she'd met him at the Rocksino in Cleveland. I knew very little else about him. I certainly hadn't known what he looked like or that Lois would react so strongly to seeing him again.

"Yes, the lying, cheating cad. What are you doing in my café?" Lois wanted to know.

I cringed. I didn't think this was how Lois imagined her first reunion with Rocksino-Guy going. I doubted she'd thought she would ever see him in Holmes County, Ohio, much less in her granddaughter's café.

Rocksino-Guy's mouth fell open. "Lois, is that really you? I never for a minute thought I'd run into you while I was in Holmes County. I should have known better. By the way you used to tell it, you ran this county."

"Lois, can you step into the café? You're letting all the warm air out." I said this because it was true, and also, I didn't want her to scare off the tourists strolling around Harvest with her shouts. There wasn't much I could do to protect the diners inside the café. Thankfully, only two tables had customers.

She stumbled forward but didn't appear happy about it. When I stepped into the café, I removed my bonnet.

"Is that a real Amish person?" the woman asked. "I've seen them on the side of the road, walking, or in their buggies, but I've never seen one this close up."

I felt my cheeks redden. In truth, the woman's rudeness wasn't uncommon. Most *Englisch* were very kind, if a little bit curious about the Amish they saw in Holmes County. However, there were others—apparently, like this woman—who saw members of my church as curiosities and oddities. I bit my tongue to stop myself from saying something rude back.

Lois wasn't in as much control of her mouth as I was. "This is my dear friend Millie Fisher, and if you look at her for one more second like she's a zoo animal, I'm going to smack that expression right off your face."

The woman sucked in a breath.

Rocksino-Guy—I realized I still didn't know his real name—cleared his throat. "Are you here for lunch, Lois? This is a lively spot. It's a break from all the heavy Amish food. I highly recommend the Valentine's pie."

The Valentine's pie was a red berry pie that was a mixture of strawberries, red raspberries, and cranberries. It had been a hit all month long for the café, and Lois was quite proud of its success. However, she didn't appear to be happy that Rocksino-Guy had eaten some.

Lois folded her arms. "The Valentine's pie was my idea. This is my café."

Darcy cleared her throat behind the counter.

"This is my granddaughter's café and therefore my family's place," Lois corrected herself.

He put a hand to his throat as if he were afraid he might choke. "Y-you made the pie?"

"No, I don't cook or bake or do any of those domestic things. I work here, serving people. However, I must say that I would not have served you if you were seated in my section."

His shoulders sagged. "Oh, thank goodness. I thought I was a goner for a moment there."

Lois put her hands on her hips. "Why are you here, Gerome?"

Gerome? Of all the names that I would have given Rocksino-Guy, that wasn't even on the list.

He grinned from ear to ear. "We're on our honeymoon. The area is charming. Don't you agree, Honeybee?"

Honeybee had to be at least thirty years Gerome's junior. She smiled at her new husband as she sipped her latte from a paper to-go cup. "It's perfect, Big Bear." She looked back at us. "We wanted a simple honeymoon. No frills and not too far from home. Holmes County was the perfect choice."

"Honeybee? Big Bear?" Lois said to me in a hoarse whisper. "It's enough to make you want to toss your cookies."

"Lois." I eyed Gerome and Honeybee—I supposed I had to think of her as such, since I didn't know her name yet—who were listening closely. "They can hear you."

Lois folded her arms. "So what if they can? I think anyone would be rolling their eyes at those ridiculous names."

I shook my head.

Gerome cleared his throat. "Maybe, Lois, you could tell us some nice places to visit while we're in the county? I remember you told me that you grew up around here."

Honeybee clapped her hands together. "We have a long list already. Let's not bother your friend when she's clearly . . ." She trailed off, as if she were unable to describe Lois's expression.

I knew what it was, though. Furious. Lois was furious. About what exactly, I couldn't yet tell.

Honeybee cleared her throat. "I want to visit the candy shop, Swissmen Sweets, for sure. I'm a huge fan of that television show. Bailey makes it look so effortless, but I know it's not. I've tried candy making so many times and failed horribly. I'm much better at selling things than making them myself, but the world needs all kinds, right?"

"Bailey is very talented," I agreed. "And her grandmother is, as well. They trained up everyone who works with them right. I'm Lois's friend, Millie Fisher, by the way. I don't think I caught your name."

"It's Paige. Paige Moorhead as of two days ago." She sighed as if she couldn't believe her good fortune. "It's a dream come true to finally call myself Mrs. Moorhead. It's an honor to be married to such an upstanding and successful man, and to know I'll be taken care of for the rest of my life. It's all I've ever wanted."

"Upstanding and successful are *not* the adjectives I would use to describe Rocksino-Guy," Lois muttered under her breath. "And I thought young women today were more concerned with taking care of themselves than finding a man to do it for them."

I poked her in her side with my elbow, hoping that would be enough to encourage her to watch her tongue.

Gerome smiled at her. "I don't know if I have ever heard a lovelier name. I'm a lucky man. I can't believe she said yes when I popped the question, and then when we recited our vows to Elvis in front of the Rock and Roll Hall of Fame, I couldn't believe my good fortune. It was a perfect winter day, too, with fresh snow on the ground and blue skies over Lake Erie."

"You were married by Elvis at the Rock and Roll Hall of Fame?" All the color drained from Lois's face. "That is what I wanted. That's what I asked to do."

"Oh, I know. When I shared your idea with Honeybee, she agreed it was perfect."

Lois's face turned an odd shade of red that wasn't far from the red-purple color of her hair. "You said that we couldn't get married there because it was too corny. Now, it's not corny any longer?"

Paige looked from Lois to her husband and back again as if it had just dawned on her that the connection between them was deeper than a casual friendship. "How do the two of you know each other exactly? Why would you be talking about a wedding?"

"Old friends," Gerome said at the exact same time Lois said, "We were married."

Of those two statements, Paige unsurprisingly latched onto Lois's comment. "You were married?" she asked with a squeak in her voice. "Gerome," she said, not calling him by her pet name for the very first time. "You told me you'd never been married before, that I was the only woman you'd ever proposed to."

"That's true," Gerome said. "Getting married was Lois's idea, not mine. We were together two days, and then the marriage was annulled, so it doesn't count. That's why I never considered myself married before."

"No," Lois said. "We were really married. It was only six months, but we got a divorce, not an annulment." She put her hands on her hips. "And in my memory, getting married was a mutual decision, not just mine. You traded in the Rolex you'd won at blackjack for our wedding rings."

"I miss that watch to this day. I have never had one I loved as much." He sighed.

Paige looked at her new husband as if she were seeing him for just the first time. "I can't believe you kept this from me. All this time, I was under the impression I was the only Mrs. Moorhead."

"Oh, honey, I was never Mrs. Moorhead," Lois said. "I stopped changing my name after husband number two. The paperwork!"

"Honeybee," Gerome said, ignoring Lois's comment. "I didn't hide this from you, truly. It was a non-issue for me."

"A non-issue, but you agreed to honeymoon in Holmes County, knowing full well that your ex-wife lives here. You brought me to *her* café!"

"I didn't," Gerome said. "I promise you, I didn't. You were the one who wanted to honeymoon in Amish Country. We agreed it was smarter to take a small trip this year so we could focus on our businesses. You suggested Holmes County because—"

"I don't care if I suggested it first," Paige snapped. "You should have told me right then about your ex-wife. What else are you hiding from me? Do you have other secret wives? Are you leading a double life? Who are you?" she cried, before rushing out of the café in tears.

"Honeybee! Honeybee!" Gerome threw a wad of bills at Darcy and pushed his way out of the door after his new bride.

Lois and I stumbled to the side to move out of the way as quickly as possible.

Darcy cleared her throat as she gathered up the bills that Gerome had tossed on the counter. "Grandma, I just have one question—what did you see in him?"

Lois sighed. "He could really throw some dice. In hindsight, I realize that's a terrible reason to get married."

Chapter Three

It was dark outside when Lois locked up the café. Hours ago, Darcy had left for the night to head off on her date with her new mystery man. She'd given her grandmother permission to close early so we could attend the spaghetti dinner at the church, which had started an hour before.

After Gerome had left, business at the café had been brisk with the dinner rush, which usually started at four and lasted until seven. Typically, the café stayed open until eight on Friday nights.

Because the café had been so busy, I hadn't had a chance to ask Lois more about Rocksino-Guy—I mean, Gerome. It was going to take me a little while to think of him actually having a given name.

Lois tested the café door to double-check it was locked, and then we walked toward the church, just on the other side of the cemetery.

I opened my mouth.

"I don't want to talk about it," she said. "It's Valentine's Day. I want to forget failed romance and concentrate on new ones."

I snapped my mouth closed and wondered what new romances those could possibly be, but thought better of asking. Lois would tell me when she was ready.

The parking lot of the church was full, which was an excellent sign for the fundraiser. People were leaving through the back door of the church with to-go boxes. If a person didn't want to eat at the church, they could pick up their order to go. After a long evening of helping Lois in the café, I wished we had chosen that option, too. After seven was a very late dinner for me, indeed. I could smell the meatballs and garlic bread from yards away.

Lois and I let an Amish couple slip out of church before we went inside. We followed the signs to the fellowship hall. Not that we needed guidance to know where to go. We'd both been in the church many times before.

Just before the doors of the fellowship hall was a table with a young woman sitting at it. She had bright red hair and a lovely smile, and even though she wasn't Amish any longer, there was a sweetness about her that many young Amish women possessed. Charlotte Weaver collected a dinner ticket from an Amish man with a grizzled beard. He appeared to be close to fifty. The back of his neck was permanently tanned from long days laboring in the sun. He nodded when Charlotte accepted his dinner ticket but didn't speak. He walked into the fellowship hall alone.

Charlotte smiled at Lois and me. "I'm so glad to see you. You're one of the last to arrive. I was afraid you might not be coming at all."

"We would never miss it," Lois said. "It's an important cause."

Charlotte nodded, her face clouded with concern.

"Is something wrong, Charlotte?" I asked as I handed her our tickets.

She glanced at the doors leading into the dinner. "I just feel so awful for him."

"For who?" I asked.

"The man who just went inside."

"Who was it?" Lois asked. "I didn't see his face. His back was to us."

"That's Elijah Smucker," Charlotte said in a low voice. "Did you hear about his son?" She looked around as if to make sure no one else was listening.

My heart ached for Elijah. "I have." John Michael Smucker was a seventeen-year-old Amish boy who'd fallen in with the wrong crowd during his *Rumspringa.* He'd died from a drug overdose two weeks ago. It was all anyone talked about in the Amish communities for days, but only in hushed voices. Many of the Amish liked to believe drugs and alcohol could not touch their children, but it simply was not the case. Evil could always find a way in. But with the support of community and the love of *Gott,* we could withstand it.

When Amish teens and young adults were on *Rumspringa,* they usually didn't go wild. Very few Amish left the faith, and very few tested boundaries to the extent young John Michael had.

"I'm surprised he's here," Lois said. "I would have thought it would be too soon for him. He must know that John Michael's death is on the minds of most people attending."

"What happened to John Michael is the reason so many Amish are here," I explained. "I think the community is finally accepting there is a problem, and the Amish have to be part of the solution."

"Let's hope that's the case," Lois said.

Charlotte shook her head. "I know it's becoming more of a problem in the county. Luke said there have been more drug-related arrests than at any other time he can think of."

Luke was Deputy Luke Little and Charlotte's fiancé. They had been engaged over a year, but as of yet, hadn't set a date for the wedding. Charlotte had just left the Amish faith when she'd agreed to marry Luke. She'd felt that she had to become accustomed to *Englisch* life before marrying an *Englisch* man. In her case, I believed this was wise. Even though the Amish and *Englisch* had lived side by side in Holmes County for over a century, there were many cultural differences between the two, and the use of technology was just the starting point.

Lois and I said goodbye to Charlotte and went in to the dinner. The church's fellowship hall had been transformed into an Italian restaurant, from the red-and-white-checked tablecloths to the glowing votive candles on the tables.

The room smelled heavenly, too, and my stomach grumbled. Even though I had been with Lois at the café most of the afternoon, I had eaten very little, hoping to save my appetite for tonight's dinner. It seemed I had been successful at that.

Margot Rawlings waltzed over to us. Typically, Margot could be found in a sweatshirt and jeans, but for this special occasion, she wore trousers and a sweater. As always, the short brown curls on the top of her head were perfectly in place. Margot was a little bit younger than Lois and me. I think I'd heard she'd turned sixty last year, while Lois and I were coming up on seventy far too quickly for my taste.

She held her hands wide. "What do you think?" She didn't even bother to hide the pride in her voice. And why should she? The place was still two-thirds full, and it was close to eight at night. Usually people in Holmes County ate much earlier in the evening, so I could only guess how great the turnout had been at five, which would have been the most popular time.

"It's incredible," Lois said. "Are you happy?"

"Very." Margot beamed. "Selling the tickets at twenty dollars each, we've raised just over ten thousand dollars. This will be a great jump-start for the center."

"That's wonderful news," I said. "And for a worthy cause. I see a lot of Amish here."

Margot nodded. "The community really turned out." Her face fell a little. "I know it's mostly because of the tragedy of John Michael Smucker, but it's proof his life was not in vain."

"No life is," I replied.

"True," Margot said with a crisp nod. "Let me show you to your table."

Lois and I followed Margot to a table in the middle of the room with seating for six. The bishop from my Amish district, Bishop Yoder, and his wife, Ruth, were already sitting there, enjoying their dessert of tiramisu. My mouth watered when I saw it. I loved tiramisu almost as much as I did blueberry pie. Almost. It was a special treat, because it was most certainly not an Amish recipe.

Bishop Yoder smiled at us. "It's *gut* to see you here, Millie, and you too, Lois."

Ruth nodded at us. "It is nice." Ruth gave a sideways glance at Lois.

Ruth, Lois, and I had all grown up together. Lois and Ruth had been at odds for over sixty years. I didn't see that changing in one meal.

A young *Englisch* girl brought Lois and I iced tea and salad to start. After she left, I said, "I'm glad to see so many Amish communities here to support a *gut* cause."

"We have to be here," Ruth said. "It is imperative we do everything we can to keep the *Englisch* youth from corrupting our children." She leaned over her plate. "You know that is the source of all this trouble."

Across from me, Lois bristled, and I couldn't say I blamed her. The Amish made their own decisions, whether good or bad.

"And with the death of John Michael Smucker, it becomes even more urgent," Ruth went on. "I have asked Deputy Little what he plans to do about the drug issue in the county. As of yet, he doesn't have an acceptable answer for me."

"Everyone has to be involved," Lois said. "Isn't

that the point of this meal tonight? We have to come together as a community to help those who need assistance putting their lives back together."

Ruth sniffed at this answer and set her fork next to her empty plate. "Dear, are you finished with your meal? I'm ready to leave."

Bishop Yoder looked down at his half-eaten tiramisu, took two big bites in succession, and nodded. He was unable to speak because his mouth was full. He stopped and sipped his water. After he swallowed, he bid Lois and me good night.

Ruth looked down at me. "Do not forget the Double Stitch meeting on Monday. We have much to talk about."

"How could I? It's at my house," I said with my most gracious smile.

Double Stitch was the quilting circle in our district. Both Ruth and I were members. Ruth viewed herself as the leader of the group, but in fact, there was no leader, at least not officially.

Ruth pressed her lips together and nodded.

After she was gone, Lois said, "Have you ever considered that she uses those quilting circle gatherings as councils of war?"

I didn't bother to respond.

Lois poked at her salad. "I don't think that woman is ever going to like me."

"I wouldn't hold my breath after all this time."

She straightened up. "Maybe I should start a campaign to make her my friend."

That sounded like a terrible idea, one that most certainly wouldn't have a happy ending.

Across the room, Elijah Smucker sat alone at a table for four, tucking into his spaghetti dinner.

He didn't speak or smile at anyone. He didn't even look up from his plate when a server refilled his water glass.

"I'll be right back," I said to Lois, and before she could stop me, I was out of my seat.

I walked across the room, straight for Elijah's table.

"Elijah?" I said.

He didn't look up when I spoke.

"I just want to give you my condolences over the loss of John Michael," I said in Pennsylvania Dutch. "Everyone in the community is praying for you and your family during this difficult time."

He glanced in my direction but didn't meet my eyes. What I saw was a man with bloodshot eyes, sunken cheeks, and a heart shattered into a thousand shards. In a gravelly voice, he said, "Prayers will not bring my son back."

"*Nee*, they won't," I agreed. "But they can lead to healing."

He looked me in the eye for the first time. "Maybe healing isn't what I'm after."

I wanted to say more, but a shout tore through the fellowship hall. A black and white blur raced by me with a loaf of garlic bread in its mouth. Juliet Brook, the pastor's wife, ran after her polka-dotted potbellied pig. "Jethro! That's too many carbs for you! Think of your headshots for Hollywood! Your diet! We're shooting next week!"

Chapter Four

Most of the year, I worked part-time at a green-house owned by my niece. Usually, I watered the plants and worked at the cash register. However, in the middle of February—with six inches of snow on the ground—the greenhouse was closed. After a busy Friday helping Lois at the café and then the spaghetti dinner, it was nice to know I didn't have to go anywhere Saturday morning. I planned to have a leisurely start. At least as leisurely as an Amish woman would allow herself. I rose at five-thirty, thirty whole minutes later than I habitually got up to do my farm chores.

I took great pride in my small farm. It was tiny by Amish standards—just shy of five acres, with a small house and a modest barn—but it was home. I'd bought it with the money I had saved over the years from odd jobs and selling my handmade quilts. Selling Amish quilts could be lucrative if you built up a good customer list and had friends, family, and past customers who were willing to spread the word. I had been blessed in that regard, and my business had grown even more since I'd moved back to Ohio after a decade in Michigan caring for my ailing older sister. This was mostly because of my close-knit quilting circle, Double Stitch. I would not be so comfortable in life without the kindness of friends who were willing to give me extra work.

Of course, comfort for a widowed Amish woman was much different from what it might be for an *Englischer*. I only needed a roof over my head, food, and peace. Well, that and a home for my two ornery goats, Phillip and Peter, plus my prim cat, Peaches, who was the newest addition to the little farm, but by far the most exacting. And lastly, my mild-mannered horse, Bessie. That's really all I required. The income from my quilts, and the little money I made helping my niece in the warmer months, made it all possible.

As always, I fed Peaches even before making my own coffee. The cat wouldn't have it any other way. The peach-colored cat buried his delicate face into his food bowl and made noises as he ate that were anything but delicate.

After two sips of coffee, I slipped on my black rain boots, winter coat, hat, scarf, and gloves to make my morning trek to the barn to let the two hoofed rascals out. I knew they would both be awake and waiting at the door for me to open up the barn for the day. It didn't matter to them that there was snow on the ground and the sun wouldn't be up for over an hour. All they cared about was busting out of the barn and romping around the yard. If they knocked something over in the process, all the better. As long as I wasn't the thing they knocked over, I was fairly tolerant of their antics.

I liked to consider myself a cheerful person, but I didn't think anyone was so truly happy as a goat when he was freed from the barn.

The goats' joy was infectious, so most days I let them romp for my own amusement. Ruth Yoder would not approve at all.

I pulled a stocking cap down over my ears. Now, had I been heading into town during the cold weather, I would have put on my large black bonnet like a proper Amish woman. However, in the privacy of my own farm, I felt it was fine to wear my late husband's old stocking cap. Kip might have been gone for over twenty years now, but I felt closer to him when I wore the hat. I also knew it would make him laugh to see me walking around in a man's cap on the farm. However, had I ever sported trousers in his sight, he would have fainted dead away.

I opened the back door to the house, and a giant gust of icy wind and snow smacked me in the face. The gust was so hard that I stumbled back and had to hold onto the doorframe to keep from falling over.

When I regained my bearings, I looked out into the snow. I had a battery-operated lantern in my hand, and it swung back and forth with each wind gust. I debated whether I should wait another hour to go outside. The goats would not like being stuck inside the barn for one minute more than they had to, but it might be too cold for them outdoors.

Just when I had decided to turn around and head back inside to make a second cup of coffee, I spotted something moving by the barn. That wasn't too unusual. The barn was one of the few structures for over a half of a mile. Many times, wild animals sheltered near it, especially in the middle of the winter. Even on the outside, there was some protection from the elements under the eaves.

But what I saw near the barn was a lot larger than a raccoon, and it wasn't shaped like a deer.

I held my lantern up higher in the hope that I could get a better look at the shadowy figure.

That's when the creature—or dare I say *person*—stood up. I yelped and dropped my lantern on the concrete slab at my feet, and the light went out. In the moonlight, the figure ran away from the barn and dashed across my small yard into a neighboring field.

I jumped back inside the house, slammed the door closed, and locked it.

I leaned against the door. What was someone doing out by my barn so early in the morning, and why did they run away when they saw me? If they'd come to me for help, that didn't make any sense at all.

Was the person Amish? It had been too hard to tell in the moonlight. I supposed it was a man. The person had been wearing trousers, so I assumed it would have to be a man, if the person was Amish.

I placed a shaky hand on my cheek. This wasn't the way I'd wanted to start my leisurely morning. Also, this was the difficult thing about living out in the country with no close neighbors. I felt vulnerable when something didn't feel right. And a person running away from my barn in the dark certainly didn't feel right at all.

It was another hour before the sun came up completely, but I soon saw the sky lightening with the promise of morning. The poor goats must have been beside themselves, stuck in the barn a full hour longer than they expected, and they must have heard the person outside the barn, too.

I picked up a cast-iron frying pan and opened the back door. My battery-operated lantern lay on the ground in pieces. That really was a shame. It had been a handy tool and much easier to use than my old oil lantern. A gift from Lois, who didn't like the idea of me living all the way out here by myself. She also knew I liked to be up before the sun, so she'd said I needed the lantern. She'd even taken the extra step and talked to Bishop Yoder about my having it for safety. It was something to be considered, because in any Amish district, the bishop was the one who decided what technology the members of his church could use.

I suppose to the *Englisch*, a battery-operated lantern would not have been seen as technology at all, but to the Amish, it was. It had a light source other than fire or the sun. We were an Old Order district, but the bishop was lenient about what could be used at work. For the Amish businesses in the district to survive, they had to have access to electricity so their shops could comply with the proper government codes, and telephones so they could do business. Some Amish even used the internet if they could make a *gut* case for it. Or at least, that's what I had heard. That wasn't true in our district. Must have been a more progressive district than mine.

Bishop Yoder was a very understanding man. His wife, not so much. Ruth meant well, but she did have a tendency to get caught up in the rules of being Amish, rather than the heart of being Amish. Ruth liked to follow rules, but more than that, she loved to enforce rules. Lois knew all this, so she had gone to the bishop without Ruth's knowledge to get permission for me to have the lantern.

I had to say, it was a smart move on her part, and the bishop had granted permission before Ruth had any idea what had happened. I also believed Lois took great pleasure in having outsmarted Ruth Yoder. The two of them were like oil and water, and enjoyed getting the best of each other.

Keeping all that in mind, I knew I could get a new lantern. Lois would know where to find one. I stepped over the broken piece and held my frying pan high, as if ready to strike. No one was around as far as I could see, but I didn't take any chances by lowering the frying pan.

I was still ten yards from the barn when I began to hear Phillip and Peter making a ruckus inside. They cried and wailed, and it sounded like they were kicking at the door in the hope of knocking it down. Those crazy goats. They were going to hurt themselves if I didn't get to them soon.

"Calm down!" I called.

The kicking stopped, but the bleating and crying increased. Phillip and Peter recognized my voice and knew they were moments away from being freed. If their protests were to be believed, I kept them locked up in the barn for days on end.

I threw open the barn door, and the goats shot out like bullets from a hunting rifle. They zipped around me in circles. Phillip raced around the entire barn, and Peter leaped in the air.

"All right. All right. Settle. Settle!" I said.

Finally, they galloped over to me and came to a stop, looking up at me with anticipation on their goaty faces. Phillip and Peter were Boer goats, and each was just shy of two hundred pounds and stood twenty-eight inches tall. They were easy to tell apart because Phillip was white and black, while Peter was white and brown. Also, even though both of them were able to get into their fair share of trouble, Phillip was usually the instigator, while Peter went along with whatever mischief his brother began.

"Calm down," I told the goats. "You are over three years old now. You should be out of this galloping kid stage."

They stood in front of me and showed me their wide goaty grins. Apparently, the kid stage never came to an end when you were a goat. It was both adorable and frustrating.

"Did either of you hear that man who was outside the barn?"

Oh, if Ruth Yoder could hear me now, speaking to a pair of goats as if they were people who could answer me, she would be beside herself and planning an intervention by the church elders. However, I knew better than to speak to my goats like this in Ruth's presence. I also knew full well they weren't going to answer me. If they did, I probably would have toppled over.

Phillip ran to the side of the barn where I had seen the man standing. He stopped in the exact spot where the person had stood.

I held the frying pan at my side. "Don't tell Ruth Yoder I said this, but it might just be that you two goats *do* understand what I'm saying."

I trudged to the spot where the figure had been. In the snow were two large, distinctive boot prints and more leading away in the direction the person had run. The prints were too large, I thought, to be those of a woman. I shivered. I had started to wonder if I'd imagined the man standing near my barn in the dim light of early morning. I thought perhaps my mind was playing tricks on me, and I hadn't seen a man at all. These boot prints proved otherwise.

However, what caught my eye was a handle sticking out of the snow. I knew it wasn't mine. I was very careful with my tools. I always accounted for them and put them away when I wasn't using them. My mother had taught me that everything must be put in its place to keep clutter away.

I grabbed the handle. It was a chisel—a wood chisel, actually. I recognized the tool because my husband had loved to whittle in the evenings. Kip would sit on the wide front porch at our old farm and chisel away at a block of wood. He would also chew the tobacco that had eventually given him cancer and killed him. It was a terrible habit he'd never been able to break, and it had cost him his life.

What was a man with a wood chisel doing by my

barn so early on a Saturday morning, in the middle of winter, no less? I tucked the chisel into my coat pocket. My intuition told me he couldn't have been up to anything *gut*. I was about to go into the barn to feed Bessie when the reflection of car headlights bounced off the side of the barn. I adjusted my grip on the frying pan. I was ready for anything.

There came the sound of a car door slamming, and the goats took off in the direction of the noise.

"Phillip! Peter!" I called, but it was no use. They were already around the side of the barn. I followed them at a much slower pace. I held my frying pan high, ready to protect myself and the goats if the need arose.

It is true that the Amish are pacifists. We don't participate in wars and try our very best to settle disputes with the *Englisch* and within the Amish community without violence, but that didn't mean that I couldn't give an intruder a fright that would encourage him to leave.

A sudden cry pierced the winter sky.

That was, unless Phillip and Peter didn't do it for me first.

I rushed around the side of the barn with the frying pan still held high and found Phillip and Peter dancing around a very irritated-looking Lois.

"Gah! If the two of you get hoofprints on my new winter coat, I swear, you'll be in my next stew!"

Possibly knowing it was an idle threat, the goats continued to dance around her.

"Millie, what on earth are you doing holding a

frying pan in the air like you're about to fling it at
my head?" Lois cried. "And call back your guards!"

I glanced at my hand, and sure enough, there
was the frying pan. "I wasn't going to throw it at
you." I let my arm drop to my side and sighed with
relief. The cast-iron was heavy.

"Likely story. And before you did, you sent your
attack goats after me. Please." She sounded offended.

"They aren't attack goats, and you know it.
Those two wouldn't hurt a fly. What are you doing
here so early, anyway?"

"I needed to talk to you, and it's a matter most
important to me. I couldn't sleep because I've
been worrying about it all night, and you know
how I love my beauty rest. I don't have this great
skin in my sixties because I take risks with my sleep
routine."

I raised my brow. That sounded serious. Lois
was very strict about getting her sleep, and she
wasn't an early riser, either. At least not by my esti-
mation. She was up at seven-thirty every day so she
could take all the time she needed to do her hair
and makeup before she headed to the Sunbeam
Café to help her granddaughter with the breakfast
rush.

"Let me just feed the animals, and then we can
go into the house to talk. I made cinnamon rolls
last night, so they will be ready to eat as soon as I
warm them in the oven."

She clapped her gloved hands together. "Oh,
Millie, you are a true friend and know exactly what
I need. Carbs and sugar are the only way I'm going
to get through this."

"If you want to go inside and pop them in the oven, help yourself. The oven is already warm, and they're wrapped in aluminum foil on the stovetop."

"Of course the oven is already warm. They would take away your Amish woman card if you had a cold oven!" She hurried toward the house.

Shaking my head, I went into the barn and fed the animals. I didn't, for the life of me, know what Lois was all worked up about. But I did know it had nothing to do with the wood chisel in my apron pocket. That was a different mystery entirely . . . or so I believed at the time.

Chapter Five

With Bessie and the goats fed, watered, and settled, at least for the morning, I went into the house and found Lois sitting at my small kitchen table with her hands wrapped around a mug.

A coffeepot percolated on the stovetop. Many Amish—including those in my district—were allowed to have simple appliances, and these were powered by a propane tank at the side of the house.

My home was two stories with two bedrooms upstairs. On the second floor, each room had slanted ceilings and was built more like a loft than a full story.

This had once been an *Englisch* home, so behind the walls, there was electric wiring. I had left it there, so the house could be sold to an *Englischer* someday, if my niece needed to do that, but all of the outlets had been covered with plain plastic plates. For the most part, I had been able to strategically place furniture in front of them, so they weren't noticeable.

The main floor itself was what the realtor had called an open floor plan. The living, dining, and kitchen area were all in the same room. That wasn't very Amish, either. Typically, in an Amish home, there were distinct rooms with specific functions.

Even though it wasn't a common Amish home, I loved the floor plan, because I could be working in the kitchen when visitors happened by, or when I had a meeting of my quilting circle, and could still speak to my guests instead of being isolated while they visited.

Lois looked up at me. To my surprise, there were bags under her eyes. Lois never had bags under her eyes. She took great care never to let it happen to her, and, I believed, great expense with fancy cosmetics she bought on trips to the mall in Canton. The last time I was in her home, there had been countless creams, lotions, and all types of makeup spread over her bathroom counter. I didn't have any idea what all of them were, or what they did. Now, I was even more concerned.

I sat across from her at the table. "Lois, my friend, what is wrong?"

I folded my hands in front of me and braced myself for the worst. She was sick. Her granddaughter was in some kind of trouble. She was moving away. All of these would be disasters. With her looking so frail and upset, I knew it had to be one of them.

She looked down at the table. "I never should have been so hard on Rocksino-Guy."

I blinked. "Rocksino-Guy?"

"Yes, yesterday when we ran into him in Darcy's café. I was rude to him and his new wife. I shouldn't have behaved that way. I haven't stopped thinking about it since we left the café. Even at the spaghetti dinner, it was on my mind. I have to do something about it. Despite everything that might have happened in our relationship, I don't want the last thing he remembers about me to be rudeness."

"What are you going to do?" I asked, a little afraid to hear what her answer might be. Lois's plans were creative, but not always wise.

"I'm going to apologize to him and his new wife. It's really the only thing I can do. It's the right thing to do."

I nodded. "I see your point, and telling them you regret the unkind things you said is a *gut* start. But how will you find them? Do you know where they are staying? Do you have his phone number?"

"No. After the divorce was finalized, I deleted his number from my phone. I just needed to close that chapter of my life. But I do know where he and his wife are staying."

"How?" I asked.

Her eyes sparkled. "I did a little sleuthing, of course. You're not the only one in this friendship who can follow the clues."

I suppressed a smile. I didn't want to encourage Lois into thinking we were detectives of some sort. We had stumbled upon a couple of mysteries, but the last time was nearly six months ago. I hoped it stayed that way. Lois hoped the opposite. "How did you find him?"

"I spent the morning calling local hotels, and I hit the right one on the third call. Very early morning is a good time to call. The staff is usually tired and bored from the late-night shift, and more willing to talk."

"The person working at the hotel told you he was staying there?" I asked in surprise. "I wouldn't think they would be allowed to do that."

"Oh, I told them I had a delivery for Gerome, and that's all they needed to hear in order to tell me he was at the hotel." She smiled. "They didn't tell me the room number, so I think the best thing to do is leave an apology note at the desk for him. I don't want to interrupt their honeymoon any more than I already have."

"That's very mature of you, Lois."

"To hit maturity at sixty-eight isn't that bad. It took a lot of trial and error."

I'll say.

"Where are they staying?"

"The Munich Chalet."

I raised my brow. I knew of the Munich Chalet. Everyone in Holmes County did. It was on Massillon Road, just outside the county seat of Millersburg. It was a large property, and it received much attention for its claim of having the largest cuckoo clock in the world. The village of Sugarcreek was just a few miles away, and had made the same claim with its cuckoo clock, which stood right in the center of the village. The village and the chalet were constantly at odds over bragging rights. Sugarcreek's clock was wider and more intricate, but there was no doubt the one at Munich Chalet was taller, as it rose thirty feet off the ground.

"I know it, of course, and I have seen the cuckoo clock from the road, but I've never been there."

Lois nodded. "I'm not surprised. The place is eccentric to the max. It's not very Amish, either. I've been there once. Parts of it were even a little too odd for me."

That was saying something.

"So I'm here because I couldn't sleep. I knew you would be up, and I also thought you'd like to accompany me on this little errand to the Munich Chalet. It shouldn't take too long. I'll apologize, and then we'll leave. Simple."

She was right. I did want to go. But she was wrong, too. It was never simple when Lois was involved. That being said, I was curious about the Munich Chalet and doubted there would be another time I would have a reason to visit. "We should at least wait until sunup to leave for the chalet. I'll make some more coffee, and we can enjoy those cinnamon rolls."

Lois removed her coat. "That's a good plan. Cinnamon rolls make everything better."

I couldn't agree more. I smiled as I took off my stocking hat and hung it from the peg on the wall.

Peaches strolled into the room with his tail held high and meowed. I knew from experience that he wanted some cinnamon rolls too. He was a peculiar cat who loved pastries. Lois claimed it made him an Amish cat.

"Were you saving the rolls for the Double Stitch meeting?"

I smiled. "I did make them for the Double Stitch meeting. But since I never know what a week will hold, I made extra just in case."

"You're always prepared, Millie. I had such a restless night, I could eat the whole tray myself."

I stood and stepped into the kitchen. I removed a metal campfire mug from the upper cabinet. The set had been a gift for Christmas from my niece, Edith, and her children. I loved the blue metal with white speckles all over it.

I refilled Lois's coffee and set cream and sugar on the table for her.

She leaned over the mug and inhaled deeply. "Mmmm, this is perfect. It's just what I needed to build up my courage."

I checked on the cinnamon rolls in the oven. "They should be ready in no time."

"Good. Because I'm starving. Guilt really makes a person hungry."

"I have heard that," I agreed.

She sipped her coffee, while the dangling snowmen earrings hanging from her ears swung back and forth. "You seem to be jumpy, and you're not a jumpy person. Is something going on?"

I bit the inside of my lip and debated whether I should mention the man I'd seen running away. I decided against it. If I did, Lois would either insist I stay with her, or she'd insist on living at the farm with me. As much as I loved her, neither of those ideas was sustainable in the long term. She wouldn't be at ease in an Amish home without her creature comforts, and I couldn't be away from my farm and the animals for long. And there was no way Lois would let me bring the goats to her home. Although I didn't think she would mind Bessie and Peaches as much.

"I slept in today," I said. "I suppose that sent me for a loop. It does make me feel a little off, I will admit."

"When you say slept in, you mean after five?"

I nodded. "I didn't wake until five-thirty."

Lois shook her head. "The Amish and *Englisch* have a different definition of sleeping in."

"Greet the dawn with enthusiasm, and you may expect satisfaction at sunset," I said.

She smiled. "Yet another one of your Amish sayings?"

"Many of them are true," I said.

"Not if I have to get up at five a.m. on a regular basis, they're not."

Chapter Six

An hour later, Lois and I said goodbye to the goats, who were romping in the snow, and headed to the chalet. As Lois buckled her seat belt, she placed her giant purse on my lap. I accepted it with a grunt. I guessed it weighed more than Jethro the pig.

"What do you have in here?" I shifted the bag on my lap so the bulky contents didn't dig into my thighs.

She started the car. "It's hard to say. I haven't cleaned it out in ages, but I know there is at least one rubber mallet if you have a need."

"Why on earth would I have a need for a rubber mallet?" I stared at her.

"Oh, I always carry one. You never know when you might need to close a paint can, or whack something back in place."

Where was Lois going when I wasn't with her that she constantly needed to close paint cans?

I tried my best not to be concerned about this. "Why'd you give me your purse?" Normally, she would have flung it into the back seat. I was convinced she was going to break the back window of her car doing that someday.

"I want you to read the note I wrote Gerome, just to make sure it hits right. It's not easy writing an apology to an ex-husband, you know."

I wouldn't know, but I imagined finding the right words would be difficult. "Your apology should really just be between you and Gerome. I don't want to intrude. It's private."

"You're not intruding if I'm asking for your help. You're the village matchmaker, aren't you? You should be able to help me navigate this relationship and bring it to a peaceful close."

Calling me the village matchmaker was a bit of a stretch. It made it sound like my position in the community was much more official than it actually was.

"Can you read the note?" Lois asked. "It's on top of the main pocket, next to the glue gun."

I wanted to ask Lois why she had a glue gun in her purse but thought better of it. Some things were best left unsaid.

I opened the main compartment, and sure enough, there was an envelope with Gerome's name on it, right next to a large glue gun. Leave it to Lois not to have the mini size when it came to glue guns. She needed the real deal. It was loaded, too.

I removed the envelope from the bag and shifted the heavy weight from my lap to the floorboards by my feet. With that, I inspected the simple white card envelope. It was unsealed. I glanced at Lois.

"Go on," she said. "Read it."

As carefully as I could, I removed the note from the envelope; it was written on a blank card with a photograph of an Amish buggy in the snow on the front. I knew the photo had been taken right here in Holmes County, because I recognized the red covered bridge in the image.

I opened the card and inside saw Lois's distinct, hurried handwriting. She'd never cared much for penmanship in school.

Gerome—

I apologize if I upset your new wife, Honeybee. No hard feels. Have a good life. Always be willing to roll the dice—Lois Henry.

I looked up from the card. "That's it?"

"That's it. I have always believed that keeping apologies short and sweet is the best approach. That way, they don't get muddled and lead to confusion. I don't leave room for interpretation in my apologies."

I arched my brow. "You referred to his wife as Honeybee. That's not her real name." I let my words hang in the air.

"Well," Lois said. "That's what he calls her. I didn't hear him call her anything else."

"But don't you think it will seem rude to use his nickname for her, and not her actual name?" I asked.

Lois drove into downtown Millersburg, and we passed the courthouse. It was a quiet Saturday morning in winter; the county seat was empty except for a pickup or two rumbling through town.

There was a dusting of snow on the statue of the Civil War soldier next to the courthouse. Lois made a right-hand turn at the traffic light onto Massillon Road. "I don't find using the nickname to be rude."

"I think you might want to change it." I paused. "And saying you're sorry that you upset his wife might sound as if you're blaming her for feeling upset."

She pressed her lips together and gripped the steering wheel as we drove out of Millersburg.

I put the card back into the envelope and set it on the dashboard. "If you don't like my opinion on the letter, that's fine, but I must be honest with you."

Her shoulders sagged. "Yes, I know, and I'm grateful. I know sometimes I come off a little brash."

That was one way of putting it.

"I can admit that I still feel a little bit of resentment toward Gerome about how everything happened. But I am also old enough to admit he wasn't completely to blame. There were two people in our marriage, and we both should have recognized marriage was a terrible idea. Instead, we were swept up in the moment."

I folded my hands on my skirted lap and thought. Lois had never told me what had happened in her last marriage. Out of her four marriages, I knew the least about the most recent one. Perhaps that was because it had only lasted a few months, but in all honesty, all I'd heard about it was that Lois had pushed Rocksino-Guy—or, as I had just learned the day before, Gerome Moorhead—into the casino pool when she'd told him she wanted a divorce. I was about to ask Lois for more of the backstory when the Munich Chalet's cuckoo clock came into view.

"Wow. It's really an eyesore, isn't it?" Lois mused. I didn't know if she was referring to just the clock or the entire property. It was a lot to take in. There were statues everywhere, including a full-sized lion, Bigfoot, and Johnny Appleseed, just to name a few.

"It that a life-size unicorn statue? Wow," Lois mused. "Stone like that is expensive. Each of these must have cost a fortune."

However, the main attraction at the Munich Chalet was the cuckoo clock. It towered over thirty feet tall with a clock on top. It was made of wood and decorated with engravings of pinecones, leaves, woodland animals, and birds. The carvings were actually quite lovely, but would have been better appreciated if there weren't so many other distractions on the grounds. Two dozen random statues seemed to pop out of the snow with no rhyme or reason. At the top of the tower, just under the clockface—which was as big as the hood of Lois's sedan—was a set of dark wooden doors. At the moment, the doors were closed, but I'd heard that on the hour, a red, black, and yellow bird would pop out and cuckoo as if its life depended on it.

I glanced at Lois's clock in the car. We were just a few minutes away from the eight a.m. cuckoo call. Lois drove past the clock to the chalet itself. As she did so, I caught a glimpse of a woman walking around the tower. I supposed it was someone staying at the chalet who wanted to see the cuckoo go off.

Lois stopped the car in the circular driveway in front of the main building. It was two stories tall and built in a traditional German style with lattice-work beams and cream-colored stucco in between them. The windows were narrow with black metal trim crisscrossing the glass. The entire building was laced with the fresh snow that had fallen the night before. It looked like a house out of the old fairy tale books I used to sneak a peek at in the library when I was a child. I never checked them out or brought them home. That sort of reading wasn't allowed for Amish children.

Lois shifted her car into park. "We'll leave the car here. This shouldn't take very long. I'm just going to give the card to the receptionist and then leave."

"You're going to give it to the receptionist as it's written?" I asked.

She sighed. "No. Can you hand the card to me and my purse?"

I handed the card right over. Yanking the purse out from under my feet proved much more of a challenge.

As I was doing so, the cuckoo sounded from the giant clock, and I knocked the back of my head on the underside of the dashboard.

Lois threw open her driver's side door and gasped. "It's going to fall!"

A scream pierced the air, and then silence.

Chapter Seven

I was still bent at the waist, rubbing the back of my head, as Lois ran from the car. I straightened up, stopped struggling with her purse, and opened the passenger door. With my winter coat and heavy wool skirt, it took me a little longer to maneuver myself out of the vehicle. At times like this, I knew why Lois loved her trousers so much.

The car was pointed in the opposite direction from the cuckoo clock, so it wasn't until I climbed all the way out of the vehicle and could turn around that I saw the horrifying scene. The doors to the cuckoo's perch stood wide open, and a set of thick cables hung out. The cuckoo itself was on the pavement below in pieces. However, that wasn't the most horrifying part. A pair of human legs stuck out from under the giant bird's body.

I covered my mouth. Lois looked back at me with the same stricken expression that must've been on my own face.

The front door of the chalet flew open, and a man came running out. He wore a uniform of traditional German lederhosen complete with a wide mustache and shoes with brass buckles, but he wasn't wearing a coat. "What's going on out here?" Then, he saw the fallen cuckoo. "No!" he cried. "Not the cuckoo!"

"Lois, we have to see if the person under there is all right!" I said.

Lois shook her head as if emerging from a deep fog. "Right."

We hurried over to the cuckoo.

"It's a woman," Lois said.

I remembered the woman I had just barely seen out of the corner of my eye moments after we arrived. She had been walking around the clock tower, seemingly waiting for it to go off. Had she just been in the wrong place at the wrong time? What a horrific accident.

The upper half of the woman's body was buried under the fallen cuckoo. Her legs weren't moving, but there was always a chance she could still be alive. "We have to try to get it off her," I said.

Lois and I pulled with all our might, but the bird was too heavy. It wouldn't budge.

"Hey," Lois cried to the man. "Get over here!"

Still looking stunned, the man ran over to us. He was young and broad-shouldered; most importantly, he was strong. His strength was what we needed.

"Help us lift this off her," Lois said. Her tone left no room for argument.

"Step back," he said, and then, as carefully as he

could, he rolled the bird off the woman. He stumbled back from what he found.

I turned my head. It was a gruesome sight. She was gone. Her neck was broken at the very least. I knew that much.

Lois removed her phone from her coat pocket. "I'm calling for help."

Before I looked away, I recognized the woman's face. I was just about to tell Lois when there was a strangled cry. "Honeybee!"

Gerome ran toward us and fell to his knees next to his wife's body. "Honeybee!"

His cries were gut-wrenching. Lois averted her eyes as she spoke to the emergency operator on the phone.

"The police are on the way," she said when the call ended. "The EMTs, too." She shook her head. "Not that they can do much at this point." Lois looked close to tears herself.

She walked over to Gerome and helped him to his feet.

Sirens soon cut through the cold morning air. The Millersburg police station was just down the street. It took them no time at all to reach the scene.

The man in the lederhosen wrung his hands. "This is terrible. Terrible. The chalet will be ruined. We will be sued." His eyes were the size of saucers.

"A woman is dead," I said as kindly as I could, but I was afraid my tone was sharp.

"Yes." He tugged on the side of his impressive mustache. "Yes, I know that. It's horrible." He glanced back at the chalet as if he were worried more about it than Paige Moorhead's death.

A county sheriff's department SUV, ambulance, and two police vehicles from Millersburg parked in the circular driveway behind Lois's car.

The EMTs jumped out of the ambulance and headed straight for Paige. There wasn't any debate about where the victim was. I glanced at the road and saw cars slowing down. Their passengers were trying to see what was going on. I didn't think the rubberneckers could see Paige on the ground, but they would certainly be aware of the cuckoo's demise.

Deputy Little climbed out of his SUV and strode toward us. He was a young, compact man in his twenties. He used to always part his hair down the side, but recently—since he had become engaged to Charlotte Weaver—his hairstyle was shorter and much more casual. Not that Deputy Little was looking casual at the moment. His mouth was pressed into a hard line. In the last year, the young deputy had risen in the ranks of the sheriff's department and was typically the one assigned to the most complicated cases. Apparently, a fallen cuckoo qualified. Even assuming it was just a freak accident and some sort of crime wasn't involved here.

"Just when you think you've seen everything," one of the EMTs said with a shake of her head.

I glanced over my shoulder and noticed the EMTs' movements had changed from urgent to methodical. It was a sure sign there was no chance of saving Paige now. Not that I'd had much hope she could have been saved, unfortunately.

Deputy Little nodded at Lois and me and then walked over to the scene. He had a hushed conversation with the EMTs. I was desperate to hear what they were saying. I knew Lois was, too, as she took a few steps in that direction. Deputy Little noticed and frowned at her.

Lois retreated to my side. "Deputy Little doesn't look happy."

"I don't think anyone would come upon a scene like this happily," I responded.

She nodded. "You have a fair point. My guess is he's not very pleased to see us here."

"Probably not," I agreed. "How's Gerome?"

"A mess."

I glanced around. "Where is he?"

"He said he needed a moment, and he was going back to his room."

My eyes went wide. "I don't think Deputy Little will have wanted him to leave."

She twisted her mouth. "No, I suppose, you're right. We'd better find him and bring him back."

"Deputy Little will want to talk to us, too. We can't leave either."

"All right, you stay here, and I'll go."

I didn't like that idea in the least. Things were always more manageable when I could keep track of Lois. "We will both go," I said. "But we have to be quick. How do we even know which room Gerome is staying in?"

"The guy in the lederhosen will know. I mean, he obviously works here. Why else would he be wearing that outfit? I saw him go into the chalet. We'll ask him, find which room Gerome is staying in, locate him, and bring him back. Simple."

So simple.

Deputy Little was speaking to two of the officers from Millersburg, and the sound of more sirens cut through the air. He was going to be busy for quite a while yet. "Let's go," I said.

The chalet had one of the largest porches I had ever seen. It had to be thirty feet deep. It was furnished with small tables covered in plastic to protect them from the snow and winter weather.

"I didn't think giant front porches were a German architectural detail," I said.

"They serve meals on the porch during the warmer months," Lois said. "I've eaten here before. They have a wonderful restaurant inside. Real German fare. Their sauerkraut is to die for."

"I think that's the first time anyone has ever said that about sauerkraut."

"It's the truth." She grimaced. "But considering this morning's events, it was a poor choice of words."

I had to agree with her.

Lois opened the chalet's heavy wooden front door, and we went inside. If we thought the exterior of the building had prepared us for the German décor on the inside, it had not. There was so much red, yellow, and black in the room. A framed German flag hung proudly over the medieval-looking fireplace.

"That hearth is large enough for a pig roast," Lois said, as if she knew the dimensions of such an activity.

"Don't ever say anything like that in front of Juliet Brook."

The man in the lederhosen, who we'd seen outside, stood behind the reception desk, pacing and pulling on his suspenders. "What am I going to do? What am I going to do?" He muttered to himself over and over again.

Lois cleared her throat.

The man jumped as if he had been shot. Grasping the counter, he caught his breath. "Welcome to the Munich Chalet. Can I help you?" he asked in a shaky voice.

"Yes," Lois said. "We are looking for Gerome Moorhead. He's a guest here. Can you tell us his room number?"

"Sorry, but I can't tell you the room number of a guest. That's against protocol."

"I'm sure it is, but this is a unique situation. We need to find him. His wife is the woman who was just killed."

"The police can ask. I can tell the police," he said, more to himself than to us. His voice dropped to barely a whisper. "What am I going to do?"

Lois looked as if she were about to say something more. I put a hand on her arm to stop her. "Sir, my name is Millie Fisher, and this is my friend, Lois Henry. What is your name?"

He opened and closed his mouth as if the question had caught him off guard. "Karl Spoke."

"Okay, Karl," I said as soothingly as I could. "We have all had a terrible shock this morning. As Lois said, we need to find Gerome. We came here this morning to visit Mr. Moorhead and his wife. Of course, we had no idea such a tragic accident would happen. We have to make sure he's all right."

"Oh yes," Karl said. "The poor man must be beside himself. I suppose in this case, I can give you the room number."

"You certainly can," I said encouragingly. "We just want to help Gerome."

He nodded and clicked on the keyboard of his computer. "He and his wife were staying in Hillside Three."

"What's Hillside Three?" Lois asked. "I don't know of any caves around here."

He cleared his throat. "It's one of the chalets built into the hillside behind the main building. You can't miss them. They stand out and are clearly marked."

"*Danki*, Karl," I said in my most soothing voice. "We really appreciate it. It's been a difficult morning for everyone. Is there anyone you can call to help you? I think there will be a lot to be done in these—" I paused. "Difficult circumstances."

"I don't have anyone I can call." He tugged on the corner of his mustache. "You're friends of Mr. Moorhead, right?"

Lois and I didn't correct him but simply waited.

"Can I ask you a question about him?"

We nodded.

"Is . . ." He cleared his throat. "Is he the type to sue over this accident?"

I blinked.

Lois, however, didn't appear surprised by the question. "You're afraid he will bring a wrongful death suit against the chalet."

The man began to sweat, and he pulled at the collar of his shirt. "I know it sounds horrible. A woman has just died, but you see, I just bought the business three months ago and have a massive mortgage on it. I can't be sued right now."

"I think being sued at any time is bad," Lois said.

"I'm sure you're right," Karl replied. "But now is the worst time. The absolute worst. I don't have any money to pay an attorney."

"Did you know the clock was in disrepair?" I asked.

"No!" he cried. "It wasn't in disrepair. I never would have purchased this place with a deadly cuckoo clock looming over the property."

Lois winced at the volume of his voice.

"No, I didn't know. I had the clock tower inspected before the sale at my own expense. The inspector said it was sound."

"Who was your inspector?" Lois asked.

"Dexter Milton. He has a great reputation, and therefore was a little more expensive. However, I was willing to pay extra to know I'd made a good investment."

Lois wrinkled her brow. "I know Dexter. He stops by my niece's café every Tuesday when he's out doing inspections. He's a decent guy. How could he have missed something so big as a bird on the verge of taking a nosedive from the clock tower? He seems very knowledgeable about his job and has been doing it for over thirty years."

"Oh, this is so awful." He bent over the desk and buried his face in his arms.

Lois tugged on my sleeve. "We should let him be and find Gerome."

I nodded and followed her out of the chalet. The whole time, I couldn't stop thinking about the cuckoo clock having been inspected just three months ago. What had happened in that time to cause it to deteriorate to the point of breaking?

It left me wondering if human hands had played a part in the cuckoo's fall.

Chapter Eight

As Karl said, the way to the Hillsides was clearly marked with wooden, hand-painted signs in red and yellow. The brightly colored signs stood out against the shimmering white snow. "It's this way," Lois said, pointing to one of the half-dozen signs.

There was a large hill in front of us that looked too perfect to be there naturally. The path wove to the left around the man-made hill.

On the snowy hillside, a half-dozen sheep in full woolen coats pawed at the snow-covered ground and nibbled on the dry dead grass they unearthed.

The foraging sheep were huddled together in small groups of three and four, and I wondered how long they had to stay outside. Despite their warm fleece, it was a cold morning. I was happy when we came around the hill to find a barn with the door wide open. The sheep could go in and out as they pleased.

One of those sheep stood in the middle of the path leading from the main building to the location of Hillsides. Usually, Lois would stop and coo over any animal she spotted. She really did have a soft heart. But this time, she was a woman on a mission, and there was no time to stop and pet the sheep.

The path wrapped around the hillside. On the other side of the hill was a large garden that must be beautiful in the summer. Even in the winter, it was clearly well cared for. I imagined it was a favorite of guests when they came to stay at the chalet.

I glanced behind me. The sheep were following us. They walked in a line on the path behind us, but when I looked, they stopped and put their heads down to graze. It might have just been me, but it was almost as if the sheep didn't want me to know they were following along. I shook my head. When I'd started speaking to my goats like they were people, I had started down a slippery slope. Now, I believed I was being followed by sheep.

The Hillsides were set into the side of the dome-shaped hill, and each doorway featured a rise in the hill, so from this angle, it looked more like a wave than one continuous hillside.

"That's taking on quite a bit of expense, to build an entire hillside," I said. "And why would they want to? Is it for the warmth?"

"Because of hobbits," Lois said.

"What?" I stared at her.

"They're in a fantasy book and movie. It's all right that you don't know about it; you're Amish."

As if I didn't know I was Amish. I wondered how

many other things I didn't know because I was Amish.

There was a number on each door. When we reached the third door, I was surprised to see it stood partially open. Maybe Gerome had just run into the room to collect himself, and he planned to come right back out again.

Lois and I walked up to Hillside Three. The sound of someone moving around hastily inside reached us.

We shared a look.

"Should we knock?" I asked.

Before Lois could answer, the door was flung all the way open, and Gerome appeared in front of us. His hair stood on end, as if he had stuck a fork into an electric socket.

"Gerome," Lois said. "Are you all right?"

He blinked at her. "You're here. I can't believe you're here. I'm so glad that you're here."

"You're glad I'm—"

Before Lois could finish her sentence, he pulled her into the room and slammed the door in my face.

My heart sank as I stared at the closed door. I immediately tried the doorknob, but it was locked, so I knocked and kicked on it for all I was worth. "Lois! Lois! Are you okay? Do you need help?"

There was no answer, and fear gripped my heart. What was going on in that room? Was Lois hurt? Up until this point, I had seen Gerome as harmless, but now I was truly afraid. I didn't like the idea of my friend being alone with him. The man's wife had just been killed.

I banged on the door harder. If Lois had been

with me on this side of the door, we could have used her cell phone to call the police for help. The best I could do was bang on the door and cry out.

I looked over my shoulder and debated running back to the chalet to have Karl call for help, but there was no telling how long that would take. I was too afraid to leave for even a moment in case Lois needed me.

"Let me in! Let me in! Lois! Lois!" I was shouting so loud, I was surprised Deputy Little or one of the Millersburg police officers didn't come running.

As much as I hated the idea of leaving Lois trapped in the Hillside with Gerome, I couldn't break in. I had to run for help.

Then, I saw a small metal snow shovel by Gerome's door, presumably left there when someone came by to clear the walk. Before I could change my mind, I picked up the shovel and swung it at the adjacent window with all my might.

The window didn't break, but there was a definite cracking sound. I hit it again.

I made such a ruckus, I got the attention of the man staying in Hillside number four, right next to Gerome's room. He was a tall African American man and blinked at me as if he had just awakened from a deep sleep. "Ma'am, is everything okay?"

I turned around with the shovel, ready to strike.

"Whoa!" He held up both of his hands. "Can I ask you to put down the shovel?"

I looked up at my hands. Sure enough, I was holding the shovel in a very menacing manner. "I'm sorry. I'm trying to break the window to get inside this room."

"Why?" he asked.

"My friend is in there. A man grabbed her and pulled her inside, and I don't know what might be happening to her. You must have heard the commotion by the clock tower."

His brows rose. "Commotion? I just woke up. It's not even nine in the morning yet. My wife and I are here on vacation."

"Oh. A woman was killed when the cuckoo fell on her."

He stared at me. "What did you say?"

I repeated my sentence a little bit slower this time. "That's why I need to get into this room. My friend is in there with the man whose wife was killed. I've been banging on the door and now the window for several minutes with no answer."

He nodded. "I'll call the front desk and have them send the police. In the meantime, I wouldn't keep hitting the window. If it breaks, you're at risk of being hurt."

"You're right." I glanced over my shoulder at the closed door. What was I supposed to do now? Just sit here and wait? Lois could be in danger.

The man disappeared back into his room to make the phone call.

Not satisfied with waiting, I was about to start banging on the door again when it opened. Lois was the one who opened it.

I stared at her. "Are you okay? I thought he was going to hurt you."

"Were you hitting the window?"

"*Ya*, with a shovel."

"Why on earth would you do that?" She stared at me in disbelief.

"To break you out. I didn't know what was happening. I thought you might be hurt."

She snorted. "Gerome would never hurt me."

"Excuse me if I assumed the worst, but his wife is dead." I let that statement hang in the air.

"You can't think Gerome had something to do with it! It was an accident."

I cocked my head, surprised at the role reversal. Usually when Lois and I were in this type of situation, she was the one insisting foul play was involved, while I cautioned her not to jump to conclusions. This time, however, I felt something wasn't quite right. A lot of that had to do with Gerome.

Before I could ask Lois what was going on, Deputy Little strode around the side of the man-made hill, followed by two Millersburg police officers and four young sheep.

Lois noticed the sheep, too. "It seems the yearlings have taken a liking to the deputy."

Deputy Little looked over his shoulder and saw the sheep there. He kept walking, and they did, too. It would have been comical if it weren't such a serious situation. A woman was dead. A young, vibrant woman who should have had her whole life in front of her.

Deputy Little didn't seem all that happy about the sheep, but seemed even more upset over seeing Lois and me.

"Millie," he said with resignation in his voice. "Lois," he added. "What are you doing back here? You shouldn't leave the scene of an incident until you are released."

"Deputy Little," Lois said. "When are we ever

known to stay in one place for very long? We are women on the move!"

He sighed. "A guest called and reported a woman trapped in one of the Hillside rooms, and another woman—an Amish one—beating the window with a shovel." His eyes slid in my direction.

"The window didn't break, if that's what you're worried about."

"What I'm worried about is the reason the two of you are back here looking very much like you're up to something."

I pulled the sleeves of my coat to cover my bare wrists. "We came to talk with Gerome and see how he's feeling. He had quite a shock this morning, and we just wanted to make sure he was all right."

"That doesn't explain the beating on the window." The deputy arched his brow.

Lois and I shared a glance.

"I might have overreacted. When we got here, Gerome pulled Lois into the room. He wouldn't let me in, and I got worried. The shovel was close, so I thought I would give it a try. In my defense, a woman had just died."

Deputy Little rubbed his forehead a little more vigorously, as if he were trying to soothe a pounding headache between his eyes. "Why did you go into the room, Lois?"

"Gerome didn't give me much choice. As Millie said, he yanked me in like a yo-yo on a string. He was panicked, but I wasn't afraid of him. He's Gerome, for goodness' sake. He's harmless. Since Gerome is my ex-husband, I felt it was my job to check on him and make sure he was okay."

"You know Gerome? You were *married* to Gerome?" He asked both questions in a slow manner, as if he couldn't form the words unless he was thinking about them very carefully.

"Yes, we got divorced over three years ago. It was never going to work. I realized that early on, pushed him into the hotel pool at the casino, and the rest is history." Lois shrugged.

"He's your ex-husband. Based on the pool comment, your marriage ended on bad terms. Now, he's here at the Chalet on a honeymoon with his new wife. Why are you here?" He looked at me. "Why are you two here? Am I losing my mind that I find that odd?" The deputy rubbed the back of his neck.

"After being a deputy for so long, I'm shocked that anything surprises you anymore. You know that interpersonal relationships can be complicated," Lois said.

"So is he your most recent ex-husband?" Deputy Little had known Lois and me long enough to have an idea of our history, and Lois wasn't exactly a private person when it came to her own life. If someone asked for her life story while sipping coffee at the café, Lois would pull up a chair and pour a mug of coffee for herself and share the whole tale.

"He's the most recent one. The gambler. Rocksino-Guy."

Deputy Little didn't seem to be taken aback by the nickname. He studied Lois. "Despite the pool dunking, the two of you split on good terms?" He asked this with some trepidation. I believed it was fair to assume Deputy Little didn't want to see Lois as a suspect, but he would if he had to. He was a good cop, and that meant looking at all the possibilities when it came to a crime.

Lois pointed her finger at him. "Don't you go suspecting I might have something to do with his wife's death!"

The deputy arched his brow. "I just find it odd you're here during your ex-husband's honeymoon."

She put her hands on her hips. "I can assure you it has nothing to do with her death. It's an accident anyway, right?" Her voice jumped up an octave on the last word. "I mean the cuckoo falling like that has to be an accident."

Deputy Little looked away.

"Deputy, if this wasn't an accident, you need to tell us," I said.

His gaze slid in my direction. "Millie, I'm under no obligation to tell the two of you anything."

"You are under a respect obligation. We're old enough to be your grandmothers," Lois said.

"That's a terrifying thought. I don't know what I would do if I had a couple of grandmothers like the two of you." He gave a half-hearted laugh.

Lois folded her arms and scowled at him.

"Okay, okay. I'll tell you what I can," the young deputy said, waving his hands. "You will know soon enough, I'm sure."

"I don't doubt it," Lois agreed. "Rarely does anything happen in this county that we don't know about."

He frowned as if he wasn't too happy with that reality. "The way Mrs. Moorhead died is suspicious."

"You don't think she was crushed by the cuckoo?" I asked. As I spoke, the image of the young woman's crumpled body came to mind. I wished the thought away. "Was she shot beforehand? Stabbed?" I searched my memory of Paige lying on the sidewalk. It was a terrible memory to revisit, but I couldn't recall any outward wounds that couldn't have been made by the fallen cuckoo. "Poisoned?"

Deputy Little closed his eyes for a long moment, as if he regretted saying anything at all. "Nothing like that. The cuckoo killed her." He shook his head, as if he couldn't believe that was a mode of death he had to deal with. "But what caused the cuckoo to fall remains in question."

Lois and I leaned in. "What do you mean?"

He cleared his throat. "It appears that the cuckoo didn't just fall on its own. Someone tampered with it very recently to make it fall."

Lois and I gasped. That would fit with Karl's claim that the clock was inspected and pronounced to be in working order just three months ago.

"Are you saying someone murdered Paige Moorhead?" I asked.

"I'm saying this investigation is much more complicated than we first thought," he said in a resigned voice. "Much more complicated."

Chapter Nine

"Was it murder, Deputy?" I asked again.

"You can tell us," Lois said as she gripped the strap of her purse until her knuckles turned bright white.

"We can't go as far as that. It seems quite a difficult way to kill someone. There are easier options."

With all the murders and crimes Deputy Little had investigated during his career, he would know. From murders to runaway cows, he had seen it all, or so we thought until this cuckoo crime.

Lois shook her head. "Murdered by a cuckoo? What are the odds?"

"Maybe Gerome calculated the odds. You said he was a gambler," he said in a casual manner, as if he wanted to gauge Lois's reaction.

Her response was immediate. Lois shook her bejeweled finger at him. "Now, see here. Just because he's the husband, that doesn't make him the killer, and you even said yourself, you don't know that there was actually a murder."

"There is clear evidence of tampering with the cuckoo in the tower."

"What tampering?" Lois wanted to know.

He cleared his throat. "I prefer not to disclose. Just know this is not an open-and-shut case."

"They never are," I said with a sigh.

A few feet away from us, Gerome spoke to a Millersburg police officer. From the way Gerome waved his arms and began to pace as if he couldn't believe what was happening, the conversation wasn't going as he had hoped.

"It looks like I should lend Officer Jenkins a hand," Deputy Little said and took a step in that direction.

"If this is a murder case," I said, "will the sheriff's department or the Millersburg police be in charge of the investigation?"

He seemed to consider my question. "We're technically still inside the limits of Millersburg, but the police department is more than willing to turn the case over to us. We have more experience with this sort of thing—with murder cases, not the cuckoo clock aspect."

That was certainly true.

He looked from Lois to me, and then back again. "Now, I'm asking the two of you—no, I'm begging the two of you—not to get involved in this case. You, especially, Lois, should stay as far away from it as possible."

Lois stuck out her lower lip. "Why are you singling me out, Deputy? Amish Marple here gets into as much trouble as I do."

He squinted in the sunlight reflecting off the snow. "I know all too well, but as far as I can see, Millie didn't have any motive to murder this woman. You did."

Lois opened and closed her mouth. "Well . . . I . . . I never."

As Lois sputtered, I realized what the deputy had said was true. If Paige's death was murder, Lois—filling the role of the bitter ex-wife—would be a suspect. I didn't believe Lois actually was bitter over her divorce from Gerome. Or at least not bitter enough that she would crush someone with a cuckoo from a clock. To me, Gerome, as the husband, looked more like the main suspect. Again, that was assuming there'd been a crime here, and not just some unfortunate, absurd accident.

"The two of you wait here. I will want to talk to you before you leave," Deputy Little said.

"All right," Lois said. "But we can't stay too long. I have to go to the café to help Darcy."

The young deputy strode to the Hillside door, and two of the sheep followed him. He looked over his shoulder and tried to shoo them away. They stopped moving toward him but didn't back off.

"The sheep really have a thing for Deputy Little," Lois mused.

"They are the most peculiar sheep I have ever seen."

When the deputy disappeared into the room, Lois and I shared a look. I knew what both of us were thinking. It was time to talk to Gerome and find out what he knew before the deputy returned.

Just a few yards away, Gerome paced back and

forth. He wasn't wearing a coat and wore bedroom slippers that were already soaked through from the snow.

Lois got right to the point. "Gerome, what can you tell us about your wife's death?"

He stared at her. "What can I tell you? Nothing. I know nothing about it."

"Where were you when the cuckoo fell?" Lois gave him a beady look. I had seen the same expression on her face when she was vintage-furniture shopping. Her scrutiny was intense.

He blinked at her. "I—I was in the trees taking pictures. I recently got into photography, and it seems I really have a knack for it. Paige doesn't like tromping around the woods, so she stayed back at the room. However, maybe she got tired of waiting and went out to explore. Truly, I didn't even know she'd left the room until I heard the scream."

"Paige's scream," I said.

He looked down at his shoes. "I can only assume, yes."

"You don't recognize the sound of your wife's scream?" Lois asked.

"Can you distinguish one person's scream from another's?" He arched a brow at her.

"Of course I can. The sound of everyone's scream is distinctive. Don't you think so, Millie?"

I gave a noncommittal shrug and glanced at his feet. "You weren't in your Hillside room very long before Lois and I showed up." I nodded at the slippers. "But you had time to change your shoes?"

He scowled at me. "My feet were cold from traipsing in the snow while I was taking photos this morning. I had to warm them up. You can lose your toes to frostbite, you know? Now my feet are freezing again. I wish I had thought to put my boots back on before coming outside."

"So while you were walking around in the woods, your wife was alone, and you don't know why she left the room," I said.

"If I knew that, I would be telling the police. I wouldn't be standing here talking to the two of you."

Lois held up her hand. "Hold on there, Gerome. We're trying to help you. That's what you asked me when we were in your room, wasn't it? The police think foul play might have been involved in your wife's death. If that's true, they'll be taking a long, hard look at you."

I grimaced. I knew for a fact that Deputy Little would not want Lois to tell their possible number one suspect his wife might have been murdered.

Gerome paled, and since he already had a fair complexion, his cheeks faded to the color of the inside of a potato.

"Where is your camera?" I asked.

He glanced at the open door of his Hillside room. "In there." He frowned. "Are the police searching my room because they think I killed my wife? They didn't say that when they asked me if they could take a look around. If I had known, I would have said no."

Lois shook her head. "For a gambling man, Gerome, you are a little too trusting. Why would they have wanted to go into your room if your wife died accidentally?"

He turned even paler, as if it finally seemed to

hit him how much trouble he could be in. There were no tears, though, no sorrow etched on his face over his wife's death. I did my best to hold my judgment at bay considering this fact. It was possible the shock was just too much for him. He might fall apart in a few hours when the reality of his wife's death finally hit him.

Deputy Little and the two officers from the Millersburg Police Department came out of Gerome's Hillside room. The deputy held a large camera in his hands.

Gerome's face turned beet red at the sight of it, and he marched over to the deputy. "What are you doing with my camera?" He pointed at the police officers. "I told the two of them that they could go in and have a look around. You took advantage of me in my daze over my wife's death."

I folded my arms and realized Gerome was right. The officers should have been more forthcoming with Gerome as to why they wanted to see his room. I didn't know if they needed a warrant if Karl, the owner, gave permission, which I assumed he had. I shook my head. If Kip could see me now, with my understanding of police investigations and warrants, he never would have believed it was his quiet Amish wife.

Deputy Little handed the camera to Gerome. "I'm sorry if there was a misunderstanding of the officers' intentions." He shot the two police officers an irritated look. "The sheriff's department will be taking over the case from here on out, and we'll do everything aboveboard."

Gerome held the camera to his chest and nodded.

"It's not like we could see any of the photos anyway. That's a film camera, not digital," one of the officers said. "Who shoots with film anymore?"

Gerome scowled at him. "I do, and so do a lot of other photographers. I'm a purist. Film gives photos character that digital cannot."

Deputy Little scowled at the two officers. "I would like you to go back to the front of the resort, confirm the scene is secure, and see if the coroner needs any assistance."

If the officers were upset at being dismissed, they didn't show it.

"Mr. Moorhead, we have reason to believe your wife was murdered," Deputy Little said.

Gerome gasped. It wasn't the first time he was hearing it since Lois had already "spilled the beans" as she would have said, but the words seemed to become more real to Gerome coming from a man in uniform. Perhaps Gerome had thought Lois was mistaken.

Deputy Little stuck his hands into the pockets of his department jacket. "The officers said you were taking pictures at the time she died."

Gerome shivered. It might have been from the cold, or from the shock of it all, or both.

"I—I was. I got up early to take photos in the woods just as the sun was coming up. With so few electric lights here, the shots are very different from the ones I snap at home. I like to capture how the sunlight bounces off the snow onto the trees and creates shadows."

"And you use that camera?" The deputy pointed at the camera in Gerome's hands.

Gerome peered down at the camera as if he was seeing it for the very first time. "Yes, this is the camera I use."

Deputy Little rocked back on his heels. "Are you a professional photographer?"

"Not a professional one, no. But I would like to be. I'm an amateur at best. However, I do dabble in vintage lenses and cameras. They give a certain character to the photograph that a modern lens with its stark exactness cannot."

Lois seemed to consider this. "Did you catch anything unusual on your camera this morning? Maybe you caught a glimpse of the killer and didn't even know it." She did little to keep the excitement from her voice.

Deputy Little shot her a look as if to say *I was going to get to that.*

"I wouldn't have caught anything on the camera. I was in the woods and then on the hillside behind my room. My lens was always pointed away from the clock tower. There is no way that anything on this camera will help with the investigation. I was nowhere near my wife when . . . when the accident happened. I didn't even know she was outside. When I left the room this morning, she was still asleep."

"That may be so, but I still want to see those images on the off chance they could give us a clue to what might have happened this morning," Deputy Little said. "We have to explore all avenues to solve this case. That includes looking at the film."

Gerome held the camera even closer to his body. "I can't give you this. The roll isn't even done yet. It's an expensive roll; I can't just waste it like that."

The deputy arched his brow. "Is it a waste to find out what happened to your wife?"

"Of course not," Gerome snapped. "But Paige knew how important photography was to me. She wouldn't want me to waste any film, either."

Deputy Little removed his hands from his pockets and folded his arms. "I can get a warrant for the camera, Mr. Moorhead."

Gerome glowered at him. "Then do it, because I'm not handing over this camera without one."

"I need to make a call," Deputy Little said and excused himself.

He walked a few feet away and placed his cell phone to his ear. The small flock of sheep followed him. Lois was right. The sheep had a thing for the deputy.

I mulled over the morning's events. Who would want to kill Gerome's new bride while they were on their honeymoon? And then, the even more peculiar question: If she was murdered, who would use such an unreliable means? And could Gerome be holding those photos back because they revealed something he didn't want to share?

Gerome grabbed Lois's arm. "Lois, you have to help me. I can't go to jail."

Lois tried to pull her arm away, but he held fast.

"Please." He was desperate. "Please. You have to help me. I swear to you, I didn't kill my wife."

Lois finally managed to gently remove her arm from his grasp. "I know you didn't, Gerome."

I glanced at her.

Lois answered my unspoken question. "Gerome won't fly, or go up a ladder, or even look out a window more than one story up. There's no way he would climb up into that clock tower to tamper with the cuckoo. He'd be too scared." She turned to Gerome. "Did you tell the police you're afraid of heights?"

"N-no, but I will. You're right. This should clear my name!"

I wished I could believe her, but with the right motivation, people were able to face their fears, even the one that terrified them the most. The question was, had Gerome been motivated enough to conquer his fear of heights in order to kill his wife?

Chapter Ten

"If it wasn't Gerome, who else could have tampered with the clock tower?" I asked.

Gerome made a whimpering sound at my question. I was becoming increasingly more amazed Lois had once agreed to marry him. He did not seem to be her type at all, his skill at dice notwithstanding.

"Maybe it was a case of being in the wrong place at the wrong time," Lois offered. "Maybe the killer wanted to murder someone else. It's possible Paige was never even the target."

"If that's true, this case will be even harder to solve than we thought," I said.

"We can do it; you're Amish Marple. No case is too big or too small," Lois said.

Gerome blinked. "Amish Marple?"

"Oh!" Lois clapped her hands. "You don't know about our cases?"

"Your cases?" His forehead wrinkled in confusion.

Lois studied him. "I thought that was why you asked me for help. Because you knew Millie and I had solved murders before."

"You've what?" he yelped.

Lois gave him a brief summary of our past experiences with murder.

Gerome paled. "I asked you for help because you are the only person I know here. I needed you to help me navigate Holmes County, and you seemed to know the deputy, too. I thought you could put in a good word for me."

"Oh," Lois said, looking slightly disappointed. She really wanted our reputation as crime solvers to be known far and wide. "We might be able to solve the murder. I'm not sure about putting in a good word, though."

Gerome's eyes bulged out of his head. I decided to jump into the conversation to smooth things over. "You might not know anyone in Holmes County other than Lois, but did your wife know anyone?" I asked. "Even a slight acquaintance would be helpful."

Gerome pulled at the cuffs of his gloves. "She had contacts here."

Lois and I shared a look. "Contacts?"

"Yes, for her family business. Her family owns a very successful furniture store chain in Cuyahoga County. You might have heard of it—Delpont Furniture Warehouse. They have four giant showrooms and are looking to open a fifth."

Lois nodded. "I've seen the commercials. They have a catchy jingle." She hummed a little tune.

I had never heard of the furniture store, but if Lois had learned of it through television commercials, I wouldn't have.

He nodded. "They buy a lot of the furniture from Amish carpenters and craftsmen at wholesale prices right here in Holmes County. Amish-made furniture commands a higher price in the city. You say that a table is Amish-made, people immediately expect it's worth more because of the quality and craftsmanship. Personally, I don't always think the work is superior to what others do, but even I can't ignore the high prices shoppers are willing to pay." He continued to pull at his gloves. "One of the reasons we chose Holmes County for our honeymoon was to appease Paige's family. They wanted her to come here on business."

"I wouldn't think appeasing a bride's family had anything to do with the location of a honeymoon," Lois said.

"While we were down here, Paige promised she would meet up with some of their Amish carpenters and craftsmen and try to find more places to acquire furniture. I didn't mind, because I planned to work on my photography while we were here. When she was off at her meetings, I would be off shooting."

"It all sounds so romantic," Lois quipped.

"We weren't the type of couple that was attached at the hip. I didn't know much about her business, and she didn't know much about mine. That worked for us. I was just happy that there was a way to keep the peace. She had a very large family, and they didn't like the idea of us getting married."

"Are her parents still alive?" I asked.

He shook his head. "No, but she has aunts, uncles, a brother, and cousins, and they're all in the family furniture business. They are constantly expanding the business to give some relative a piece of the company."

"Why didn't her family want you to marry?" I asked.

"The age difference, for the most part. I'm technically old enough to be her father, but love doesn't see age, you know?"

I made no comment, because as a matchmaker, I'd witnessed successful relationships with large age gaps. However, such marriages came with their own unique challenges. If two people in a relationship were at different stages of life, they might want different things, which could lead to conflict. That being said, there was conflict in every marriage. It was unavoidable. I found it suspicious when there was no conflict. Usually it meant one of the spouses was not making his or her needs known to the other.

"You need to tell Deputy Little all of this," Lois said.

"Why?" Gerome asked with a scowl. "He tried to take my camera."

"You need to tell him because this information shows there are other potential suspects in the county. That's good news for you."

"That's ridiculous! Why would any of the Amish

carpenters kill Honeybee? They want to be in business with her family, not kill the person who could make that happen for them."

Lois threw up her hands. "I don't know, but from our experience"—she gestured between us—"the more suspects, the better, as far as keeping the police off your back. And off my back. I'm a suspect, too."

His mouth fell open. "You? Why?"

She rolled her eyes, as if she couldn't believe he was so dense. "Because you and I were married. The angle is I'm a jealous ex-wife."

"That's ridiculous," Gerome muttered.

"I appreciate the vote of confidence," Lois said.

He rubbed the back of his head. "I'll have to call her brother and tell him what's happened. He's closest to Paige in the family, and with her parents gone, he's the next of kin. Well, other than me, as her husband." He shook his head. "We were only married for two days before she died." His voice caught.

For a second, I thought he was about to break down and cry, but he gathered his composure. His eyes remained clear.

"I think you will want to be the one to tell her brother instead of the sheriff's deputy. It's going to come as a shock," I said.

"It will. It will send the family reeling. In many ways, Honeybee was running the show. She was the one who always knew the next move to make, and without her, the company would never have grown so much in the last couple of years. She took over the helm when her father died."

"Because she was the oldest?" Lois asked.

"She's actually younger than her brother, but much better in business. Her father recognized that before he died and left the leadership of the company in her hands. He couldn't have picked a better person. Since Paige has been at the helm of the furniture company, their revenue has doubled."

"What did she do to make the revenue double?" I asked.

He looked at me. "Well, I—I don't know. Like I said, her business was her business, and my business was mine. I believe it's healthier if a husband and wife have their own jobs to care about."

I considered this. It certainly wasn't the intertwined community thinking that I had been raised with. In the Amish world, the whole family worked together whenever possible, and in many cases, the whole district worked together, too. Being separate was frowned upon.

"Well, there's a second suspect for you," Lois said triumphantly. "A jealous older brother who feels passed over for his little sister."

"But he's not in Holmes County," Gerome said.

"Oh," Lois muttered.

"What's her brother's name?" I asked.

"Ronan."

"I will pray for you and Ronan during my evening devotions. You've both suffered a terrible loss," I said.

He studied me as if trying to decide whether I was really telling the truth or not. "You're as kind as Lois said. When we were together, she talked about you all the time. I always wondered if you were real. I just could not wrap my head around the idea that her closest friend was Amish, since she and I met at a casino. But here you are in the flesh."

"Opposites attract," I said with a smile. "Just as much in friendship as they do in romance."

"I suppose so. I thought it was the case with Paige and me. We were opposite in a lot of ways, too. She was so organized and had a good head on her shoulders. Every decision she made was carefully thought out and reasonable. I can't say I have lived my life like that." His face crumpled. "I can't believe she's dead. What will I do without her?"

It seemed the finality of his wife's death had at last hit him full in the heart. He covered his face with his hands and ran into his room, slamming the door behind him. The deadbolt slid home.

"What do we do now?" I whispered to Lois. I wasn't sure why I was whispering, since it was only Lois and the sheep who could hear me now.

She folded her arms. "The only thing we can do. Solve the case."

"You make it sound like it will be easy," I said.

"It should be easy for us. We've solved trickier cases than this."

I wasn't so sure about that. A cuckoo clock murder sounded extra tricky to me.

Lois sensed my hesitation. "Millie, listen to me. I know my marriage to Gerome was short, but I have to know I wasn't married to a killer. It would tear me up inside to think I once loved—okay, *love* might be too strong a word—that I once cared about a man who could take a life with so little thought. Will you help me?"

I nodded. There was nothing else I could say. Lois was always there for me. I needed to be there for her. "Let's get to work."

"That's just what I hoped you'd say, Amish Marple." She wrapped an arm around my shoulders.

I groaned. I couldn't seem to shake the nickname as far as Lois was concerned.

Chapter Eleven

"What do we do first?" I asked after we settled into her car a few minutes later. Deputy Little had made it abundantly clear he wanted Lois and me to leave the chalet. However, I knew he was aware this wasn't the last he would hear from us about the case.

"I need to go to the café. I'm late for the breakfast rush as it is, but I texted Darcy. She knows I'm with you."

I chuckled. "So she is assuming we're getting into trouble, then."

"Well, aren't we? Dead bodies do tend to bring trouble," Lois said. "If you need to go home, I can take you. It's Saturday, so the breakfast service may last until lunchtime, and then we are into the lunch rush. It goes on and on Saturdays."

I thought about the quiet day at home that I had planned. I knew I wouldn't have the quiet day I wanted as my mind raced over what might have happened that morning at the Munich Chalet. I had so many questions about Paige Moorhead's death and even more about Gerome, her husband and my best friend's ex-husband. I knew that Gerome had made Lois upset enough in the short time they were married that she'd pushed him into the hotel pool, but that was all I knew. I'd never asked for the reason that she wanted the divorce. I never expected to meet Rocksino-Guy, so there had been no reason to press the issue. However, now seemed like the time to ask.

"*Nee,* I'll go with you into town," I said. "It's been a rough morning. I could use some of Darcy's blueberry pancakes to calm my nerves."

Lois shook her head. "You and blueberries, Millie. It's an obsession."

"It's *gut* to know what you like and what you don't. I'm decisive, not obsessed."

Lois snorted.

When we were settled in her car and pulling away from the chalet, I said, "It's also *gut* to have as much information as possible as we enter this investigation. Some of that information I need from you."

She took her eyes off the road for a second and glanced at me before returning her attention to driving.

I thought she would just tell me the story at that point, as she would with any other story in her life, but it was not to be. "What happened with you and Gerome? Why did you divorce so soon after your wedding?"

Her shoulders shifted up and down, making her earrings swing from her ears. Today, she had traded the pink and red heart earrings for jolly snowmen. "I was wondering when you would ask. To be honest, I'm surprised you've waited this long. Your patience is legendary."

I waited.

"Just a few months after we were married, I saw Gerome canoodling with a waitress at the casino where we met."

"Canoodling?" I tested the word. It wasn't one I had heard before.

"Flirting and kissing her hand. Behaving in a way that a married man should not with another woman." There was hurt in her voice still. "It wasn't like I caught him in the act of adultery or anything, but I took it as a bad sign that he would behave like that so soon after we'd said *I do*." She gripped the steering wheel. "I couldn't remember feeling that insignificant since I was a child."

I reached for her arm and gave it a brief squeeze. Lois hadn't had the best home life growing up. That was why we had spent so much time together, even though we were from two different worlds. When things were hard at home for her—and they often were—she stayed with my family. Even with her zany *Englisch* ways, my parents welcomed her onto our farm and let her stay as long as she wished. They knew she needed a safe place to go.

She smiled at me, and I dropped my hand onto my lap.

"When I left my parents' home when I was eighteen, I promised myself I would never let anyone make me feel that way again, and I didn't. At least, I hadn't until I met Gerome Moorhead. I knew I had to get out before it got worse. This was my new husband, and he already seemed to have forgotten that we were married."

"Oh, I was afraid it was something like that." I placed a hand on her shoulder.

She took a deep breath. "Flirting with another woman when we weren't even married a year was a red flag. My beloved second husband—God rest his soul—would never have done that to me. The moment we met, he never even looked at another woman. I knew I deserved more. I didn't confront him when I spotted them. I was too embarrassed, to be honest. I felt like he would have downplayed his actions in front of this other woman. I didn't want to be more humiliated than I had been. After I calmed myself down a few hours later, I caught up with him at the hotel pool. When I told him what I'd seen, he said I was blowing it out of proportion. I took the only reasonable action: told him I wanted a divorce and pushed him into the water. It was very satisfying, if I do say so myself. I would do it again in a heartbeat."

No one could say Lois wasn't decisive. Sometimes that trait worked in her favor. Other times, it worked to her detriment. However, I was in full agreement with her in this case that Gerome had treated her poorly.

She'd told him she wanted a divorce because of his actions. If she had been Amish, it might not have been that simple. To get a divorce in the Amish faith without an extremely *gut* reason—and I'm not sure the church elders would see what Gerome did as a *gut* enough reason—was next to impossible. Many times, the community would do whatever it took to keep a couple together.

"And this was three years ago?"

"Thereabouts."

I pressed my lips together.

She glanced at me again. "You're wondering why I treated Gerome so poorly when I saw him at the café."

"I was," I admitted. I saw no reason to keep this a secret from my friend.

"It was the shock. It was the first time I had seen him since the divorce was finalized. I never dealt with what happened. Even if I wasn't at fault, I felt ashamed . . . ashamed I was dumb enough to marry him in the first place. Being a hopeless romantic is not as free and easy as Hollywood would have you believe. I've made my share of mistakes because of my romantic outlook, and I have a string of marriages to prove it."

I would have to take her word on it, because I had no idea of Hollywood's opinion on this matter or any matter at all.

"Even so, our relationship was long over. I shouldn't have been rude. What I should have done was greet him nicely and get on with serving customers at the café. Sometimes my emotions get the best of me."

She could say that again.

"That's why I hatched this plan to go to the chalet and apologize to him. It felt like I would finally get some closure. I never for a moment thought that his wife would end up dead."

That was a relief.

"I can't see why you would."

"And even if I did—since we have been involved in a handful of murders—a cuckoo clock would not be my first choice for a murder weapon. How absurd!"

Absurd was a good word for it, but didn't lessen the fact it was the method by which Paige Moorhead—a young woman, in her prime, and newly married—had been killed. It was a tragedy on all levels.

I removed my gloves and laid them across my lap. "After all that has happened between you and Gerome, why do you want to help him now?"

"I told you why, Millie. So I can reassure myself that I'm not capable of falling in love with a killer. Yes, Gerome was a flirt, but I can't believe he would hurt anyone. If he did kill Paige, it calls into question my judgment. I can't have that. It will cause me crippling self-doubt."

Yet she had already admitted to bad judgment when she'd married him. I had more questions, but I could sense Lois was becoming increasingly upset, and pressing her would go nowhere. Amish women learned from a young age when to push and when to back off. Gender roles were very traditional in Amish communities. It was an aspect of my culture Lois did not care for and complained about often. However, I knew this was a time to take a step back from the conversation. I knew Lois; she would tell me the rest eventually.

One of my Amish proverbs came to mind: "Patience is a virtue that carries a lot of wait."

Even so, I hoped that she would finish her story sooner rather than later.

"What we need to do is focus on the case," Lois

said. "And it really doesn't have anything to do with me."

I wished I was convinced Deputy Little felt the same way. However, as much as Deputy Little liked Lois, he had to be considering her as a suspect. She was Gerome's ex-wife. Witnesses, whom he would surely find at the café, could share how Lois and Gerome had had a public fight the day before Paige died. Even I had to admit, Lois came out of the conversation looking like the jealous ex-wife. The deputy wouldn't be able to ignore those facts. That was the reason we needed to find the real culprit as quickly as possible.

Lois tapped her cheek with a brightly painted red nail, which included a pink heart decal in the middle. The design was for Valentine's Day, of course. "Could it be that someone followed Gerome and Paige here from Cleveland? He'd told us that Paige had come here partly on business, looking for Amish carpenters—and I have those carpenters, whoever they may be, on my suspect list—but Cleveland is only two hours away. It's not impossible someone followed them with foul play in mind."

"That's true," I agreed. "However, it just makes our job more difficult. Because if that's the case, the killer must have left the area by now. He or she would have no reason to stay." I frowned. "And I don't see us having much luck following this case to Cleveland. Deputy Little and the local authorities might give us some leeway over snooping about, but the Cleveland police won't do that."

She parked her car in the corner of the church parking lot. The church allowed locals to use the parking lot, as long as it wasn't a Sunday, or the church wasn't hosting an event. As we exited the car, I wondered how the fundraiser had fared, which made me think of Elijah Smucker. His son's life had been cut short like Paige's. Every loss was a tragedy.

"Millie, are you coming?" Lois was already on the sidewalk, making her way to the café.

I hurried to catch up with her. "I'm sorry. My thoughts wandered to John Michael Smucker."

She nodded. "And his poor father, I would imagine."

I nodded. His poor father. At the spaghetti dinner, Elijah Smucker had been a broken man, and I wondered, not for the first time, why he had been at the dinner. It had been brave of him to go. *Ya*, that was true, but it was rare that Amish men would show up in a public place so visibly stricken as Elijah had been. Emotions were dealt with in private. Sometimes even kept hidden from their wives and family.

We had almost reached the café when Lois snapped her fingers. "I have an idea."

The way she said it made the hairs stand up on the back of my neck. "An idea?"

"Oh, and it's a good one, too!"

We reached the café. The place was busy, and a small group of people stood near the front, waiting to be seated.

Lois opened the door. "It's even busier than I thought." She glanced at me. "We will have to talk about the case later. After the crowd dies down. I will tell you my idea then. It's brilliant! Absolutely brilliant."

Brilliant felt like trouble.

She took off her coat and hat and flung them on one of the pegs on the wall. "You are going to love it. I'm sure of it."

I was going to need a double order of blueberry pancakes to survive the wait. That was the only thing I was sure of.

Chapter Twelve

As anxious as I was to hear Lois's plans for the investigation, I still enjoyed my double stack of blueberry pancakes, fresh from Darcy's griddle. I ate them with just a bit of butter. I didn't want maple syrup to overwhelm the deliciously tart blueberry taste.

I had a forkful halfway to my mouth when I heard a sharp voice. "Millie Fisher, what is this I hear about you finding a dead *Englischer*?" The words came in Pennsylvania Dutch, so at least the tourists didn't know what the bishop's wife, Ruth Yoder, was asking me.

Today, Ruth wore a plain gray dress, the same color as her hair, with a black cloak and black bonnet. She removed the large bonnet and hung it on the pegboard by the door. The pegboard held a mixture of Amish cloaks and *Englisch* ski jackets. Anywhere else in the country, the collection of outerwear might have appeared odd, but in Holmes County, it was the norm.

"Are you going to answer my question?" Ruth walked over to my table and folded her arms as she glowered down at me.

I popped the forkful of blueberry pancake in my mouth, because it gave me time to think.

Ruth tapped her prayer cap to make sure it was still perfectly in place on top of her head. It was, of course. Her prayer cap wouldn't dare move even an inch. She scowled at me. "Well?"

I knew I shouldn't have sat by the window. As much as I loved the bright, white winter sunshine pouring over my table, there was a price for it, and that price was being easily spotted from the street. I knew it was the only reason Ruth had come into the Sunbeam Café.

Typically, she stayed away from the café, unless we held a quilting circle meeting there. Ruth avoided the Sunbeam Café because of Lois. They'd had a strained relationship ever since we were all in pigtails, and Ruth had made it more than clear on several occasions that she didn't approve of my close friendship with an *Englischer*—and such a nontraditional *Englischer*, at that.

When I was younger, it used to bother me, and sometimes I had wondered if I needed to end my friendship with Lois in order to protect my Amishness. Now, I was too old to care much about what Ruth thought. We had been having the same disagreements for over sixty years, and I didn't see that changing anytime soon. I wouldn't be the least bit surprised if Ruth took her grievances all the way to Heaven.

I sipped my coffee and decided it would be best if I just answered her before she made a scene. "Ruth, why don't you have a seat, and we can talk about it?"

She pulled out the chair and fell into the seat across from me. "So it is true." She folded her hands on the tabletop. "I was really hoping it was a rumor. You know how people in this county like to talk, and not everything they say is right."

I did know that.

"What were you told?"

Ruth crossed her arms and sat back in her chair. "That you and Lois—" She paused and looked around the café. Lois was in the back, chatting and refilling customers' coffees. She was easy to spot and hear. Lois didn't do anything quietly. "That you and Lois found a dead body at the *Englischer* chalet."

"That's kind of true."

Ruth pinched the bridge of her nose and closed her eyes as if she were fighting a piercing pain in her head. "Please tell me what happened."

I didn't see any point in keeping it from her. I knew the Harvest rumor mill would already be churning out multiple versions of the story. "Lois and I were at the chalet this morning and were there right when the giant cuckoo from the clock tower fell on one of the guests."

"The cuckoo fell." She gasped.

I nodded.

She pressed her lips together. "I always knew that eyesore would come to no *gut*. But because it was in Millersburg, there wasn't much the Amish community could do to have it removed."

I knew what she meant. In Holmes County, some of the many small towns had more Amish than others. In Harvest, over sixty percent of the population was Amish, but in Millersburg, there were far fewer Amish.

"Why on earth were you even there? It's not a place for Amish," Ruth accused, and then looked across the café at Lois, who was refilling water glasses. "It was *her* idea, wasn't it? You can't tell me that you wanted to go there. This has Lois written all over it."

I looked down at my plate. I couldn't deny that it was Lois's idea to go to the chalet, but I wanted to answer in such a way that I didn't bring up Gerome and his history with Lois. I didn't want my dearest friend's possible guilt to become the topic of speculation in the village. At the same time, I could not lie. "We were there to see a guest who had visited the café the day before."

Ruth frowned and didn't look the least bit satisfied with that answer. "Which guest?"

I sipped my coffee. These questions were becoming more uncomfortable by the second. I regretted telling Ruth anything at all.

"You can't keep it from me. I'm the bishop's wife, and you are a member of my husband's district. You must answer me. It's your obligation out of respect for my position in the community."

I set my mug down and scowled at her. It was true that she was the bishop's wife, and as such, she should be respected. However, she wasn't the bishop. If he had been asking me these questions, I would have to answer. I didn't have to answer her.

As annoyed as I was at her veiled threat, I wasn't

too concerned about the repercussions if I said nothing. Ruth constantly threatened to tell her husband this or that. Very little came of it. When it came to real problems, Bishop Yoder was far more discerning than his wife. If you asked Ruth, our district was constantly on the brink of collapse, and every *Englischer* was plotting against the Amish. Bishop Yoder knew that wasn't true.

It may have been his age; he was much older than his wife. However, I think it had more to do with his *gut* sense. He knew when to intervene and knew when Ruth was just trying to assert her place in the community. Not that he would ever accuse his wife of such behavior. He loved Ruth and was devoted to her despite her alarmist tendencies. Lois claimed that was the biggest mystery in Holmes County—how such a kind man could be so devoted to such an irritable woman.

Ruth was irritable and strict, but underneath her prickly exterior, she was a caring person. She wanted what she believed was best for the people of the district, and in her mind, that could be achieved by following the district rules to the letter, staying out of trouble, and being the best Amish person possible. She didn't understand anyone who wouldn't or couldn't follow the rules and found anyone who questioned their Amish upbringing suspect.

"I cannot believe you agreed to go there of all places. Millie, I would have thought you knew better." She furrowed her brow to the point that her eyebrows made one solid silver line across her face. "The chalet is a disgrace and an embarrassment. It makes a mockery of the Amish's Swiss

German heritage. We don't run around in lederhosen, eat pretzels, or drink beer all day, but that's
what the chalet would like you to believe."

"I don't think the chalet is trying to be A—"

"Don't argue with me on this. The only reason
that it's here is because of the tourists who come to
Holmes County who want to experience our culture. The owners of the chalet are taking advantage of that to make money," she said, as if making
money was next to adultery in the Ten Command-
ments.

I bit my lower lip to keep from saying what I was
thinking: Everyone, *Englisch* and Amish alike, took
advantage of the tourists who came to Holmes
County. That's where everyone's income came
from. Without the Amish culture, we would just be
another rural county in Ohio with very little com-
merce to be found. The Amish brought people
here, and we and the *Englisch* knew it. Sometimes
that led to odd attractions in the county as some
entrepreneur piggybacked off the popularity of
Amish Country, but that was to be expected. In
Berlin, there was a crystal New Age shop, art gal-
leries, and a community theater hall. None of
those were Amish, but had sprung up because of
tourists.

Ruth relaxed her face, and I was relieved to see
she had two eyebrows once again.

"At least," she said, "the location of this death
proves that it has nothing to do with the Amish.
It's an *Englisch* problem, and we should leave it at
that. No *Gott*-fearing Amish person would be
found in such a place. Well, except for you, but we
all know that's Lois Henry's influence."

I frowned at her. "That may not be true. The woman who died, Paige Moorhead, was here in Holmes County for her honeymoon, but she was also here on business, business with the Amish community. We can't count every Amish person out of the sheriff department's investigation."

Ruth's perpetual frowned deepened. "What kind of business could she have had with the Amish community?"

As concisely as possible, I told Ruth about the furniture business Paige was in.

"You can't possibly think that an Amish craftsman is somehow involved in this woman's death just because she wanted to buy a few pieces of furniture. That is ridiculous. First of all, Amish people are non-violent, and second of all, it would make no sense to kill someone you hoped to work with."

I would grant her the second point, but not the first. As much as she might deny it, Ruth knew as well as I did that Amish people made as many mistakes as *Englisch,* and some of those mistakes included murder.

"The husband was there. He should be the main suspect." Her tone was matter-of-fact.

"*Ya,* but Lois doesn't believe he did it."

"Why not?" Ruth wanted to know.

"Because he's my ex-husband," Lois said as she stood beside our table with a pot of coffee in one hand and her other hand on her hip.

Ruth looked at Lois. "What are you talking about?"

"It's Rocksino-Guy, my last husband. You must

remember me talking about Rocksino-Guy from time to time."

"Unfortunately, I cannot forget," Ruth grumbled. "What are the two of you going to do about this? Lois, you have to be a suspect."

What a long way the bishop's wife had come, I marveled. She was talking about suspects. A few years ago, she probably had never even uttered the word.

"We're going to solve the murder," Lois said with certainty. I wished that I had her confidence.

Ruth stood up. "Not by yourself, you won't. You are too close to the case. We need outside thinkers." She buttoned up her cloak. "We will have to discuss this at the Double Stitch meeting. You're going to need our help."

"You're going to ask your quilting circle to help me?" Lois's mouth fell open.

"What else can we do?" Ruth said, as if she thought it was the most ridiculous question she had ever heard. "We have to solve this murder and make sure Lois stays out of prison. I won't have her going to prison." She marched to the door, grabbing her bonnet off the peg as she went. "Unfortunately, we can deal with this no sooner than Monday. Tomorrow is the Lord's Day. There is no sleuthing on the Lord's Day." She gave us a beady look, as if she dared us to investigate on Sunday. When Lois and I didn't argue with her, she left the café.

Lois set the pot of coffee on the table and dropped into the seat Ruth had just left. "Well, look at that. Ruth Yoder just might care about me."

I smiled, folded my napkin, and set it by my empty plate. I was full, but that didn't mean I wouldn't eat a few more pancakes if they were presented to me. Blueberries really were my weakness. "When are you going to tell me your great plan?"

Lois stood and picked up the pot of coffee. "After my shift. You will love it!"

I groaned. "I'm going to need more pancakes if I have to wait much longer."

"I'll let Darcy know to fire up the griddle," she said with a wink.

Chapter Thirteen

As much as I wanted more pancakes, I refrained and finished my black coffee. Thankfully, I received the coffee from Darcy, so it was served just the way I liked it. Black, no cream or sugar. Had Lois made my coffee, it would have been full of sugar, flavoring, and enough cream to float a ship. I would much rather spend my calories on pancakes than a sugary drink.

When the coffee mug was empty, I told Lois that I was going to go for a walk until it was time for her shift to end. As more and more customers came into the café, all she could do was wave. Even before I left the room, my little table at the window was taken.

When I stepped outside into the wintery air, I shivered. I dug into my coat pockets and came up with a pair of mittens so big they could have passed for blades of shovels. The fact they were mud brown didn't help, either. However, I loved them because they were a gift made by my niece, Edith. She was better with plants than she was with yarn.

"Jethro!" a voice cried as a white and black blur flew by me on the sidewalk.

Bailey King ran down the sidewalk after the pig. It seemed she was on pig-sitting detail again. "Hi, Millie!" She waved at me as she ran by.

I stood there for a moment and wondered if I should help. However, I believed Bailey knew how to handle Jethro better than anyone, even better than his mistress, Juliet Brook. Still, I thought perhaps I should lend a hand.

I followed the sound of Jethro's shouted name, and found my way to the playground next to the café.

Bailey and Jethro were squaring off. The pig was behind the swing set, and Bailey stood in front of it, pleading with him to cooperate.

"Jethro, please, let's go. Don't you want to see Nutmeg and Puff?" She said the names of her cat and rabbit, who were improbable friends of the little pig. "I'm sure they miss you. Come on, buddy."

The pig seemed to consider her words, but then, as if someone had pricked him with a pin, he suddenly took off again. He peeled around the swing set and appeared to be running straight for the road.

"Jethro!" I cried in my sternest voice. "Stop!"

The pig froze in his tracks and fell to his side in the grass as if he had been shot.

Bailey rushed over to him and scooped him up. While the pig was in her arms, she looked him over for any signs of injury. Apparently satisfied that the pig was all right, she turned to me. "H–how did you do that?" Bailey asked, staring at me with something close to awe.

"How do you think I keep Phillip and Peter in line? When talking to animals, you have to speak with conviction. Be firm, and they will show you respect."

"This is why Puff hops all over me," Bailey lamented. "I don't speak to her with conviction. She knows she can get away with just about anything."

"That could very well be the case." I patted the top of Jethro's head. The little pig, who was about the size of a toaster, breathed heavily after his exertion and buried his snout in the crook of Bailey's arm.

"Why were you chasing Jethro?" I asked. "I thought the two of you got along fine."

"We do. Most of the time," she added. "He got spooked. I took him to the jobsite, and the bulldozer rolled in to clear the land. Jethro was terrified. He took off like his tail was on fire. It was all I could do to keep up with him. It's crazy how fast that little pork chop can run." She let out a breath. "I need to work out more if I'm going to be spending more time with him."

"What about Juliet? He's her pig. Why will you be spending more time with him?"

"Juliet's church work continues to expand. She is there as much as Reverend Brook is now. It's not always appropriate to have a pig with her."

"But it's appropriate for you?" I arched a brow.

She chuckled. "I didn't say that."

"What's this jobsite you're talking about?" I asked.

Her face flushed. "We're breaking ground on

my new candy factory this week. I still can't believe it's finally happening. The contractor said the ground was soft enough to start digging, since we had a mild winter. I had expected to start in April, but when the weather cooperated, I couldn't pass up the chance to get started." She pressed her lips into a thin line. "It's exciting and terrifying, all at the same time. It's such a huge undertaking. Even though I have signed on the dotted line, and there is no going back now, I'd be lying if I didn't say I was nervous. I'm nervous, extremely nervous."

"I'm sure you are, but it is high time you did it. Your family's candy business has outgrown Swissmen Sweets."

She nodded.

"And how is your grandmother taking this?"

Bailey's happy expression faded. "She's adjusting. It's not very Amish to be so ambitious." She sighed. "It's hard to walk the line of pursuing what I want and what is acceptable to the Amish district."

I could imagine. Ruth Yoder, for one, had some choice words about Bailey's candy factory that I had heard on more than one occasion. None of those words were *gut*.

"I'm trying to handle everything myself, so she just has to focus on the candy shop, which we are keeping. I would never lose the storefront. It was my *daadi*'s pride and joy. However, there's an unbelievable amount of work involved. I would not be able to do it without Charlotte. I've been so distracted that I didn't even know about the cuckoo clock accident until Charlotte told me. Deputy Little told her that you and Lois were there when it fell."

I nodded. "It was terrible."

Tears gathered in the corners of her eyes. "That poor woman. What an awful accident."

"I don't think Deputy Little told his fiancée everything. It wasn't an accident. The deputy is thinking it was murder."

Her mouth fell open. "Murder. How could you murder someone with a cuckoo clock?"

"It looks like it was tampered with, or that's what Deputy Little told Lois and me."

"Even so. It seems like a stretch. You'd have to be very precise to kill someone in such a way, or you would have to be there." Bailey knew a thing or two about murder investigations, just as Lois and I did.

Her last comment caught my attention. Until that moment, I had never considered that the killer might have been present when Paige was killed. Bailey was right; the killer might have been there to make sure that the cuckoo fell at the perfect time.

"Who at the scene would have wanted her dead?" she mused.

I swallowed as only two people came to mind. Gerome . . . and Lois. I knew Lois hadn't done it. She had been with me the entire time, but that didn't mean others wouldn't suspect her, including the young deputy.

I considered telling Bailey my fears that Lois would be a prime suspect as Gerome's ex-wife, but I held my tongue. I trusted that Bailey wouldn't say anything, but the fewer people who saw Lois as a murder suspect, the better, and she was Charlotte's boss, cousin, and very close friend. Charlotte was engaged to the deputy. It seemed prudent under those circumstances to keep my mouth shut.

Bailey shook her head. "I have to get back to the jobsite. I was meeting with the foundation contractor when Jethro made a break for it. I now know I have to hold onto the pig the entire time when I'm around big machinery. The little bacon bundle startles easily."

"It's probably wise," I agreed. "Before you go, I was wondering if Aiden said anything to you about John Michael Smucker."

Her face clouded over. Bailey's boyfriend, Aiden Brody, happened to be Juliet's son—which was why Bailey was constantly stuck pig-sitting Jethro—and was also an Ohio Bureau Crime Investigation officer. He'd started working for the organization last summer. Before that, he had been a deputy in the county for over a decade. I knew Aiden would be aware of any drug investigations in the county.

"That's another sad story," Bailey said with a downturned mouth. "John Michael died of an overdose."

"What kind of overdose?"

"Opiates and meth, I'm afraid. Aidan said that is becoming a serious problem in the county. It's the third death this year, and it's only February."

"Who were the others?" I asked.

"I don't know their names, but they were two Englishers from Millersburg."

"Does Aidan think drugs are becoming a worse problem among the Amish?"

"He does." She frowned. "It's rarer among the Amish, but they are not immune. The BCI and the

DEA are looking into ways to deal with the problem. The fundraiser last night for the counseling center brings hope, too. Drug use is up and dangerous everywhere, but rural Ohio just doesn't have the treatment options to help people like the bigger cities do. People have to drive over an hour for help, and if the person is Amish and can't find the transportation they need, it's even more complicated. I'm glad Harvest is stepping up. The counseling center is not going to help just the village, but the whole county. It will even benefit the state. That's why BCI is involved."

"How will it help the state?"

"According to Aiden, meth used to be a drug found more often in rural areas. Now, it is being moved from rural counties, like Holmes, to be sold in the bigger cities. Slowing it down here will keep it from reaching other corners of the state." Her shoulders sagged. "But the problem will never completely go away. From what Aiden said, the drug dealers are constantly finding new ways to move their products. They keep law enforcement on their toes."

I nodded. "Lois and I were at the dinner last night, but we came toward the end of it, because Lois closed the café for Darcy."

"Aiden and I were there earlier. He was able to come up from Columbus for the fundraiser but had to go straight back after we ate." She smiled. "It was nice to spend Valentine's Day with him, even if his visit was short. I'm glad you were able to go, Millie. It's very important that both the English and the Amish get behind this idea of the counseling center."

"I agree," I said. "Lois and I both felt we had to be there. I was surprised to see Elijah Smucker there, too. He was alone."

"John Michael's father?" She raised her eyebrows. "I'm surprised, as well. From what I've heard, he's barely left his home since his son died."

"He was there," I said. "I hope that's a good sign for him, too."

"I hope it's a sign that he's doing better. I can't imagine how he feels. Many parents blame themselves in these situations, but the younger Amish I know who were friends with John Michael said he was beyond help. I don't know if I believe that anyone is beyond help, but it would have been very difficult for his father to reach him without some major intervention."

"I'm sorry to hear that."

Jethro wiggled in Bailey's arms. "I was, too." She looked down at the pig. "I should take him back and finish up that meeting with the contractor. To be honest, I feel I'm in over my head with this whole thing. There are so many decisions to make, and I'm learning as I go."

I patted her arm and then scratched Jethro's head for good measure. "You'll be just fine. You have a level head and make wise decisions."

She gave me a half smile as if she wasn't so sure of that. "I appreciate the vote of confidence."

After Bailey left, I continued my walk around town. I had told Lois that I didn't mind going with her to the center of the village when we left the chalet, but now, I wished that I had been dropped off at home when I'd had the chance. I felt at loose ends, which was a feeling I hated. Amish women were people of action. Being idle felt wrong.

Lois had plans for the investigation, but that didn't mean I couldn't make some plans of my own while I waited for her to finish up at the café. I might not be able to investigate the murder at the moment, but that wasn't the only problem in Harvest keeping me up at night. Walking by the church for a second time, I knew just where to start.

Chapter Fourteen

The *Englisch* church on the square was always open during the day. There had been a time when the congregation considered keeping the church locked because of the increase of crime in Holmes County, but Reverend Brook would not allow it. He strongly believed that the church building should be open as much as possible to the *Englisch*, Amish, and people of all walks of life.

Reverend Brook's compassion and caring for the community were two of the characteristics I most admired about him. He carried out his ministry in his own quiet way. He was a timid, soft-spoken man, who wasn't shouting from the pulpit every Sunday morning. He cared about his flock.

I realized as I opened the large purple door at the top of the church steps that he was much like Bishop Yoder from my district. Both were steady and quiet leaders, and both had married women with strong opinions and big personalities. The comparison between Juliet Brook and Ruth Yoder made me smile, but I decided to keep that conclusion under my bonnet. I didn't think Juliet or Ruth would appreciate it.

As I stepped into the church, I stood in an entryway. To my left was the hall that led to the stairs. At the bottom of those stairs was the fellowship hall, where the spaghetti dinner was held. There was still a faint scent of marinara in the air, and even though I had eaten more blueberry pancakes than I cared to admit, the smell made my mouth water. As an Amish cook, spaghetti wasn't something I ate often, so it had been a real treat.

Directly in front of me were the blond wood double doors with large windows that led into the sanctuary. I opened one door and slipped inside, taking a moment to look around the room.

Even though the Amish did not worship in church, I couldn't deny its beauty. The thirty-foot walls were pristinely white, and huge blond wooden beams crisscrossed the cathedral ceiling. At the front of the church was a wide platform with a pulpit, altar, and small lectern on the opposite side from the pulpit. Behind all three was the pipe organ. Its façade was the same color as the wooden beams. I imagined Charlotte Weaver on that bench seat playing the organ. Her love of music was what had initiated her decision to leave the Amish faith. The district she'd grown up in was much more conservative than mine and didn't allow musical instruments.

A door behind the pulpit opened, and Reverend Brook came out through it. He was staring at a stack of papers in his hands and frowning at them.

"*Gude mariye*," I said.

"Oh, Millie!" Reverend Brook juggled his papers, saving them from falling onto the platform. "I didn't see you there. I was too absorbed in my work." He chuckled. "Is there something that I can help you with? Were you looking for Juliet? She's leading a women's Bible study today in the church library, but I can tell her when she's finished that you were here."

I removed my bonnet and held it lightly against my waist so that I would not bend the brim. "I actually stopped by to ask about the drug counseling center. The spaghetti dinner was such a success, and there were many Amish there. I wondered how our community could be involved."

His eyes lit up. "Oh, well, that's so nice to hear. We have been overjoyed with the outpouring of support for the center." He stepped off the platform. "Would you like to see the space?"

"I'd love to," I said.

He led me out of the sanctuary and down a hallway I had never been in before. "This is the Sunday-school wing of the church," he explained. "Ever since I took over this pulpit, I have wanted to use it for something else during the week. It seems a shame that all this space stands empty six days a week."

"So you hit on the idea of the counseling center?" I asked as I admired the brightly colored valentines that lined the wall. The congregation's children must have made them.

"Not at first. I have been doing substance abuse counseling myself at a county community center. I see the impact it has on people's lives, and I wanted to bring that to Harvest. After speaking with the church leadership team about it, we agreed that this was a bigger issue than just our congregation could manage, so we threw out a wider net to include the village proper and all the Amish districts, including yours, that wished to be involved. The counseling center will be using our space, but is not officially affiliated with the church. We wanted people from all faiths to feel welcome."

He stopped in front of a door and opened it. He stepped back and allowed me to go in first.

The space was not at all as I expected. I had thought it would have a clinical doctor's office feel to it, but it wasn't like that at all. The room was cozy. Large couches were placed around the room. Curtains hung on the windows, and colorful throw pillows were everywhere. A giant beanbag chair, which could have held four adults, sat in one corner. There was a large conference table in another, but it was made homier with a bouquet of pink and red carnations in the middle. It felt like someone's living room.

"This is the main room for group meetings and staff planning, but we have three much smaller, private rooms that we will be using for one-on-one counseling."

"It's very nice. I think it would be a comfortable environment to talk."

He smiled. "That's what we are hoping for. The counseling center where I was volunteering before was very sterile. A more welcoming environment will help clients open up."

"It all looks very nice and will benefit so many people. How can the Amish community help?"

He smiled. "It's so kind of you to ask. Bishop Yoder has been very involved already, and I'm grateful for his support, as he is one of the most influential bishops in Harvest, if not the entire county. What we really need is education about the dangers of drugs and alcohol abuse for the Amish. We need it for everyone, of course, but English kids hear it in school. It's not a taboo topic to discuss in the English world, at least not as much as it is in the Amish world."

I had to agree with him there. I knew many Amish who wanted to believe that drugs and alcohol could not touch their children because of their faith, but that just wasn't the case.

"With the recent increase of drugs in the county, this is becoming more and more of a problem. So our plan is two-fold—education of the general population, especially young people, and counseling for addicts to help them back onto the right path."

I nodded. "I was surprised to see Elijah Smucker at the spaghetti dinner."

"I think a lot of people were, but Elijah is quite interested in the center. He came to me on more than one occasion to talk about his concerns for his son. It does break my heart the center was not open in time to help John Michael. I suggested other options for help, but I got the impression that Elijah wasn't comfortable with any help outside of Harvest. He's a quiet man who was torn between what he felt he could do as an Amish man and what he wanted to do as a father. I was very glad to see him at the dinner and supporting the center in that way, especially when it could be argued that we failed him."

"You didn't fail him. You just weren't open yet."

"I'm afraid that feels like the same thing." He shook his head.

"Did Elijah ever go to his bishop about his concerns for his son?" I asked. The Smucker family weren't members of my district, and I didn't know how progressive or conservative their community was in comparison to mine. My district was Old Order Amish, but since Bishop Yoder had taken over the helm after his late father, he'd made many changes that put us more in line with progressive communities. Most of those didn't have to do with technology, but had to do with his concern for the church members. He gave women more of a voice; I guessed that Ruth had had something to do with that, as well as the tragic death of Galilee Zook forty years ago. He was also more willing to address the problems in the community like drug abuse, which would never have been spoken about before.

Elijah's district could be quite different from mine.

"Not that I know of. My guess is no. His district is very conservative. I'm not even sure if his bishop would approve of him being at the spaghetti dinner last night."

Reverend Brook walked me back to the church door. I was glad of that; I never would have been able to find my way out through the maze of hallways and classrooms I found in the Sunday school wing. As we went, he pointed out the smaller rooms that would be used for one-on-one counseling.

"And this is just a start," he said with enthusiasm. "I envision more community use of this building during the week. What better way to do God's work than invite people into the church? We don't have to preach the Gospel to share it."

"It sounds like a wonderful plan," I agreed.

At the door, he said, "I'm glad you stopped by, Millie. It will be Amish like you who will make a difference to your community on this matter, because you will let others know about this resource. We have to look drug abuse straight in the eye to fight it. It's when we turn away that evil wins."

Chapter Fifteen

I walked back to the Sunbeam Café, thinking over all that I had learned. The counseling center did sound like a great addition to the community. It was going to help a lot of people. However, I couldn't help being a little sad that it hadn't been in place fast enough to help John Michael Smucker. Would he still be alive if it had been open?

I took a breath and reminded myself it was not my job to question. An Amish proverb came to mind. "It is better to hold out a helping hand than point a finger." That's what I intended to do.

As soon as I stepped inside the café, I spotted Lois with her coat on, large purse slung over her shoulder, and her hands on her hips. "It's about time you came back. We have a murder to solve."

I cocked my head. "I wasn't gone more than an hour. I thought you'd be busy well into the afternoon."

"I thought so, too, but Iris came into work early. Heavens knows, I was grateful to see her!"

I saw Iris Young in the back of the café, filling coffee mugs and chatting with customers. She was hard to miss with her auburn hair and delicate features. She was one of the most beautiful women in the district, though she didn't seem to know it.

I waved at her, and she waved back. Iris was a lovely wife and the mother of one teenaged son. I had matched her and her husband Carter Young two decades ago, and the couple was a great success. Iris was also a *gut* friend of mine and a member of the quilting circle.

Iris filled one more coffee cup before winding her way through the café table to reach us. "Millie, it is so nice to see you. I'm glad that I was able to steal away and come to work today. I knew that you and Lois would have some . . ." She lowered her voice. "Investigation to do."

I raised my brow. "You know about the murder?" I whispered.

"Oh *ya*! Ruth came to my house and told me that it will be a main topic of conversation at the Double Stitch meeting. She was even the one who suggested I work at the café today."

"Will wonders never cease," Lois mused.

I should have known. When Ruth Yoder says she's going to do something, she does it.

Millie went into the kitchen to tell Darcy we were leaving, and Iris touched my arm. "Millie, when you have a private moment, I would like to talk to you."

My eyes went wide. "What about?"

"I can't tell you here."

I wanted to ask her more, but a man held up an empty coffee mug. "Miss, can I get a refill?"

Iris gave me a pained expression and then grabbed the coffeepot from the counter.

"I'm ready to roll," Lois said, coming out of the kitchen. "Darcy and Iris have got this."

I wondered what Darcy thought when she heard her grandmother was on another case. I didn't have time to ask, because Lois ushered me out the door.

When we were outside and walking toward her car, she said, "When I was between customers, I called Gerome." She unlocked her car, and we got in. "I asked him for the list of the furniture makers Paige had planned to see this weekend. He found her work files and gave it to me." She removed a piece of scratch paper from her pocket and handed it over. "The police can focus on Gerome while we work the Amish angle like always. It shouldn't take too long. There are only three names."

I must have looked unsure about this plan, probably because I was.

"What?"

"I'm not sure how much of an Amish angle this case has. Paige wasn't Amish, and neither is Gerome."

"And that's exactly what Deputy Little and the sheriff's department will be thinking. They might ignore those leads because they're too far-fetched. We won't fall for that. We investigate the more unlikely leads."

Lois was right. We did have a tendency to follow leads, even if they seemed ridiculous.

"We have to go now, because we can't wait until tomorrow to follow these leads. All the shops will be closed."

She was right on that account. Holmes County virtually shut down on Sunday. Just a handful of *Englisch* businesses stayed open, but all the Amish ones were closed in honor of the Lord's Day.

I peered down at the list in my hand. In Lois's hasty scrawl were three business names. Smucker Dressers, Swiss Carpentry, and Elon's Warehouse. The business that jumped out at me was Smucker Dressers. I pointed at the name. "Is this related to Elijah Smucker?"

She shrugged. "I don't know, but the thought struck me, too. I was hoping you would know since he's Amish."

"He's Amish, but not a member of my district. I know very little about him, except for what happened to his son and what I learned from Reverend Brook."

"You were doing a little sleuthing without me?" She gasped.

"I wasn't sleuthing. I didn't know about this lead and still don't know if Smucker Dressers is related to Elijah. There aren't that many Amish surnames, you know. Many of them are very common."

Lois nodded. "Tell that to every Yoder."

"I went to the church to see how the Amish community could help with the counseling center. My visit didn't have anything to do with Paige or Gerome."

"Is Ruth going to like that you were asking how the community could be involved? Counseling doesn't sound all that Amish to me."

"Ruth is not in charge of the district. Bishop Yoder is."

She snorted as if she didn't believe that.

"The only way to find out if Elijah and Smucker Dressers are connected is to go there," I said. "Are these businesses in Harvest?"

"No," she said. "They're peppered around the county. Charm, Millersburg, and Berlin. I looked up the addresses on my phone before we left. We're headed to Elon's Warehouse first. It's the closest, located in Berlin. I'm not sure we'll make it to all three before closing time, since they are so distant from each other."

As if on cue, her phone squawked, telling her to turn onto a county road.

I nodded. Of the three businesses, Elon's Warehouse sounded the most familiar to me. If it was in Berlin, that could explain why. I might have seen the shop's sign. Downtown Berlin was the busiest and most touristy part of Holmes County. There were so many shops, signs, and commotion; it could become overwhelming if a person preferred peace and quiet as I did. I rarely went there and even chose to take the long way home while traveling around the county to avoid driving through it.

Before long, Lois inched her car into the traffic of Berlin, and I was on the lookout for signs to indicate the direction of the warehouse. I knew Lois's phone would direct us, but like any sixty-something Amish woman, I didn't put much trust in such contraptions. Besides, I couldn't forget the time when Lois's phone had tried to direct us into a lake because it was the shortest distance between two points. Technology wasn't foolproof.

On a corner featuring a dress shop and a Christmas store, there was a hand-painted sign on the right pointing toward the turn for Elon's Warehouse.

"I think it's that way," I said, pointing to the sign.

Lois glanced at her phone, which was tethered to the dashboard with a slim piece of plastic. "My phone is telling me to go straight."

"The sign is telling you to turn. I believe the sign," I said, still pointing.

"Okay, we will do it the old-fashioned way and follow the signs. I know you're still chafing at the GPS over the lake incident," she said, as if it had been nothing to worry over.

"We could have drowned!"

"Oh, I wouldn't have driven into the lake." She paused. "At least, I don't think I would."

I didn't find that particularly comforting.

Lois's phone yelled at her to make a U-turn, but we pressed on down the road, led by the signs. Before too long, another sign appeared as we drove farther away from the congestion of downtown. This sign indicated a turn on a gravel road and that the warehouse was three miles away.

"Turn left," the phone said.

"It seems my GPS and your signs are finally in agreement," Lois said happily.

"Finally," I said with a relieved sigh. Personally, I found it more than a little concerning that the GPS was that off.

The warehouse was huge. I guessed it was the size of two fifty-foot pole barns put together. It was on a large, open piece of land, and appeared to be a newer construction.

Lois parked the car in the gravel lot. "Wow, this place is massive. What do you think is inside there?"

I shrugged. Anything could be hidden in a building so large.

We got out of the car, and before we could even make it to the huge open garage door of the warehouse, a young Amish man came out to stop us. He couldn't have been a day over eighteen. He was tall and slim, and looked as if he was used to chasing people away.

"You can't park there," he said in English. "We don't sell directly to customers. We are wholesale." He had a frown on his face as he pointed to a sign indicating just that.

Lois read the sign, but then turned back to the young man. "We're not here about buying for ourselves. We want to talk to someone about the sale you planned to the Delpont family for their large chain of stores in Cleveland." She gave him her best disapproving elder face.

"Oh! I didn't know you were from the Delponts."

We weren't from the Delponts, but neither Lois nor I corrected him. I tried not to think of silence as a sin of omission.

His face cleared. "I'm so sorry. Please come in."

We stepped into the large building and suddenly, I was hit with the overpowering scent of an Amish furniture store. It was a mix of sawdust, lemon oil, and polyurethane.

"I'm sorry we don't have anywhere for you to sit. Please wait here, and I will get my father. He has been waiting for you. He's very appreciative of the partnership."

"It has been lucrative for both parties," Lois said.

"Lois," I hissed. "It seems to me the young man thinks you represent the Delpont family in some way."

"I know," she said with a gleam in her eye. "What a great stroke of luck that is! We will get a lot further with them if they think we come from a wealthy furniture empire. Money talks."

Before I could tell her what a bad idea it was, a tall, thin Amish man with a black beard walked toward us. He was followed by the young man we'd met earlier. Seeing them so close together, it was obvious they had to be father and son.

"I expected you to be younger," the older man said with a slight frown at Lois, making it clear that although he'd done business with Paige, he'd never met her face-to-face.

Someone who wasn't accustomed to Amish ways might have found such a comment offensive, but it was not unusual for Amish—men in particular— to be blunt. Lois knew this and was unfazed.

"People tell me I have a young voice," Lois said.

He frowned. "*Ya*, I suppose so. I am Elon Troyer, and this is my warehouse. You have already met my son Joshua." He cleared his throat. "We're so very glad you're here. It's *gut* to finally meet you in person. We loved the ideas of your new designs. Our craftsmen and carpenters are already hard at work on some samples for you."

I hid a cringe. It seemed that Elon not only

thought Lois worked for Paige's company, but he thought she was Paige.

"Yes, I was hoping to see those samples," Lois said in her most businesslike voice.

"*Ya,* of course. Let's go look at them now, and then we can discuss terms and prices. You mentioned you were thinking of a five-hundred-piece order? It's going to take some time. I have dozens of carpenters working on your project, but it will still take time."

"Five hundred pieces!" Lois gasped.

He paled. "Isn't that what you said? I am certain that's what I heard."

"Oh." Lois gathered herself. "Oh, yes, that number sounds right."

I frowned as I noticed Lois taking care with her words, and not directly claiming she was Paige. However, she was doing little to discourage Elon's assumption. In truth, I did little, too.

Elon began to walk through the warehouse. "Your specifications have been quite unusual, so it's taken a little bit of time to explain to the craftsmen what you wanted and why. However, I think you will be happy with the results."

What were those unusual specifications? We would soon find out.

Chapter Sixteen

The warehouse was a maze of furniture. There were thousands of pieces, all organized by like items. All the dressers were together, and all the desks, as well. Most were made in the traditional Amish style of maple, polished to a high sheen and then sealed with polyurethane or another sealant. However, there were more surprising pieces, too, in both dark and bright colors.

"I didn't expect so much variety," Lois said.

"*Ya,*" he said. "Our craftsmen can make any piece of furniture you want in any style. We don't have to stick to the Amish look. We're about to make a big push to export our items out of state. We have orders for store chains as far away as Texas and Florida. It's an exciting time for our business."

Lois removed her gloves and dropped them in her purse. "I hope this new venture will not distract you from the work you've been making for the Delpont family."

He paled. "Oh no, it never would. Your family is an essential client to our business. We always place your orders at the head of the line."

Lois nodded as if she were a bishop and a member of her church had pleased her.

"Is the warehouse fairly new?" I asked.

He glanced at me. If he was wondering why Lois had an Amish companion, he didn't say anything. Though the Amish could be blunt, they didn't pry into strangers' affairs. I, of course, was an exception to this Amish trait.

"It has been here less than a year. It was finished last April. In that time, the business has grown and surpassed our expectations. Exporting across state lines is proof of that. A few months ago, we wouldn't have considered such a lofty goal, but now we can think even bigger. We're looking to export into Canada as our next move. The paperwork is tricky, but we will get there."

"You keep talking about growing and expansion; this surprises me," Lois said. "It doesn't seem like a very Amish approach. Usually the Amish work to be comfortable, but not much beyond that. What you're describing sounds like building an empire."

"I would not call it an empire, but I see it as a service to my community. Whether we like it or not, we Amish have to play the *Englisch* game when it comes to business if we are to survive. The *Englisch* are not going to wait for us. They never have."

It seemed to me his goal was to get ahead. In the

Englisch world, that attitude would be widely accepted and even praised. In the Amish world, it was different. Getting ahead and personal success weren't as important as being a *gut* church member, friend, and neighbor. Putting yourself second was the desired behavior.

He went on, "I like to think I'm making it possible for those who want to live a traditional Amish life to also make a decent wage. The larger our reputation grows, the more we can charge for our pieces. I pass the increase on to the craftsmen. They do the real work to make this business run the way it does."

I supposed in his own way, Elon was taking care of others by providing this service, but I expected he was doing very well, too. If he was a member of my church district, I could only guess what Ruth Yoder would have to say about it. Actually, that wasn't true. I knew exactly what Ruth would say, and none of it would be welcomed by Elon.

"It is our plan to make further connections between Amish craftsmen and *Englisch* sellers. We're a bridge between the two. The Amish create the pieces and bring them to us to then sell. There are many craftsmen who would like to avoid dealing with *Englisch* sellers. They just want to make their wares and be left alone. I can't say I blame them. Sometimes, I wonder why I stick with it. The *Englisch* sellers can be demanding at best and rude at worst."

We walked by an office, where we could see a computer and printer through the window. Lois pointed it out. "Do you have any English working for you?"

"*Nee,* I'm New Order Amish, and in my district, I'm permitted to use a computer for work. I would not be able to make this business so successful without it. I even went to a few years of business school when I was in *Rumspringa,* before I committed to the faith. That experience was invaluable. However, I always planned to commit to the Amish way. My *Rumspringa* just made it possible for me to learn enough about the *Englisch* so I could make a successful business model, advantageous for both the *Englisch* and the Amish."

"How did you get into furniture selling?" I asked.

Again, he gave me a look that asked why I was there, but he answered. "My father was a carpenter and would sell his furniture to stores one by one on consignment. I watched as time and time again, he would become overwhelmed by working with *Englisch* shopkeepers. Many of those shopkeepers took advantage of his *gut* nature. I knew there had to be a better way to protect artisans like him, because I believe people who make furniture are true artists. They put as much love and heart into a stool as a painter puts into his painting."

"I think it's a wonderful concept, and I know the Delpont family is looking forward to partnering with you on this new project," Lois said.

"And I am with them. We have the models of the pieces you requested in the back room, if you would like to take a look."

"You bet I would," Lois said with gusto.

At the end of the large warehouse was a metal door that looked like it would withstand a tornado.

Before going through the door, Lois whispered, "I feel like we are going into a bomb shelter."

I had never been in a bomb shelter, nor did I ever want to, so I would have to take my friend's word for it.

The door led us into a smaller room that was as plain as the main warehouse, but was empty except for three pieces of furniture: a desk, a small table, and a dresser.

"Here they are," he said with great pride, as if he were showing us the most beautiful piece of furniture he had ever seen.

Lois and I shared a look. I knew we must have been thinking the same thing. To be honest, the pieces were a little underwhelming. There was no question they were well-built and sturdily made. Lois could have danced on top of each one and they wouldn't have even squeaked, but they had no character, Amish or otherwise, to them.

"This is what the Delpont family ordered?" she asked.

Elon's face fell. "You sent us plans down to the letter, and we followed them. We made all of the special requests."

Lois raised her brow. "Can we see those special features?"

"Of course." He walked over to the desk and tapped the side.

Nothing happened.

Lois and I shared a look.

He then walked to the other side of the desk and tapped in the same way.

To our amazement, the middle of the desktop

popped open. Inside was a small, empty, velvet-lined compartment.

Lois stepped forward to have a better look. "This is incredible," she said. "You can't see the seams at all."

His color returned to normal. "Yes, our craftsmen are very talented. Honestly, when you asked for this secret compartment in the desks, I didn't think it could be done without at least a hint that something might be hidden in the piece. However, our talented artisans proved me wrong. It was confirmation to me that I was working with the very best furniture makers in the county."

"Why did the Delpont family request this secret compartment?" I asked.

He glanced at Lois as if he expected her to have the answer.

"You can go ahead and tell her. I would like to hear your interpretation," she said, as if she already knew.

"Well, Paige"—he glanced at Lois—"told me many of their clients have valuable possessions they plan to keep hidden from home invasion. It could be jewelry, money, or papers. Anything at all. They need a place to hide these items where a burglar would never look."

"Wouldn't it be better to put it all in a safe or the bank?" I asked.

"I was told that the customers asked for this," Elon said, looking at Lois again. She gave a slight nod of her head, as if what he'd said was right in line with what she was thinking. However, I knew this information was as new to her as it was to me.

Elon closed the secret compartment by pressing

down on it. "I have learned not to question the whims of the *Englisch*. They change too frequently."

Lois ran her hand over the top of the desk. "Not a single sign. How does it work? What are the mechanics you used?"

"There are a number of levers inside the desk that trigger the door. It is much like a clock."

A clock. My heart constricted. Did he mean like a cuckoo clock? Like the one that killed Paige?

"It's really an ingenious design," he said. "The Amish craftsmen assigned to the work were impressed with how much thought went into it."

"Where did the idea come from?" I asked.

He glanced at me. "Haven't the two of you talked about this before? If you know each other, shouldn't you both know?"

"I wanted Millie's honest opinion on the pieces with no input from me," Lois said. "So I told her nothing about these secret compartments."

Elon nodded. "I suppose that makes sense. Paige said she found jewelry boxes made by a local artisan with secret compartments, and she wanted to expand the idea into furniture. When she shared the idea with me, I knew craftsmen who would be perfect for this challenge." He looked at Lois. "I hope we've exceeded your expectations."

"I've never seen anything like it," Lois said. "We should go to our next stop. Now we know what we're looking for."

"Next stop?"

"There are two more furniture sellers who have made similar items. We are paying them a visit next."

"There are other companies you're talking to?" His expression turned dark as he leaned against the side of the desk. "Why would you do that? We were in agreement that I was the best person for the job and for—" He looked at me as if he wasn't sure he should say more. "And for the other project."

Before I could ask what the other project was, Lois said, "You weren't in agreement with me. This wasn't my idea."

He gasped. "But you contacted me. This *was* your idea. Everything was your idea."

I inched toward the door in case Lois and I had to make a run for it.

"Oh, I'm not Paige. My name is Lois Henry, and we are here because Paige was not able to come."

His face turned red. "Not able to come? Why not? Why didn't she let me know? We have been working tirelessly to meet her strict deadline. The designs she requested are deceptively simple, but the secret compartments are challenging to create. It's an insult after all our work that she wouldn't even bother to show up."

"I can see you're upset," Lois said. "But Paige isn't here for a very good reason."

He folded his arms. "I would like to hear what that good reason is."

"She's dead," Lois said without preamble.

He slid off the side of the desk onto the concrete floor.

Chapter Seventeen

"**A**re you all right?" Lois asked, peering down at the Amish man splayed on his back.

He groaned and got to his feet without acknowledging the hand Lois offered him. "Dead? How is she dead?"

"That's the interesting bit," Lois said. "It was the cuckoo clock that got her."

I suppressed a sigh. From Lois's tone, I could tell she had been waiting a while to use that line.

Confusion covered his face, and I thought I had better speak up before Lois said something else to make matters worse. "She and her husband were staying at the Munich Chalet. From what her husband said, she had every intention of seeing you this week. Unfortunately, this morning, there was an accident. Part of the cuckoo clock fell and killed her."

"How awful. Where does that leave me with her

family's furniture store? She was my only contact with the business."

I noted that his first thought had been for himself and his own troubles, not with Paige or her friends and family.

"I'll be your contact going forward," a deep voice said from behind us.

A stocky *Englisch* man with a full blond beard and dark eyes stood in the doorway.

"Who are you?" Elon asked.

"I'm Ronan Delpont. Paige was my sister."

"How did you get in here?" Elon asked.

"The garage door was open, and when I asked for the owner, one of your Amish workers said you were in here."

Elon scowled, as if he didn't like the idea of his staff giving up his location so easily. "They just told me your sister is dead. Is that true?" He shot a glare at Lois as if to say he wouldn't be surprised to find her lying to him about Paige's death.

"It is. I can't believe it. She was more than a sister to me; she was my best friend." Ronan's voice cracked. "Her new husband, Gerome, called me not long after it happened. I left immediately to come here. It's only a two-hour drive, even with traffic. It made sense for me to come, since I was the one who worked the closest with her, but I'd be lying if I said it was easy." He closed his eyes, as if he were holding back tears. "I'm sorry. I thought I got all my crying out on the drive here."

"We are so sorry for your loss," I said. He was the first person we'd met who demonstrated profound sadness over Paige's death. Not even her husband was so broken up over it. It made me feel a little bit better that she had meant something to her brother, at least. At the same time, I reminded myself not to judge Gerome and the way he grieved.

"Shouldn't you be talking to Gerome?" Lois asked. "Aren't there arrangements to discuss? I'm surprised this would be your first stop."

He cleared his throat. "It's not. I've already spoken with Gerome, for whatever it might be worth. Not much, I can assure you. He'd been married to my sister for two days, and she's already dead. My only comfort is he won't see a penny of her money."

"Oh?" Lois said, as if she only had a mild interest in these details. I knew different. She wanted to know everything, just as I did.

Ronan looked at Lois and me. "Who are the two of you and how do you know my sister? How do you know Gerome?"

Lois shifted back and forth on her feet.

"You don't know them?" Elon asked. "They work for your company. I've just been going over the order Paige made with us."

"No, they don't," Ronan said. "I've never seen them before in my life."

Elon wrung his hands. "But they arrived and said they were here in Paige's place."

Lois held up one finger. "No, we never said that. First, you assumed I was Paige, and then you assumed I was here on her behalf."

"But that's what you said," Elon argued.

"No, it's what you thought I said. I said I came because she could not. It's very different."

I took another step toward the door. I thought the white lies were going to end badly for Lois, and me by extension.

Elon's face was red as canned sweet peppers. This was definitely not going to end well. It was time to make our exit.

"We should let the two of you talk business. Again, we're so sorry for the loss of your sister. You have our condolences." I grabbed Lois's hand and turned to Elon. "Your furniture is beautiful. *Danki* for the tour, but we should be going."

Ronan jumped in front of the doorway. Unfortunately, it was the only way in or out of the windowless room. "You're not going anywhere until you tell me how you knew my sister. Someone killed her, and I want to know who it was. If either of you know, you have to tell me."

Lois adjusted her large purse on her shoulder, and for the briefest second, I feared she would whack him with it. I didn't believe violence would help our relations with the Delpont family at all.

"Paige was married to my ex-husband, and we were at the chalet when she was killed. We're just trying to help the police sort it out. In a case like this, there's no time to waste. Trust me, we know."

"Two old women are helping the police?" Ronan asked, as if it were the most ridiculous thing he had ever heard.

This comment rubbed Lois the wrong way, and she lowered her purse from her shoulder into swinging position. "I will have you know Millie and I have solved *several* murders in Holmes County. Google us if you need the facts. The streets are safer here because of us. When you got crime, you call us."

It really didn't work that way at all, but I wasn't going to correct her in front of these men.

"Super grannies?" Ronan asked, as if he might laugh.

Lois adjusted her grip on the purse strap. "If the name fits. Like Millie said, we are sorry for your loss. We would love to talk more about your sister. We will have a better chance of solving her murder if we know more about her. We can be found at the Sunbeam Café, and if we aren't there, we will be soon."

A strange look crossed Ronan's face. It was a mix of disbelief, sadness, and something else. Worry? Fear?

"Thank you again, Elon. We're so sorry for the misunderstanding," I said as I ushered Lois toward the door. "Have a *gut* afternoon."

Thankfully, Ronan stepped out of the way, and I was able to maneuver Lois through it before she hit anything or anyone with that purse of hers.

When we'd reached the main part of the warehouse, Lois was seething. "Super grannies? Who does that young man think he is? He should have more respect for his elders."

I kept hold of Lois's arm and propelled her to the large open garage door. Two Amish men were unloading dining room chairs from a wagon and stared at us as we came out of the building.

Once we'd reached the safety of Lois's car, I finally let out a sigh of relief. "We really should not be impersonating other people. That could get us into trouble. Honestly, I'm surprised they took it so well."

She started the car. "He made an assumption. It's not my job to correct everyone who makes the wrong assumption."

I leaned my head back against the headrest.

"Where should we go now?" Lois asked as she directed the car out onto the gravel road.

"Of the two businesses left, Swiss Carpentry is the closest. It's in Charm. I don't think we'll make it to the third business before five, when everything closes for the weekend."

She sighed. "Probably not, and that's disappointing, because I had wanted to speak to Elijah Smucker the most."

I had to, especially after my conversation with Reverend Brook.

Lois idled at a stop sign at the end of the road. "We'll have to wait until Monday to visit Smucker Dressers. I hate to put off sleuthing."

"It's for the Sabbath tomorrow." I thought of Elijah Smucker. "And the Smucker family has been through enough recently. Waiting an extra day won't be a bad thing."

"Very well. You're right as always. It's an infuriating quality," she grumbled, but then her face cleared. "But Swiss Carpentry, here we come. Let's see what other trouble we can find."

I groaned.

Chapter Eighteen

The drive between the warehouse and the carpentry shop was twenty minutes, but we were slowed down by the traffic in Berlin. Even in cold February, the village was busy with Saturday afternoon shoppers. I had to remind myself it was still Valentine's weekend, and many of the tourists might be in Holmes County for a romantic getaway. After we'd made our way through the congestion downtown, Lois hit the gas, and we made it to Charm in record time. I must admit that I had to close my eyes a couple of times when she made turns.

Charm was much smaller than Berlin, but it also had a good number of popular shops and a handful of restaurants, all near its main street. Unlike Harvest, which had the square, there was no central focal point of the village.

However, the village quilt shop was one of my favorites. The proprietress, Netty Dienner, found some of the most interesting-patterned fabrics. I knew as an Amish quilter, I was expected to make plain quilts of solid-colored blocks, but I secretly loved it when customers asked for a pattern. Flowered fabric was my favorite. It was so soothing to work with a bright, cheerful flower-covered fabric on a cold winter's night. It reminded me that spring always came like the proverb said, "No winter lasts forever; no spring skips its turn."

Lois and I drove by the quilt shop, and there was a sign in the window announcing a Valentine's Day sale. Lois saw it, too. "We should pop in there," she said.

"Do we have time?" I asked, even though I very much wanted to stop into the quilt shop to see what new fabric they had in stock. "It's almost four now."

"We can make the time. I see that gleam in your eye when you see fabric. I get the same look when I see vintage furniture."

This was true. Lois collected furniture and had dozens upon dozens of pieces crowding her small rental house in Harvest. In fact, she could barely walk through her own living room because there were so many chairs in it. It was a point of contention between her and her granddaughter, Darcy. Darcy wanted her to get rid of all of it, but Lois couldn't part with a single piece. Each piece had a story about where she'd found it, and how much she'd saved when she'd made the purchase. There might come a time when she wouldn't have anywhere to put the pieces she found. Who knew what she would do then?

Lois parked in the last open parking spot in front of the quilt shop.

"Let's go to the Swiss Carpentry first," I said. "If there's time, we will come back to the quilt shop."

Lois nodded.

Before we even got out of the car, the quilt shop door opened. Netty Dienner stood in the doorway. She was a plump, petite woman with pink cheeks and a bright smile. "Millie Fisher, I haven't seen you in months. You come on in right now."

I glanced at Lois as if to ask her what we should do. It would seem rude just to walk by Netty when she called us into the shop, but we only had an hour before Swiss Carpentry closed.

"We won't be long," Lois said. "We'll get to the woodworker's shop before it closes."

I hoped she was right.

Lois and I walked up to the door.

I grinned. "Perhaps because I bought so much fabric the last time I was here, I still haven't used it all. I bought too much."

"You can never have too much fabric," Netty said with a sparkle in her eye.

The cozy warmth of the potbelly stove in the corner of the shop filled the room. There was a coffee service area with coffee and quilt-pattern sugar cookies right next to it. Netty did everything she could to make her customers as comfortable as possible when they stopped by her store. I wondered why it had taken me so long to come back, too much fabric notwithstanding.

Lois made a beeline for the cookies. "I'm starving! Millie and I have been sleuthing all day, and it really works up an appetite. I need the strength to continue with the case."

Netty followed Lois over to the coffee station and poured her a paper cup of coffee. "Would you like one too, Millie?"

"Yes, please, but no cookies for me. I already had my allowance of sweets this morning in a double stack of blueberry pancakes."

Lois swallowed her bite of cookie and shook her head. "I don't believe in a sweet allowance. I'm two years from seventy. That means my sweets are unlimited."

"Same here," Netty said, taking her own sugar cookie with a rolling block pattern of icing on it. "You came at the perfect time. A tourist busload of quilters just left. I was about to sit down with a cup of coffee and cookie myself to recover. Those buses are good for my piggy bank but remind me that I'm not a spring chicken anymore."

"Who wants to be a chicken in any season?" Lois asked.

Netty laughed. "What are you two up to today? Sleuthing, did you say?"

Not wanting to start that conversation with Netty, I asked, "Where's Faith? Wasn't she here to help you when the bus arrived? I'm sure you needed the extra help. Those bus tours can be demanding."

A frown creased her usually cheerful face. "*Ya*, so many ladies want to buy fabric they will likely never use, but then again, everyone coming into a quilt shop believes—even if just for that moment—she is a quilter. Whether they use the fabric or not, it's *gut* for my business."

I was surprised not to see Netty's granddaughter Faith in the shop. Faith was almost always around to help her. Last year, Faith's parents and younger siblings had moved to a new Amish settlement in Wyoming. Netty's son was enticed by the chance to have land of his own. In Holmes County, large swaths of land were hard to come by, as they were passed down from generation to generation. The family had wanted Netty, who was a widow like me, to go with them, but she had said she was too old to start over or leave her beloved shop. As a compromise, they'd left their eldest granddaughter, Faith, behind to live with and help Netty. I'd never been under the impression that either Netty or Faith was unhappy with the arrangement, until now.

"She wasn't here. She has been very preoccupied lately." Netty looked at the wood-plank floor.

"Is something wrong?" I asked.

"In a way," Netty said. "I'm glad you stopped by the shop today, Millie. It's a real answer to my prayers. Faith needs help. The kind of help only you can provide."

"Oh?" I stopped studying the heart-patterned Valentine's linen on display.

"She is twenty now and with no prospects for a husband. At least, there are no prospects she is interested in. I'm worried for her."

"Twenty is young," Lois said. "The right guy will come along. Or the wrong guy. In either case, she'll snag a proposal."

I shot Lois a look. Talking about the wrong guy was not the best way to comfort a *grossmaami* worried about her granddaughter's future.

"That's the *Englisch* way of thinking," Netty said hotly.

"She does have time," I said soothingly. "Twenty is still young for marriage. Why is there any urgency?" I asked.

"She's growing more and more distant from me. I'm afraid she might leave the Amish way if she doesn't have a husband to hold her to the faith."

Beside me, I could feel Lois tense up, and I couldn't blame her. However, I said a quick prayer in my head that Lois wouldn't say anything to upset Netty more. It was clear she was very worried about her granddaughter.

"Finding a husband should not be the single thing tethering a young woman to the Amish faith," I said as kindly as I could. "In fact, it should be Faith's relationship with *Gott* that holds her in the community. A husband has no part in that."

"I know it's true, but many young women feel the pressure to marry or think they must leave." Netty sipped her coffee.

I couldn't say Netty was right that *many* young Amish women felt this kind of pressure, but I had known of several who'd left the Amish way because they couldn't find a match within the community. They felt the rejection, and in turn, rejected their upbringing. However, Faith Dienner had always been dedicated to her community. She had been baptized at age sixteen. If she left now, she would be shunned. Her grandmother would be required to shun her, so Netty's fear of losing her granddaughter was legitimate.

"You said there are prospects she isn't interested in. Who are they?" I asked.

Netty walked over to the potbelly stove, where four paddle-back chairs sat in a circle. "I think we had better sit down to talk about this."

It looked to me as if this conversation with Netty was going to take time. I glanced at Lois, who gave a slight nod. We were lifelong friends—she knew by my expression alone that I was asking if we could stay. However, if we remained too long, we would miss out on Swiss Carpentry and not be able to follow the lead until Monday.

I was relieved when my dearest friend gave the nod. Netty needed a compassionate ear right now.

"*Ya,* there is a young man who has expressed his interest more than once. Hosea Flaud. His father owns Swiss Carpentry, and Hosea is apprenticing there now. It would be a *gut* fit for Faith. He's a member of our district and has a stable future. There's not much more a *grossmaami* could want for her granddaughter."

Lois perked up. "We were just on our way to Swiss Carpentry."

Netty's eyes went wide. "For sleuthing? You said the two of you were up to sleuthing again. I pray it doesn't involve Hosea."

"Swiss Carpentry was on a list of businesses the murder victim planned to visit over the coming days," Lois said, as if she were telling Netty the weather.

Netty set her coffee cup on a side table. "Murder victim!"

I inwardly groaned. There went my plan of not talking to Netty about the murder. "A *possible* murder victim," I clarified. "Did you hear about the accident at the Munich Chalet?"

"I did! Several customers came in talking about it. What a terrible thing to happen. So, this woman's death is what you are investigating?"

"We were there when the cuckoo fell," Lois said dramatically.

Netty covered her mouth with her hand. "How terrible! And you think the Flaud family is involved? I can't see how. They are kind and upstanding people. Model Amish, truly."

"If they are such a great family, what's Faith's issue with the match?" Lois leaned forward in her seat.

"She won't tell me. Believe me; I have tried to talk to her. In recent weeks, she has become increasingly upset whenever I've brought it up. I'm afraid of pushing her farther away, so I stopped pushing. I have tried another tactic. To be honest, I thought that's why you were here, until Lois mentioned the sleuthing."

"What new tactic was that?" I asked.

"I told Hosea to talk to you." Netty's eyes shone with tears. "You're the best chance for Faith to see this is the right decision about her future. I had thought you were here because he talked to you, and you had come up with a plan to convince Faith marrying Hosea is the right path for her."

"I haven't heard from Hosea," I said. "I haven't even met him."

Netty sighed and folded her hands on her lap. "That is disheartening indeed. He promised me he would contact you. I'm sure he will soon, but if the two of you are going to the carpentry workshop, you can talk with him then. A few encouraging words of advice from you, and I know he will be able to convince Faith they are a perfect match. If that doesn't work, perhaps you can speak to Faith, as well, and set her straight about the best course for her future. This marriage has to happen. It's the only way I can see to keep Faith in the Amish way."

Contrary to what some *Englischers* believed, the Amish did not have arranged marriages. It was our firm belief the best and most successful marriages were built on a mutual love between man and woman and an unwavering belief in *Gott.*

"I'm happy to speak with Hosea and Faith, but as a matchmaker, it isn't my job to convince two people to fall in love and to marry. I can recognize when they are right for each other and counsel them through their courtship. However, they both have to want that relationship."

Netty sighed. "I was afraid you'd say something like that."

We heard the sound of a door opening somewhere in the back of the shop, and a moment later, Faith stepped into the main room. She was a lovely young woman with shining brown hair and a pink complexion similar to her grandmother's. Her cheeks were made even rosier by the cold bite in the air outside. She nodded at Lois and me, removed her coat, and donned an apron from behind the counter. All the while, she didn't once look at her grandmother. The tension between them was palpable, where before, there had always been affection.

I sensed Netty tense up beside me. There was a deep hurt between *grossmaami* and granddaughter, and I didn't know if it just stemmed from the situation with Hosea, or something else. I wished I could say this was the first time I'd seen something similar injure a familial relationship, but it wasn't. When the elders in a family wanted a certain life for a young relative and the younger refused, there was always tension.

"If you will excuse me," Netty said upon standing, and then she went over to speak to Faith. Netty and Faith went into the back room.

Lois and I stood, as well.

"Do you think we should leave?" Lois asked. "If we want to see the carpenter before his shop closes, we need to go, like right now."

Heated voices came from the back room, and the words were in the Amish language of Pennsylvania Dutch. Lois gestured at me to go nearer to the closed doorway and eavesdrop. However, I didn't need to be any closer. Their voices came through loud and clear.

"You called the matchmaker to deal with me?" Faith asked in a high-pitched voice.

"*Nee, kinder, nee.* Millie is only here to shop like she always does."

"I know that's not true." Faith's voice was sharp. "Hosea told me you are in agreement with him about the match. What about what I want?"

"You were speaking to Hosea?" Netty didn't even try to hide the hopefulness in her voice.

"*Ya,* only because you put this wild idea in his head that I might be willing to marry him. I had to say something to discourage him. He follows me wherever I go. I can't stand it."

"What did you tell him?" Netty asked. Her voice shook with emotion.

"That I didn't want to be courted by him. I asked him to leave me alone."

"Many Amish girls dream about having a young man so devoted to them. You should take this opportunity while you can. Another one might not come along."

"I'm not many Amish girls. I have told you what I want, and you don't listen to me. You are no better than my parents, who abandoned me here. They left to pursue their dreams. Why can't I pursue mine? Because you won't let me."

Netty gasped. "Do not speak to me in that way."

"Don't try to run my life!" Faith cried. The back door of the quilt shop slammed shut.

I shooed Lois back to the coffee station, and the two of us fell into our seats just as Netty reappeared with tears in her eyes. She tried to collect herself. "I'm sorry. Faith had to leave suddenly. Millie, perhaps you can talk to her about Hosea another time when she's less emotional."

I nodded, but I didn't think Netty would like to hear what I really thought of the situation. To be married when your heart is adamantly against it is a recipe for disaster. The only thing it would guarantee was a miserable marriage, and there were few things in life so terrible.

Chapter Nineteen

Shortly after Faith left the shop, Lois and I made our exit, as well. If we had any hope of arriving at Swiss Carpentry before it closed, we had to be on our way. The carpentry shop was just up the street from the quilt shop, so we opted to walk. It would be easier than circling the village looking for a parking spot on a busy Saturday afternoon.

Lois shook her head. "It doesn't seem like things are going well between Netty and Faith. It's such a shame. I had always thought the two of them were close."

I'd thought the same.

"I don't know what I would do if a similar rift developed between Darcy and me. It would break my heart." She pulled her red beret out of her massive purse and settled it on top of her head. "I understand Netty wants her granddaughter to have a husband and a family, but is it right to encourage the girl to marry someone she's not certain about?" Lois asked. "I can speak to bad marriages. They are hard. In fact, I can't think of anything about the single life that's as awful as a bad marriage. Netty wouldn't want that for Faith."

"She wouldn't," I agreed. "But there is this thought in the Amish community that love will come. Even if two people don't love each other deeply when they marry, it is believed love and affection will come in time. To some extent, it is true. In a healthy relationship, love grows and changes with time. Marriage is very much a living thing in that way."

"But you can also grow in the opposite direction. My life is a perfect example," Lois said with a downturned face.

I studied her closely. Usually when Lois spoke about her failed marriages, it was with a smile and hint of jest. She rarely showed the pain I knew she must have experienced when dealing with divorce.

Lois secured her hat in place with hair pins. "All I'm saying is Faith seems like a sweet girl. Let her make up her own mind."

"That is a tenet of the Amish faith: Every person in the community has to make up his or her own mind," I said.

"From what I've seen, it hasn't always been put into practice." She dropped the extra hair pins into her purse. "There's a lot of pressure to do what your family or the community wants."

I couldn't argue with her there.

Swiss Carpentry was little more than a large shed at the end of the road, next to a small brick building that looked like it had been there since the Amish settled in Holmes County well over one hundred years ago.

The CLOSED sign hung from a nail in the middle of the door. Lois checked the time on her phone. "Hey, it's not five o'clock yet. We had four minutes."

I shrugged. "I guess they didn't think anyone would stop by so close to quitting time."

"That's false advertising," Lois complained. "The door says ten to five on Saturday."

"Can I help you?" A tall, broad-shouldered young man came around the side of the shed. He wasn't wearing a coat or hat, even though it had started to snow. He shoved his hands deep into his trouser pockets.

Before Lois or I could answer him, he said, "Oh! You're the matchmaker." Worry creased his face.

"Have we met before?" I asked, doubting we ever had. The young man had to be close to six and a half feet tall and was built like those football players I had occasionally seen on the television in the Sunbeam Café. As he was Amish, I knew he didn't play football.

He clasped his hands together. "You're here about this morning, aren't you? I'm really sorry I scared you. I got spooked and knew I was making a mistake. Did you find my chisel? I think I dropped it, and it was a favorite of mine."

"Hold the phone," Lois said, and then thought aloud. "Okay, that's probably not the best expression to use since both of you are Amish and don't have phones. What I mean is, wait up. What are you talking about?"

I ignored Lois's rambling. "You were the one outside my barn this morning? You nearly scared me to death." However, even as I said it, relief flooded through me. I would never admit it, even to myself, but I had been worried about going back to the farm in the cold and the dark that evening with a stranger possibly lurking about. The goats weren't exactly top-notch security.

"*Ya*, it was me. I was just so eager to talk to you. I realized it was far too early to make a house call after I'd already arrived at your farm." He kicked at a clump of snow on the ground. "I'm sorry I scared you. That was never my intention. I just really needed to talk to you."

"Why did you want to talk to me?"

"Netty told me to." He gave the snow another light kick.

"Are you Hosea Flaud?" I asked.

Lois stamped her foot. "Would someone please tell me what's going on? You had a stranger at your house and didn't tell me?" Lois gave me an accusing look.

Hosea looked up and down the street, though it was all but deserted on this winter evening. "We should talk inside." He unlocked the door to the shed and stepped through.

I glanced at Lois with my brow raised.

"That's one way to get in," Lois said. "Let's go."

The inside of the shed was much more spacious than it looked from the outside. Everything was organized and in its place. The back wall had a pegboard with tools hanging on it that ran from one side to the other, from ceiling to floor. I had a feeling the Flaud men rarely misplaced a chisel.

Lois sat down on a stool in a way that suggested she wasn't planning to get up until she had some answers. She folded her arms as if to announce her intention.

I sighed and sat on a chair a few feet away. My feet were tired from all the walking, and it felt nice to sit down. "Hosea, this is my friend, Lois Henry."

"Friend?" he asked. "I thought she was your driver."

It was an understandable assumption. Many Amish had *Englisch* drivers whom they relied on to drive them to appointments or even take them into town during poor weather. However, it was not the right thing to say to Lois.

"Driver? You think I'm just her driver? I'm Millie's best friend, her partner in crime, her co-sleuth," she said hotly.

His face clouded in confusion. "What's a co-sleuth?"

"It doesn't matter," I said quickly before Lois said too much. We still needed information from Hosea about Paige, assuming he had any to share.

I spoke to Lois, "Early this morning, I was headed to the barn to let the goats out."

"Which is the equivalent of releasing the hounds," Lois quipped.

I gave her a look. "And before I reached the barn, I saw what I thought was a man standing next to it. The man ran away."

The light dawned on Lois's face. "So you were that man."

He swallowed and nodded. "I didn't mean to scare you, really. I had worked up my courage the night before to speak to you, and then realizing

I'd come at the worst time possible, I ran. I'm not proud of it."

Lois studied him. "Take a seat. We don't want you going anywhere, since you have a reputation for fleeing. We have business to discuss."

"You have business with me?" He looked as confused as ever.

"We'll get to that in a second," Lois said, as Hosea perched on another wooden stool next to a workbench across the room. "You wanted to talk to Millie about Faith, I take it. That's why you were at her home early in the morning?"

He looked around the small room as if searching for an escape, but the only way in or out was through the door we'd entered earlier. Lois had strategically positioned her stool in front of it.

"I did," he said finally. "Everyone in the district, even her grandmother, believes we are a *gut* match, but Faith won't even give me a chance. I'm at the end of my rope. I don't know where else to turn."

"You know that's really creepy behavior? Sneaking around Millie's house in the early morning. Had you been at another farm, you would have been reported as a prowler. Or worse, shot at."

Hosea paled, as if he had never considered the possibility.

"Why are you so sure Faith is your match?" I asked.

"We're from the same district. Our businesses are next door to each other. We're both of age and unattached." He spoke as if he were checking off a list. "It makes sense."

Lois wrinkled her nose at this answer. "That's not the most romantic thing I've ever heard."

"Do you love her? Do you feel affection for her?" I asked.

"I can love her." He picked up a screwdriver from the table and tapped the handle of it on the edge. "That's all she really needs to know. I will make a *gut* husband for her. Everyone agrees, even her *grossmaami*. She would be blessed to be called my wife."

Lois muttered something under her breath. I placed a hand on her knee to calm her. I wasn't sure how well it worked. Comments like that were sure to get Lois's hackles up.

"That's not the same as loving her now," I said gently and dropped my hands to my lap.

"It's marriage. It's not about feelings. It's about building a life and family." He spoke in a way that made me believe the words were something he simply parroted from someone else—the bishop in his district, perhaps.

I shook my head. "It's very much about feelings. Although you are right that love can't be the only factor to consider when you choose to marry. Had you come up to me this morning, I would have told you the same thing. A love match is the best way to a happy marriage. There will be difficult times ahead in married life, but through those hard times with your wife, you can fall back on the love you have for each other. Without love, what do you have to cushion your fall when it comes? Because it most certainly will."

He blinked at me as if he had never looked at it that way. "Netty said you would help me convince Faith."

I shook my head. "I never talk one person into

marrying another, or tell anyone whom to love. That would be wrong. I have an ability to recognize when two people belong together, and when I can, I help them navigate the ups and downs of their courtship."

"Do you think Faith and I belong together?" His voice had a pleading quality that I hadn't heard before.

"The only way for me to know would be to see the two of you together. But if Faith has been vocal about not liking the idea of the match, that should be your answer. Usually, a young woman wants to spend as much time as possible with the person courting her, not run away."

The expression on his face was pained.

"We have another matter to discuss with you," Lois said.

Hosea's broad shoulders went up and down in a pronounced sigh. "What about?"

"Paige from Delpont Furniture Warehouse."

He scratched the back of his neck. "Why do you want to talk about her?"

"She died this morning, and she had a list of places she wanted to visit in Holmes County. Your workshop was on the very top of her list."

Hosea paled. "She died? How?"

Lois gave him a quick summary. "We want to know why she was planning to see your shop while on her honeymoon."

"She was on her honeymoon? I knew that she planned to be in the county on business, but not that she was also just married. Why would she spend her honeymoon here?"

"I suppose she planned to mix business with

pleasure while she was here," Lois said. "What business did she have with you?"

"All I know is she wanted to speak to my father about building more jewelry boxes. That's why I'm still here. My *daed* wanted me to make at least one more box tonight. He was disappointed when Paige didn't arrive. She pays very well. We could use the money." He looked away and cleared his throat. "*Daed* would like to expand and build a larger structure for the shop so the business will support me and my children. He worries about when he's not here. He hasn't been . . ." He shook his head, as if he thought better of what he had just been about to say. "Unfortunately, competing with other furniture makers in the county means we've never been able to do that. Working with Paige was our chance. My father is going to be so upset when he hears the news that she's gone. I don't know where we will go from here."

"Tell us more about these jewelry boxes. Why are they so special?" I asked.

"Would you like to see one? It will be much easier if I just show you."

We nodded.

"I just finished one. This might be my favorite yet. I was thinking of giving it to Faith instead of selling it. My father wouldn't like that idea." He hopped off his stool and walked to the back of the shed, where shelves lined the walls. He removed a shoebox-sized jewelry box from the shelf. He set the box in the middle of the worktable.

Lois and I stood up to take a better look at it. It was beautiful, made from oak and freshly sanded. The top was decorated with intricately carved flowers. There were roses, daisies, and irises that were so well done, the flowers looked as if you could pluck them right off the box and tuck them into a vase.

"It's gorgeous," Lois said.

"It is," I agreed.

Hosea smiled. "*Danki.* I will oil it tomorrow. I just finished carving the top before I met the two of you outside."

"How much does this cost?" Lois asked.

"We sell them retail for eighty dollars. Paige was planning to buy several at fifty dollars apiece. She planned to make an initial order of thirty in total. We can make three boxes in a single day's work, so it would be a good profit for us."

"You could probably charge more than that," Lois said. "This level of craftsmanship is hard to find."

He nodded. "I have told my father this, but he likes a price most people can afford. He even feels eighty is a little too much, but we have to sell at that price to make a profit."

"It's a beautiful box," I said. "But what about it makes Paige want so many?"

"For this reason." He pressed the middle of the daisy on the top of the box. A compartment on the back of the box popped open.

"A secret compartment," Lois said.

He nodded and smiled. "It was something I came up with. At first, my father didn't like the idea. He said it wasn't the Amish way to hide things, but when he saw how popular they have been with *Englisch* customers, he asked me to make more."

"How did Paige find out about them?" I asked.

"I suppose it was five or six months ago. She and another man—I believe she said it was her brother—stopped in the shop to look around. That's when I showed her the jewelry boxes. She said they were perfect and bought three right there on the spot. A few weeks later, she called to say she wanted to make a wholesale order and planned to come see us in person this weekend. My father and I couldn't believe our good fortune."

I wrinkled my brow. Certainly, I could see why Paige had been impressed by the jewelry boxes. They were lovely, and the secret compartment was clever. The box had been so well-made, it was impossible to tell where the compartment was located until the daisy was pressed just so. Why did Paige like the secret compartment so much? As we'd discovered earlier in the day, she had also commissioned furniture makers to include secret compartments in their pieces. Maybe I should have been asking what exactly did Paige have to hide?

"Can I buy this jewelry box from you? I'll give you a hundred for it," Lois offered.

"We only ask for eighty," Hosea said, confused.

"Consider the rest a thank-you for taking the time to talk with us."

He shrugged. "It's not oiled yet."

She waved away this concern. "That doesn't matter to me. I refinish furniture myself, so I know what to do."

"All right, if that's what you want." His voice jumped an octave, as if he couldn't believe she would pay him so much.

Lois reached into her purse and came up with a stack of bills. "That should cover it."

He counted the money and nodded. Lois picked up the jewelry box and tucked it under her arm. "Ready, Millie?"

I said goodbye to Hosea and followed her out the door.

It was dark now, and the temperature had dropped several degrees. Neither of us spoke until we were inside Lois's car and she had started the engine. She turned the heat all the way up.

"We need to find out why Paige was so fascinated with secret compartments," Lois said. "Because it might just be the reason she was killed."

My thoughts exactly.

Chapter Twenty

As an Amish person, I didn't have church every Sunday. Church gatherings were every other week at a member of the district's home. The home changed every time, so everyone in the district hosted a church service at least once a year. The off Sundays were meant to be family time, when the immediate family gathered together for family devotions and a meal in a time-honored tradition. The devotions were led by the father, and the meal was prepared by the mother. It was a well-thought-out idea to ensure both emotional and spiritual closeness in a family unit.

However, it didn't take into account the Amish who lived alone . . .

In the summer, I would spend these Sundays with my niece, Edith, and her children. But in the winter, I stayed home, due to the cold and the possibility of unpredictable weather, common to

Holmes County during the chilly months. It was easy to feel isolated and blue on these Sundays.

I stared out the window and sipped my coffee. Peaches sat on the windowsill and watched the goats romp through the snow. I smiled, wishing I had a little bit of the enthusiasm my two Boer goats possessed.

I turned back to the kitchen counter to refill my coffee and spotted Hosea Flaud's chisel on the counter. I needed to return it to him. However, Sunday wasn't the day for such an errand.

The *beep, beep* of a car horn sounded outside. I returned to the window and saw Lois's car being jostled about on my long gravel driveway. I removed a second mug from the cupboard.

Screeches and yells came from outside, and I guessed Lois was out of the car and trying desperately to make her way to the house around the goats. By the sound of it, she wasn't having much luck.

I set my coffee mug on the counter and went to the front door. Peaches followed close on my heels. He always enjoyed a show, and he especially liked it when the goats got into trouble.

I opened the door, put two fingers in my mouth, and whistled for all I was worth. It was a trick Kip had taught me when were teenagers, and it was the only noise that told the goats I meant business.

Phillip and Peter froze mid-frolic around a very harried-looking Lois. They set their hooves on the snow-encrusted gravel and looked at me with big brown eyes as if they could never possibly be naughty. I knew otherwise.

"Get back to the barn, you two goofs!" I shouted.

They looked at each other as if to ask whether I was serious.

I whistled again, and they took off toward the barn. I felt bad for my horse, Bessie. I knew they would make a ruckus in the barn, too, and wake her up from her morning nap.

Lois adjusted her purse on her shoulder and rubbed her right ear. "You're going to make me deaf with that whistle."

"It was either that or let the goats torment you all day," I said as I led her inside the house.

She grunted. "Coffee?"

"I already pulled down a mug for you." I walked over to the pot and filled the mug for her. She sat in a rocking chair near my quilt frame. As I handed her the coffee, I asked, "What are you doing here?"

I didn't usually see Lois on Sundays. She knew I took the Sabbath seriously, and therefore did very little on the Lord's Day, as the scripture directed. Since she was here, I knew she had to have at least what she thought was a very *gut* reason. Lois and I weren't always in agreement about what constituted a *gut* reason.

"What do you think?" She held the coffee under her nose and inhaled. "We have a crime to solve. We are on a case, after all."

"We can't do anything about it today. It's Sunday."

"Sure, we can. Amish Marple never sleeps!" She raised her fist.

"The Sabbath is a day of rest. I can't work on

this day. Besides, you said we were working the Amish angle. We can't talk to any Amish today about the murder."

"Do you think being a detective is your *job*?" she asked with a raised brow.

I frowned. She had me there. If I said it was my job, it would be a victory of sorts for Lois. She had wanted us to hang out our shingle as a private detective duo ever since we solved our very first case.

I shook my head. "*Nee*, it's not a job."

"Then, it's not work," she said happily and drank her coffee. "Besides, we aren't going to follow up on an Amish angle today, so no one from your district will know you are out and about on Sunday, not even Ruth Yoder."

"What kind of angle are we following then?"

"The cuckoo kind," she said with a grin.

An hour later, Lois and I were back at the Munich Chalet. To be honest, it didn't look very different than it had the day before. Except for the bright yellow crime scene tape wrapped around the cuckoo clock like a winter scarf.

The cuckoo itself was gone. I assumed Deputy Little had taken it away as evidence. And of course, Paige Moorhead's body was no longer there. The crime scene tape was the only indication something nefarious had happened on these grounds.

I looked up at the clockface, and it was frozen at eight, the time in the morning the cuckoo had fallen. Something about the clock being frozen at the exact time Paige had died was chilling. The chilly feeling had nothing to do with the weather.

"Why are we here?" I asked. "To talk with Gerome again?"

"That's not a bad idea. We might do that before we go." She pointed at the clock tower. "We're here for that. We're going up."

"Do you see the yellow tape? It says, 'Police line. Do not cross.' I'm thinking that's more than just a suggestion."

"It probably is," she agreed. "But we'll be up and down before anyone is the wiser."

I had my doubts.

"Don't you want to see how the cuckoo was tampered with?"

She knew me well, because I did very much want to see what had been done to the cuckoo.

We got out of the car, and there didn't seem to be anyone around. Except that wasn't completely true. I didn't see any humans around. There were sheep, and they stood close to the clock tower. They eyed us as if assessing their odds against us. Since they didn't move, I guessed they believed that they could take Lois and me down if need be. I hoped that it wouldn't come to that. They were very odd sheep, indeed.

Lois slid a pair of gloves over her hands. "Those sheep are always watching. I feel that if we make one false move, they'll pounce. It's unsettling. At least with your goats, I know what to expect. They always pounce."

This was true. I didn't tell Lois that I was thinking the same thing. She would just become more convinced the sheep couldn't be trusted.

I stared up at the clock tower. The door the cuckoo popped out from stood open and swung eerily in the winter wind. Karl, the owner of the Munich Chalet, might want to do something about it. He surely wouldn't want anything else plummeting to the ground from the tower.

"Millie, come on," Lois said. "We have to get in and out before the sheep snitch on us. I can tell they are tattletales. Just look at them."

"Baa!" one of the sheep cried.

I had to admit, it sounded mildly threatening.

Lois disappeared around the back of the clock tower. I straightened my bonnet ribbons and followed her.

I found Lois standing at the back door, grinning from ear to ear. "It's locked!" she said with glee in her voice. "You know what that means."

I grimaced, because I did know.

"I finally get to use my lock picks!" She shook with excitement. "I've been waiting for this moment my whole life."

Lois wasn't one to avoid hyperbole.

"Lois," I whispered, just in case someone was on the grounds. Or maybe I was whispering because of the sheep. They did look like they would tell tales on us. "I don't think you should break into the clock tower. Deputy Little will be able to tell if the lock is damaged."

"I won't damage it," she scoffed. "I have been practicing by locking myself out of my house for months. The only way I can get inside is to use the lock picks." She already had the lock picks out of her purse.

I wished I could say this surprised me.

"Time me," she said, and thrust her cell phone into my hand.

"What?" I juggled the cell phone and was able to keep it from falling to the ground.

"I started the timer. You just have to hold it." She was already working on the lock.

I stood there dumbfounded, watching the little numbers flicker by on the phone screen. I could only guess what Ruth Yoder would have to say about this situation.

"Got it! Time!"

"Uhh, one minute, two seconds."

"Huzzah!" she cried. "My best time yet, and on a foreign lock, too." She took the phone from my hand and pointed at the open door. "After you, Amish Marple."

I took a deep breath and went through the doorway.

Chapter Twenty-one

The inside of the clock tower smelled damp and dank like a root cellar and was constructed from plain, cold cinder block. Above us, light poured in from the open cuckoo door.

To our right, a metal staircase wound its way up to the open door above. Lois hiked her purse on her shoulder. "Let's go. There's no time like the present."

She started up, and after a couple of beats, I followed. The steps were steep and winding. I soon had to stop, and I pressed my hand against the bare cinder block wall as I tried to catch my breath.

"Oh, good," Lois said, turning around. "This means I can rest, too. I was afraid you were going to barrel ahead. You've always been in better shape than me. Whose idea was it to make the steps so far apart from each other, anyway? Someone young, I would guess."

After several breaks, we reached the top. The platform leading to the open door looked precarious at best. Lois stepped onto it as if it were built of solid granite.

"Be careful," I warned. "We can't get hurt up here. It would be difficult for anyone to rescue us. We need to remember we aren't twenty any longer."

"We haven't been twenty for decades, but we've never let that stop us before," Lois said. "I'm still twenty in my heart."

The gears of the clock were above our heads. They were massive. The larger gears, I suspected, weighed more than Lois and me combined. They weren't moving right now, as evidenced by the frozen clockface on the outside.

An Amish proverb came to mind: "One thing you can learn by watching the clock is that it passes time by keeping its hands busy."

I swallowed. Not this clock. Not these hands.

"Deputy Little said the clock had been tampered with. We just have to find out how, and we can leave," I said. The sooner we got out of there, the better.

Lois looked up at the gears. "If those were tampered with, I wouldn't even be able to tell. Not to mention the size of them. They're as tall as I am." She touched one. "Ouch!"

"Are you okay?"

"I'm okay. It didn't break the skin. I didn't realize how sharp they would be."

I winced. "Please be careful."

"I know, I know. No one can hear us scream up here."

I inched closer to the open door from which the cuckoo had fallen.

The two bright blue double doors hung from their hinges. By the looks of it, either one could tumble to the ground at any moment. I would have to tell Karl he needed to do something about it, or he might have another tragedy on his hands. I didn't think the young man could handle the fear of possibly being sued by two different families.

I gripped a nearby two-by-four and held on for dear life. I wasn't a fan of heights. One summer, not long after we were married, Kip and I had taken the train out to see the Grand Canyon. It had been a thrilling trip, and the farthest I had ever been from home, or traveled since.

I had been so excited about seeing the Grand Canyon, and when we had finally arrived at the edge, I'd leaned way over the side. I had been struck with a wave of dizziness and almost tipped over into the canyon. I would have fallen if Kip hadn't been there to catch me. Ever since, I had been leery of edges, and I was even more careful now. As I'd told Lois, we weren't twenty any longer.

"I found it," Lois said behind me. "This is where the killer cut the cuckoo free." She pointed at three sets of cables. From the looks of them, they'd held the cuckoo on its platform when it popped in and out of the tower. Attached to each cable were giant springs as thick as my waist. I imagined they stretched out when the cuckoo made its hourly appearance.

"These springs are huge," Lois said. "They could kill someone if they snapped." She cocked her head. "Should I be worried that I see murder weapons everywhere now?"

I shook my head. "Don't think about it too much."

She pressed her lips into a thin line and walked over to the open door.

"Lois, please be careful," I said.

Her foot caught on a loose board. "Ahh!" She grabbed onto the side of the doorway and then righted herself.

My heart was in my throat. "Oh my! Are you all right?"

"I'm fine. Just a moment of vertigo there. It happens to me sometimes when I look down from a height."

I pulled her away from the edge. "Then why do you look down?"

"I like to test my limits."

I shook my head, and as I did, I saw a thick cable near the track the cuckoo ran along. The cable had been cut clean through. Crime scene tape marked the end of the cable. There was also powder on the cable.

Lois saw it at the same time and joined me along the track. "That black powder is for fingerprints. I've dabbled in that. You can buy it fairly easily online."

"You dabbled in fingerprinting?" I asked.

"You never know when we might need a new skill for an investigation." She leaned over the powder. "I can't tell if the deputies were able to pull any prints. In this weather, it's very likely the perp was wearing gloves. We both are." She stepped back. "That cable didn't break from wear and tear.

It was cut clean through. A pair of bolt cutters is my best guess. They'd snip through the cable like butter. I used to carry some in my purse, but they just made my bag too heavy. The bolt cutters or the brick had to go. I kept the brick because it's more versatile." She removed her phone from the pocket of her coat and snapped a picture of the cable.

"The cut looks recent," I mused. "Whoever killed Paige knew she was below the cuckoo when he or she cut the cord. It was a murder."

"Most definitely, but how did the killer know she would be under the cuckoo when he was up here ready to cut the cable?"

Lois and I stared at each other as the idea struck us at the same time.

"This wasn't just murder," I said. "This was premeditated murder. Whoever was up here knew that Paige would be under the cuckoo, because he planned for her to be at the wrong place at the wrong time. He planned for her to be killed."

Lois's mouth made an *O* shape as she absorbed this news. "You have to be right," Lois said.

I knew I was right. But I still didn't know who the killer was or how he had convinced Paige to stand under the cuckoo at the appointed hour. The only person who'd been around to tell her to wait there was her husband, Gerome.

I bit my lip and kept the thought to myself. I knew Lois wanted to believe Gerome had nothing to do with Paige's death, because if he did, Lois would have to question her own judgment since she had loved—or thought she'd loved—Gerome once.

"Well, we came and saw what we needed to see," Lois said. "It's as clear as day why Deputy Little is looking at this case as a homicide. How could it be anything else? We should talk to Gerome again and see if he remembers anything more about yesterday morning."

I nodded.

Lois and I slowly made our way down the stairs of the clock tower. When we reached the bottom, I let out a sigh of relief. My knees wobbled a bit. I hadn't even realized how nervous I'd been at the top until we were back at ground level.

When we left the clock tower, Lois made sure the door was locked and the crime scene tape in place, just as we'd found. There was no sign we had been there. Only the nosy sheep knew different.

As we followed the path to Gerome's Hillside room, the sheep followed behind us.

"That's really beginning to be unnerving," Lois whispered.

I had to agree with her, and I was used to being followed by animals. But the goats were always excitable and bounced about. The sheep lurked and watched. It was a tad unsettling, to say the least.

Lois and I walked toward Hillside Three and were just a few feet from the door when it flew open. Gerome and a tall, blond, bearded man came out.

Lois grabbed my arm and pulled me behind two of the sheep. Since we were much taller than the sheep, I didn't think they would hide us all that well.

"It's Paige's brother, Ronan," Lois said in a loud whisper.

I nodded.

"Please tell your family how sorry I am. I loved your sister dearly. I'm broken over this," Gerome said.

Ronan, who was starting to walk away from Gerome, spun. "If I find out that you know something about my sister's death, you'll be sorry for it! You're not going to see one cent of her money, either."

Gerome flinched. "I'm not hiding anything. I swear to you. I don't know anything about how Paige died. I'm only telling you how upset I am over losing my wife. I loved her. I didn't marry her for her money."

"Your wife? Your wife for two days. She was my sister for a lifetime. I will find out what happened to her, and if I learn you contributed to her death in any way, you're going to prison for the rest of your life." He stomped away.

Ronan brushed past us on the path and gave no indication he had met us the day before at Elon's warehouse. His face was so flushed with anger, I don't know if he saw us standing there at all.

Gerome pulled at the collar of his white and blue button-down shirt, looking as if he might be sick.

"Are you all right?" Lois asked as she hurried toward him. She almost tripped over two sheep in her haste.

The sheep baaed their irritation. I gave them a wide berth as I made my way over to Gerome and Lois.

Gerome's Adam's apple bobbed up and down. "Lois, what are you doing here?"

"We're here doing what you asked of us," she said. "We are trying to find out what happened to Paige."

He nodded and scanned the grounds, as if he were afraid Ronan might reappear.

"That was Paige's brother, wasn't it?" Lois asked.

Gerome stared at her. "How did you know that?"

"We met him briefly at Elon's Furniture Warehouse yesterday."

"W-what were you doing there?" He wasn't wearing a hat and wiped sweat from his brow with his gloved hand.

"It was on the list of businesses you gave me. The ones Paige wanted to visit. It seems she's been asking Amish craftsmen to make furniture and jewelry boxes with secret compartments to sell in her family's furniture stores in Cleveland. Did you know anything about that?"

Gerome pulled on his collar more. "No, I don't know anything about her business. Her family might believe that I married her for her money, but it wasn't like that. I loved her."

His eyes darted away. He was lying. It was clear on his face. Was he lying about not knowing about her business or about loving her? I didn't know.

Gerome looked around again. He certainly seemed afraid Ronan or someone else would come for him. Why? I supposed I could understand Gerome being nervous around Ronan after witnessing how angry Paige's brother had been at him. But was he truly worried about that only?

"Gerome," I said. "You said you were up early yesterday morning taking pictures. Can we see those pictures?"

"No." His answer was quick and decisive. "I haven't had the film developed yet. I just finished the roll. I don't plan to have it developed until I get home. There are no overnight developers here like there are in Cleveland."

"Honestly," Lois said. "I'm surprised there are any overnight film developers at all."

"There are," he said in a such a way it seemed to suggest he was offended she thought this medium was obsolete.

"Don't the police want your film?" I asked.

"Yes, we do," Deputy Little announced as he came over the hill. "And I have a warrant to take it."

A string of sheep followed him in a fluffy white line.

Gerome placed a hand on his chest, as if his heart might give out.

Chapter Twenty-two

"**D**eputy!" Lois cried. "You're as sneaky as those sheep."

"What sheep?" Deputy Little asked. He turned around, and the flock ducked their noses to the snow as if they hadn't been stalking him. Shaking his head, he turned back to us.

"You heard us talking about the camera from over the hill?" I asked.

"Lois's voice tends to carry," the deputy said.

I couldn't argue with him there.

Deputy Little reached into his coat pocket and removed a folded piece of paper. "Mr. Moorhead, this is a warrant to take the film you shot yesterday morning around the time your wife died."

"You can't have my film," Gerome said, shaking his head like a defiant child.

"I can and will," the deputy said.

Lois took the piece of paper from Deputy Little's hand and read it. "It says here you need to hand it over, Gerome. If not, you could be charged with an offense."

Gerome clutched his chest. "You don't know how difficult this is for me!"

"It will be made even more difficult if we have to take you to the sheriff's department for disobeying an order of the court," Deputy Little said.

Gerome's face paled, and then he went back into his room. A moment later, he reappeared with a camera case and roll of film in a plastic canister. "Here. Take it. Just be careful with the camera. It's old, but it's worth a lot of money."

Deputy Little accepted the camera case and film. "Thank you. I will have the forensic lab look over the camera and film. If there's nothing of interest here, I'll return the camera to you right away. You have my word." He turned to go, but then stopped. "Millie and Lois, would you mind walking to my car with me?"

Lois and I shared a look. It sounded like we were in trouble.

We said our goodbyes to Gerome and followed the deputy back over the hill. Unsurprisingly, the sheep followed.

Deputy Little glanced over his shoulder. "Do those sheep strike you as odd?"

"Those sheep?" Lois asked. "Nah, they're totally normal."

He shook his head. When we reached his departmental SUV, he removed an evidence bag from the back of it, put the film inside, and wrote on the label. Then he put the camera in a second, larger bag and wrote on that. When he was done, he set both on the back seat and then turned to face us. "What are the two of you doing here?" His eyes slid to me. "And Millie, I would have thought you'd be at church on Sunday."

"It's not a church Sunday," I said.

He sighed and rubbed the back of his neck.

"When were you going to tell us the cuckoo's cable was cut, and that's what caused the murder?" Lois asked.

"How do you know about that?"

"We have sources," Lois said.

Deputy Little looked up at the clock tower and the open door rocking in the wind as if he knew exactly what those sources were.

"How would the killer know Paige would be there at the precise moment he or she caused the cable to snap?" I asked. "The killer had to have arranged it. The killer couldn't sit up there all day in the hope that Paige would walk by."

"That's what we're thinking, too. As of yet, there's no evidence of an arrangement," the deputy said. "You would assume there'd been a text or call on her cell phone, but there is nothing."

"Told her in person?" Lois guessed.

"What would the murderer even say? 'Can you stand under this clock so I can kill you?' It doesn't seem likely." Deputy Little shut the passenger door of his car.

Lois rolled her eyes. "I'm sure the killer didn't say it *that* way."

"In any case." Deputy Little folded his arms. "The two of you have to be careful. This was a terrible murder, and a premeditated one at that. If someone could orchestrate killing another person in such an elaborate scheme, then they're not the kind of individual you want to trifle with. I'm asking the two of you to stay out of it."

We didn't say anything.

He gave a long-suffering sigh. "I had to at least say my piece."

"Of course you did, Deputy," Lois said encouragingly. "It's part of your job, and we would never get in the way of your doing your job."

"There is something that's been bothering me," I interjected.

Lois and the deputy both looked at me.

"How did the killer get away?" I asked.

"What do you mean?" Deputy Little asked.

"The killer had to cut the cable at the precise time Paige stood under the cuckoo. It meant he had to be up in the tower at the time she died. How did he get away without anyone seeing him?"

"Maybe he didn't," Lois said. "We were preoccupied with Paige at the time, but there might have been someone else on the chalet's grounds who saw something."

Deputy Little nodded. "I'll ask one of my deputies to question the guests again."

"And the manager, Karl, too," Lois said. "You can't forget Karl."

"How could I?" he muttered and leaned back on his car. "Since I know the two of you have been snooping, is there anything else you would like to share with me?"

"Yes, in fact, there is," Lois said, and then she told him about our trip to Berlin and Charm yesterday afternoon to talk to Amish craftsmen who were building furniture and jewelry boxes for Paige's store. "They all have secret compartments made to Paige's specifications."

A strange look crossed the deputy's face. "What were the names of these businesses?" he asked a little more forcefully.

"Elon's Furniture Warehouse and Swiss Carpentry were the ones we visited yesterday. There is a third, Smucker Dressers. We haven't been to that one yet."

"I have to go," he said abruptly. "The two of you be careful. Extra careful." With that, he ran around the front of his car, jumped inside, and then drove away.

"What do you think got into Deputy Little?" Lois smoothed the scarf around her neck.

"I don't know," I said, but I guessed it was important.

A gust of wind blew across the grounds, and the open door high on the clock tower banged against the side of the structure.

"That's a hazard," Lois said. "Before we go, we need to tell Karl he has to do something about it. If he doesn't, he might have another lawsuit on his hands."

"Lawsuit? Do you think Gerome will sue him over Paige's death? Or Paige's family might?" I held onto the sides of my bonnet as the wind caused them to hit my cheeks.

"It's hard to say."

I followed Lois to the chalet's main building. We walked up to the front door and stepped inside. As we stood in the red, yellow, and black room, I took the opportunity to bask in the warmth.

I hadn't realized how cold I had gotten from standing outside until I was indoors again.

No one stood at the desk, but a bell was set on the counter with a sign: RING FOR SERVICE.

I did just that.

No one came.

I rang it again, and again we waited. Nothing.

Lois hit the bell a third time, a little bit more insistently.

"I'm coming," a grumpy voice said, emanating from down the hallway. A moment later, Karl appeared, and he didn't look *gut.* Dark circles smudged under his eyes, which were also bloodshot, and the suspenders of his lederhosen were slipping off his shoulders. There was a sharp scent of alcohol when he entered the room. I would guess Karl had been doing more than a little bit of drinking since Paige had died.

He pulled up short when he saw us. "What are the two of you doing here?"

"Hello, Karl," Lois said in her cheeriest voice. "We just stopped in to suggest you do something about the door at the top of the clock tower. It looks like it's getting ready to fall clean off. You don't want another person getting hurt at the chalet."

He buried his head in his arms on the desk and said something we couldn't make out.

"What was that?" Lois asked. "We can't hear you."

He looked up. "I just asked when this nightmare will ever end. Half of my reservations for the week canceled because people read about the accident in the Sunday paper. It's February, too. It's not the height of tourist season. I was counting on those reservations to keep me afloat until spring when travel picks up again. I need every reservation I can get, and I lost so many. Even if I'm not sued, this could ruin me."

"The nightmare will end for you when the killer is caught. That's why we need your help," Lois said, as if it were as simple as that.

Maybe in her mind it was that simple.

"You're going to find the killer?" He rubbed his eyes.

"Sure," Lois said, without an ounce of false modesty. "We do it all the time."

He stared at her as if she were speaking a foreign language.

"Did you see anything out of the ordinary yesterday morning?" Lois asked.

"Yes, a woman died under my clock tower." He sniffled.

"No, no, before that. Were there any odd characters about? Any unexpected events? Anything at all you might have stopped and wondered at?"

"No—wait, yes. There was a guy walking through the woods with a camera. I couldn't see him well because of the trees, but I assumed he must have been a guest. I just found it weird because it was so early. I like to take pictures as well, you see, and I know the woods are dense. It might have been too dark in there to get decent shots."

Lois and I looked at each other. Lois's face was pinched.

Chapter Twenty-three

Late Monday morning, I tethered Bessie and my buggy to the hitching post in front of the Sunbeam Café. After the breakfast rush at the café, Lois and I planned to visit the last Amish craftsman on Paige's list, Smucker Dressers.

On the buggy ride into town, the dreary skies had released a cold rain, which had since turned into a steady drizzle. Through the raindrops, I spotted Margot Rawlings in the village gazebo struggling with the Valentine's Day garland that had been wrapped around the gazebo's pillars. She stood precariously on a ladder and with all the motion of her efforts, I thought she was sure to topple over.

Knowing it would be several minutes before Lois was free—and despite the rain—I crossed the street to the gazebo.

"This good-for-nothing—" Margot grumbled as I drew closer. "Why won't you come loose?"

"Margot, do you need some help?" I asked.

She looked up from the garland she was thus far unsuccessfully trying to yank from the pillar. "Millie, yes. Can you lend me a hand?"

I hurried up the steps of the gazebo, relieved to be under the roof and out of the rain.

Her ladder shook, and I grabbed on to steady it. "It looks like the garland is nailed to the bottom of the pillar," I said. "I think that's why you're having trouble getting it off."

"When I asked a volunteer to hang the garland, I told him to use tape, not nails. Do you know how many times we've had to have nail and staple holes filled and painted on this gazebo? Too many for me to count is how many. It's ridiculous. It seems I'll have to tell everyone again not to use them. Harvest isn't made of money to buy paint."

I would have to take her word for that. I bent over and pried the nail from the pillar. It hadn't been hammered very far into the wood. Once I did, Margot pulled, and the garland came loose.

She climbed down from the ladder with the water-logged pink garland in her hand. "Hosting these events on the square was a lot easier when Uriah Schrock lived here."

At her mention of Uriah's name, I felt a little pang in my chest. It was something I always felt when Uriah was brought up. I reminded myself that he'd made the decision to leave Harvest to be closer to his children. He should be with his children. They needed him. They needed him more than I needed him. At least, that's what I told myself.

"With Uriah, I never had to worry about a thing. We have a young Amish man who took over the job, and he means well, but Leon's not quite up to Uriah's standard. Uriah knew what to do and handled everything with little supervision. I never had to wonder if a concert would be set up on time or if the twinkle lights on the trees would be hung straight for Christmas." She sighed. "I hope this new boy gets his act together soon, or I will have to find someone else."

"I think Leon just needs a little more time. He hasn't even been through a full year of events on the square. He did very well with the parade and live nativity scene at Christmas. For the other holidays next year will be better; he will know what to expect."

"I sure hope you're right. But I didn't work this hard to put Harvest on the tourist map, only to have our reputation slip away because of dumb mistakes."

I stepped farther under the gazebo's roof to keep out of the rain. Snow in the winter could be a nuisance, but winter rain was just downright depressing in my opinion. At least when it snowed, it brightened everything up. In the rain, the square was dreary and gray. I longed for springtime, but unfortunately, it was still weeks away.

"How did the spaghetti dinner go? Did you raise the money you needed?" I asked.

The annoyance on her face fell away. Margot loved nothing more than to talk about one of her successful events. "It went so well! We raised well over our goal for the drug counseling center. Reverend Brook said the church has the space ready to go, so we might be ready to open as soon as April if we can find the right people to work there."

"Reverend Brook gave me a tour of the rooms in the church. They are very welcoming. It sounds like it's a great collaboration between the village and the church and the Amish and the *Englisch* in Harvest."

She beamed. "It is. This is going to really help people in our community who are struggling with addiction, or family members and friends who have loved ones affected by drugs. I was glad to see you and Lois there."

"We wouldn't have missed it."

Margot removed her stocking cap, and the mop of short curls on her head sprang in all directions. She tousled her curls before replacing the hat.

"Elijah Smucker was there." I let the words hang in the air.

She moved her ladder to the next pillar so she could start removing another strand of garland. "Yes, I was surprised to see him, to be honest. He really hasn't been one to come to village events, and to attend one so soon after his son died of a drug overdose . . ." She shook her head. "Maybe he just wanted to lend his support."

"Reverend Brook said he's shown interest in the counseling center."

"I didn't know that, but any interest we receive is welcome. We are trying to get the word out the best we can. I'd be interested in knowing how he would like to help. We can use all the help we can get."

"Lois and I plan to visit him later this morning. We can ask."

She removed the nail holding the garland in place and climbed up the ladder again. "Is it a sympathy visit?"

"No, actually, it's about the woman who was killed by the cuckoo."

"In Millersburg?" she asked. "I heard about that. They say Lois's ex-husband is the killer."

"He's a suspect. Not the killer." At least as far as we knew, I added in my head. However, I couldn't get out of my mind how reluctant he'd been about handing over his film and camera to the police. I could understand that he didn't want those items harmed, but his wife was dead. Wasn't it more important to find his wife's killer than protect a camera?

"What does Elijah Smucker have to do with Lois's ex-husband?" Margot wanted to know.

"Paige—the woman who died—had written a list of places she planned to visit in Holmes County while she and Gerome were on their honeymoon. Apparently, her family owns several large furniture stores in Cleveland, and they were looking to commission pieces from Amish craftsmen to buy wholesale. Smucker Dressers is on that list. All the pieces she commissioned had secret compartments."

Margot stared at me from the top of her ladder. "Did you say secret compartments?"

"*Ya*, we were told Paige claimed her customers needed to hide their valuables in case of home invasion."

"Or a place to hide their drugs." She climbed down from the ladder.

"What did you say?" I asked.

"Haven't you heard the news? I thought the Amish grapevine was better than that."

My heart beat faster. "What news?"

"I assume Lois is in the café, so I'm sure she must know by now. When the sheriff's department was investigating John Michael Smucker's overdose, they found a wooden box in his home with a secret compartment."

"How did they find the compartment?" I asked. "The pieces I saw were so well-made, you would never know the compartment existed just by looking at it."

"Apparently, it was left open after the last time John Michael used it. It's where he did his drugs." Her expression fell at the very idea.

"That doesn't mean it's what all the furniture is for. John Michael may have used it for such, but he is just one person."

She shrugged and dropped another piece of wet garland on the gazebo floor. "Maybe. Or it could be just the tip of the iceberg."

I wanted to learn more about John Michael's box, and I knew the best place to start would be talking to Lois about what she'd heard on the news. However, before I headed over to the Sunbeam Café, I helped Margot remove the rest of the Valentine's Day garlands from around the gazebo. I couldn't leave her outside in the rain to do the job alone.

All the while, I thought about what I'd learned. Could John Michael Smucker's death and Paige Moorhead's murder somehow be tied together? If a person had asked me twenty-four hours ago, I would have said "*nee.*" However, I realized now that answer was shortsighted. The Smucker family business had been on Paige's list of places to visit in Holmes County. There had to be a connection between the two, however tenuous.

I helped Margot pile all the garland into a box. Once she'd picked up the box, Margot said, "Millie, I'm not usually one to say anything to you, but if this Paige woman's death is somehow connected to drug use in our county, I'd advise you to stay as far away from the case as possible. People who take drugs, or worse, who sell drugs, are not playing around. They can be desperate to keep their secrets safe. You don't want to be involved with something so dangerous."

She was right. I didn't want to be involved in any of it. But Lois and I were in too deep to quit now. I knew we would both want to see this through to the end.

I left Margot on the square and walked across the street to the Sunbeam Café. I went inside the building, and a bell over the door sounded my entry. The inside of the café was warm and inviting, smelling like fresh cinnamon rolls and coffee. It was almost like being wrapped in a cozy blanket.

"Millie!" Lois cried. "I have news!" She hurried around the counter, wiping her hands on a tea towel as she went.

"Is your news that John Michael Smucker was hiding drugs inside a wooden box with a secret compartment much like the ones we saw on Saturday afternoon, made by Amish craftsmen?" I asked.

Lois threw her tea towel on the counter with so much force, the elderly man seated at the end jumped and nearly knocked over his coffee.

"What?" she cried. "When am I ever going to be able to tell you breaking news? I never get the scoop. Who told you?"

"Margot, on the square just now, so you were very close to getting the scoop," I said, hoping that would make her feel better.

"As if that's some kind of consolation," Lois grumbled. "Darcy," she called into the kitchen, "Millie and I are leaving now. Iris is on her way in to help you. We are off to catch a killer."

"Okay, Grandma," was Darcy's sweet reply.

Chapter Twenty-four

I filled Lois in with what Margot had told me. She nodded. "That's what I learned from the newspaper this morning. I still don't understand how it all fits together. Hopefully, Elijah Smucker will have some answers."

If Elijah would talk to us. I wasn't sure he would.

Smucker Dressers wasn't in a village or town like the other two businesses. It was located on the Smucker family farm, along an isolated gravel road that had no signs or edging between the gravel and the grassy ditches on either side of the road. The only indication of the business was a small, hand-painted sign by the driveway reading, Smucker Dressers.

The farm appeared quiet. This time of year, there wasn't much farm work happening out in the pastures and fields. This was planning time. In February, farmers made strategies for the coming year. They thought about what care they would need to give their livestock in the spring, what crops to grow, and what fields would need to be rotated on their property to keep the land fertile.

The rain had stopped by the time we reached the house, and I was grateful for this small gift. I stepped over a puddle as I got out of Lois's car. Most of the snow had melted due to the rain, leaving behind gray slush and mud.

Lifting my skirts, I took care as I followed Lois toward the house.

The building appeared completely dark. There wasn't so much as a candle in the window. Before Lois could knock on the door, I called to her. "Lois, the shop is around the back."

Another hand-painted sign at the end of the porch pointed behind the house. It read, DRESSERS THIS WAY.

Lois looked at the door as if she still wanted to knock on it.

"If there's no one in the shop, we will come back and try the house," I promised.

"Fine," she said with a sigh, and proceeded to walk with me around the home. At the rear, there were two barns; one a traditional structure, likely where the family kept their animals and buggies. The second housed the carpentry shop.

The barn door to the shop stood open, and light flickered, most likely from an oil lantern judging by the movement of the shimmering light.

"You go first," Lois said. "Usually, Amish men are more welcoming if you go first. I think you remind them of their Amish grandmas."

I shot her a look, but I did as she asked.

I stepped through the door and called hello in

Pennsylvania Dutch. It smelled and looked much the same as any other Amish man's woodshop I had been in. Particles of sawdust floated through the air, and the scent of fresh-cut wood and varnish burned the inside of my nose.

The walls were bare except for an impressive collection of tools hanging on them. Directly in front of me stood a tool bench, at least fifteen feet long. On top, screws, nails, tacks, and washers were carefully organized in glass canning jars.

Despite the sawdust in the air, there was nary a speck of dirt on the concrete floor. It appeared to have been recently swept and possibly even polished.

"Hello?" I called again.

The creaking sound of a door opening preceded a man's voice calling in Pennsylvania Dutch that he would be right there.

Hearing this, Lois stepped into the building. She looked around. "Does it seem overly organized to you for a woodshop?"

Before I could answer, Elijah Smucker came into the woodshop from the back corner. He looked much the same as he had Friday night at the spaghetti dinner. His face was drawn and his eyes downturned.

"Can I help you?" Elijah asked.

"I hope so," I said. "I'm Millie Fisher. This is my friend Lois Henry. You and I have met before. I spoke to you at the spaghetti dinner."

He furrowed his brow and then nodded. "I remember. Are you here to buy a dresser then?" he asked.

I was about to say we were not when Lois spoke

up, "Yes, I have heard so much about your dressers that I had to see one for myself. I happen to be a collector of unique furniture, and I hear yours are very unique."

Elijah's expression didn't change in the slightest with the compliment. "I can show you what I have. They are over here."

Lois and I walked across the clean floor, nearing five dressers in a range of sizes, positioned in the corner of the shop. At least two were small and likely intended for children's or even infants' clothes.

"I heard," Lois said, "that your dressers are special because they have secret compartments in them for keepsakes. Are any of these like that?"

"*Nee.*" His brow furrowed.

Lois had tried in her way to convince Elijah Smucker to talk with us. Now it was my turn. "Perhaps it was something your son John Michael was working on."

"He was not." His tone left no room for argument.

"We heard the police found a wooden box with a secret compartment that had drugs inside it," I said.

He glared at me. "My son had a problem. I admit that, but I don't understand why the two of you are here talking to me about it."

"Where did he get the box?"

"I don't know. My son was talented. Maybe he made it. When the deputy showed it to me, it was the first time I had ever seen it, and I never want to see it again. I told him to take it away." He spoke as if the words were catching in this throat. "I don't want anything that reminds me of my son's troubles in my home." He looked away.

Lois and I were quiet for a long moment to let him collect himself. He let out a deep breath.

"I was glad to see you at the spaghetti dinner. I'm sure it was difficult." I trailed off.

"It was not easy. I am a widower. John Michael was all I had. Cooking for one is pointless. I was happy for a warm meal."

I could understand his sentiments about cooking for one. I had felt much the same many times also. It wasn't uncommon for me not to bother and simply have a piece of fruit and bread for supper. Only because eating was required, not because I enjoyed the food.

"Do you know anyone by the name of Paige Moorhead?" I asked, changing the subject.

He shook his head.

"Maybe you know her as Paige Delpont," Lois piped in. "She was very recently married."

Elijah scowled. "I don't know a woman by that name, but I do know of a man named Ronan Delpont. He has come to my shop several times, trying to convince me to make dressers with secret compartments like the ones you mentioned. I was not interested. I have enough work here to support myself and my son . . . now only myself."

"Did John Michael ever talk to him?" Lois asked. "Perhaps Ronan shared the idea with him."

He scowled. "Why would he? It was my decision as to who we did business with. There would be no reason for my son to speak with anyone. When he was alive, it was his job to make furniture. That was all." He frowned. "If you are not interested in any of the pieces we have here, I need to get back to work. I'm sure there is someone in the county who can make the dresser you are looking for."

"We aren't just here for a dresser. We want to help you," I said. "And we want to help other young people in the community like your son. Do you know how he might have gotten the drugs he overdosed on?"

Elijah glowered at me, and for a long moment, I didn't expect him to answer.

"I can assure you I don't know. And if I did, I would have found the person by now and . . ."

"And what?" Lois asked.

He shook his head. "Please." There were tears in his eyes. "Let me return to work. It's the only solace I have."

My heart ached for him. Lois looked as if she wanted to ask something more, but I touched her arm, shaking my head. We said our goodbyes and quietly slipped out of the workshop.

A few minutes later, Lois and I pulled away from the Smucker farm in her car, and Lois whistled under her breath. "That poor man."

I nodded, as I was thinking the same thing.

"What do you think Elijah would have done if he found the person who gave his son drugs?"

I shook my head. "I don't know. I'm not even sure he knows what he would do. There could be hundreds of different ways that John Michael could have stumbled across them."

"He made the choice to take them."

"He did," I agreed. "I don't think many Amish young people are educated on the dangers of drug use. At least that's what Reverend Brook told me when I toured the new counseling center. Part of the center's goal is to change that."

Lois's shoulders sagged. "It's just so terribly sad, and I don't know if we learned anything that will help us find Paige's killer."

I didn't know, either. I rubbed my forehead. "I just can't understand how this all fits together or if it even fits together. The Delponts asked for secret compartments to be built in furniture after Paige discovered the jewelry boxes that Hosea Flaud made. Paige told Elon of Elon's Furniture Warehouse that those compartments were to hide valuables, but John Michael had a similar box and used it to hide drugs. Finally, drug use is on the rise in the county. Paige Moorhead was killed by the cuckoo for what reason? We still can't find a clear motive. Does it fit together at all?"

Lois shrugged and frowned. She looked as confused as I felt. There were so many threads in this case that we didn't even know which ones belonged and which were extraneous. Investigation was nothing like a well-made quilt, where everything came together so neatly. In this case, I felt that nothing was coming together, and I was beginning to wonder if we should follow Deputy Little's advice and just leave it up to him to solve Paige's murder.

"When we get back to the café, I'll have to take Bessie and go home to prepare for the quilting circle meeting. I know that Ruth will be eager for an update on the case. I wish I had more to tell her and the other ladies."

"Shoot, I wish I could go with you," Lois said. "But with both you and Iris at the meeting, I need to stay back to help Darcy. I wish you were holding the meeting at the café, so I could hear it."

"We can't talk about murder in the café," I said.

"Why not?" Lois asked, honestly confused. "I do it all the time."

Chapter Twenty-five

I untied Bessie from the hitching post by the square, and she shook her head in protest.

I scratched her nose. "Sorry, girl," I said. "I didn't know that I would be leaving you here tied up so long. Lois and I got carried away with crime solving again."

Bessie hated to be left attached to the buggy for too long. She especially hated the rain, even though I'd put a horse blanket on her.

"You get two giant carrots when we get home to make up for it. How does that sound?"

She blew hot air out of her nostrils. I took that to mean she liked the idea.

I grabbed the reins and was about to climb into the buggy when someone called my name.

Iris Young walked down the sidewalk from the direction of the café. "Millie, can I have a ride to the meeting? Carter dropped me off at the café this morning, and I planned to ask you for a ride. I forgot until just now."

"*Ya*, of course," I said. "I'm glad that you caught me."

She smiled and climbed up on the wooden bench seat next to me.

"I don't know how warm it still is or if it has any heat left at all, but there is a brick at your feet. It was red hot this morning."

"*Danki*." She smoothed a lap blanket over her legs. "I'll be fine."

I nodded and flicked the rein. "Go home, Bessie."

That was all the horse had to hear, and she knew exactly what to do. I set the reins in my lap, holding them lightly. Bessie knew her way home better than I did.

Iris stared out the windshield of the buggy.

"What did you want to speak to me about earlier?" I asked.

She glanced at me with a smile. "I was just working up the courage to bring it up. It's about my son, Carter, Jr."

"Is he all right?" I asked. "Is he ill?

"*Nee, nee*, he is fine." She looked down at her hands. "He's our only child, and maybe because of that, we worry too much about him, but we are concerned about him finding a match. You did so well matching my husband and me; I hope that you can do the same for Carter Jr."

"Carter Jr. is quite a bit younger than you and your husband were when I matched you."

"Not that much younger. We were eighteen.

Carter is sixteen now. Before too long, he will want to marry and have a family of his own."

I watched Bessie's head bob up and down as she made her way along the road. She was going at a good clip, too, which was even more proof to me that she wasn't happy about standing outside in the rain for so long. I thought I would give her three big carrots when we got home instead of two.

"Has he said that he's concerned about it?" I asked.

"He hasn't. He was just baptized into the church last month. I don't think he's thinking of much of anything right now but how to be an upstanding adult in the community."

I patted her hand. "Then that is where we should leave him until he is ready."

She squeezed my hand and smiled. "I know, but I worry that he won't find the right match. I want him to settle down."

It made me think about Netty and her worries over Faith's future. It seemed that parents and grandparents couldn't help but worry about their children.

I set my hand back on the reins as Bessie made a turn. "He is only sixteen. There has to be more to it than this."

She gripped her hands together on her lap until her knuckles turned white. "He was friends with John Michael Smucker."

I looked at her. "Oh."

She nodded. "I am worried about him because of it."

"Did he know that John Michael used drugs?"

She nodded again. "And he feels horrible about not telling anyone. He feels like it is his fault John Michael died."

"It is not his fault. No one would say it was his fault."

"It is what he believes. I thought a courtship would give him something else to focus on."

I bit my lip. Thoughts of what I wanted to say—but knew I shouldn't—flashed across my mind. "I don't think it would be wise for Carter Jr. to jump into courtship if he's upset about his friend's death. There are other ways for him to recover."

She looked at me. "Like what?"

"He could help with the drug counseling center at the church," I said. "I am sure there are many tasks that need to be done before it can open."

She nodded. "He might like that. At the very least, it will make him feel that he is doing something to make a difference." She bit her lip. "But I don't know if the bishop would allow him to do that. Counseling sounds like *Englisch* work."

"The counseling part of it is *Englisch* work, I am sure. However, Reverend Brook said there is a need to educate Amish youth about the dangers of drugs and alcohol."

"But what would Bishop Yoder say?"

"The Bishop was at the spaghetti dinner to raise money for the center. Lois sat at his and Ruth's table."

She laughed. "I'm sure that was interesting."

"Why don't you send Carter Jr. to the café tomorrow, and I will introduce him to Reverend

Brook. That way, he can decide if he's interested before talking to the bishop. Why get Ruth worked up if it turns out not to be the right thing for him?"

She clapped her mitten-covered hands together. "*Danki*, Millie. I will do just that. I knew you would have a solution." Her face clouded over again. "Will you not tell the ladies that Carter Jr. was friends with John Michael? I—I don't want anyone in the district to be looking at him oddly."

I knew what she meant. She didn't want Ruth Yoder to be suspicious that Carter Jr. might use drugs as his friend had.

Bessie turned down my long driveway, and the goats must have sensed us coming, because they stood at the end of the driveway, jumping up and down in joy that we were home.

"I have never seen such happy goats," Iris mused. "And since most goats I've met are happy, that really says something."

I agreed that it did.

In the yard beside the house, a large buggy was parked.

"Uh-oh," Iris whispered. "That's Ruth's buggy."

I grimaced. It was, in fact, Ruth Yoder's buggy. Hers was one of the easiest to pick out, since it had an extended cabin. She claimed that she had such a large buggy so that Bishop Yoder could take church members places if the need arose. However, most of the members in the district believed it was because Ruth wanted the biggest and the best buggy. I thought it might be a little of both.

Ruth lowered the window of her buggy. "I have

been sitting out here in the cold for thirty minutes waiting for you. Where have you been? We have a quilting meeting soon."

I climbed out of the buggy. "I know that, Ruth. That is why Iris and I are here now. I didn't expect you to arrive an hour early."

"Always expect I'll arrive early," she said in a huff. "If a person is on time, I consider that late. We have much to discuss, and we can't dillydally."

"There will be no dillydallying," I promised her. "Let's go inside and get settled."

"I can't even get out of my buggy because of your goats."

Sure enough, Phillip and Peter danced around the Yoders' buggy like school children playing Ring Around the Rosie.

I put my fingers in my mouth and whistled. The two goats made a mad dash for the barn.

"Ornery rascals," Ruth muttered as she climbed out of her buggy.

"But I love them still," I said with a smile.

Chapter Twenty-six

Whenever the ladies came to my home for a Double Stitch meeting, I always made sure there were plenty of snacks and the quilt frame was set up, ready for the next project. Today, I wasn't ready. In my defense, Ruth was early.

Thankfully, Iris got right to work setting up the quilt frame while Ruth and I put out the snacks. At least I had prepared all the food before going to see Lois that day. Today, I'd decided to do something a little different with the snacks. Typically, I would bake something, but after running around Holmes County all weekend with Lois, trying to find a killer, there hadn't been time. So I had opted for cheese and crackers from the cheese shop and a fruit tray from the market in Harvest.

"I'm so grateful that we will be working on my quilt today," Iris said. "It's a big project, and with the extra hours I have been working at the café, I wasn't sure I would get it done on time for my customer. It's for her niece's birthday in March."

Ruth looked up from the cheese and crackers that she was arranging on a plate. "Extra hours? What's this about?"

"Oh!" Iris said, looking at me with panic in her eyes.

"It's all right, Iris. Ruth knows that Lois and I are investigating Paige Moorhead's murder. It will be the main topic of discussion this evening, will it not?" I asked Ruth.

Ruth grunted. That was as close to an agreement on the topic as I was going to get.

"I'm happy to be working on your quilt, Iris. You do impeccable work."

Iris blushed as she tightened the corners of the quilt frame.

What I said was true. Her work was impeccable. My stitches would never be as tiny or precise as hers. Although we were all expert quilters, Iris was the most naturally talented in the group.

"I'm ready to stretch the quilt out," Iris said.

I wiped my hands on a tea towel, making sure they were clean and dry before I joined her at the quilt.

We set to work stretching the quilt on the frame. It was a large quilt frame—eight by eight feet—and practically filled my entire living room. There was just enough room for the ladies to sit around the quilt to work and occasionally sneak into the kitchen to grab a snack from the counter.

After framing the quilt—a delicate pinwheel pattern—Iris walked over to the food. "There are blueberries on this platter, Millie. I'm surprised you hadn't eaten them all before I got here."

My love of blueberries was well known by my friends, and really by the village at large. I chuckled. "I would never eat all the blueberries. At least, I don't think I would."

The front door opened, and Raellen Raber waved from the doorway. Before she stepped inside, she shook the rain from her bonnet. Raellen was a small, dark-haired Amish mother of nine and my closest neighbor. She and her husband owned a sheep farm about a half of a mile away. We shared a shed phone located on her property. Since she lived at the farm with her husband and nine children, as well as one hundred sheep, it made sense to keep the phone closer to her. She was much more likely to make emergency calls than I was.

Leah Bontrager calmly came into the house right after Raellen. Leah was just a couple years older than Ruth and me, and we had all gone to the small one-room schoolhouse. She had steel-gray hair and pink cheeks, and was one the most unflappable women I had ever met. I could vouch that she had always been like that. She wasn't even excitable in her schoolhouse days.

"Iris," Raellen exclaimed. "Your quilt is gorgeous. Not that I had any doubt it would be. You are the most talented quilter I know." She turned to me. "Millie, I heard you found another dead body. How *do* you have the knack for such a thing?"

Raellen was excitable, and sometimes it was difficult to keep up with the way her mind jumped from topic to topic. It didn't surprise me she knew of Paige's death; nor did it surprise me she'd asked about it in such an abrupt way.

"I'd like to know that, too," Ruth Yoder said as she put the finishing touches on her cheese tray. "Millie Fisher, we need to discuss what you and Lois have been up to the last several days. I have heard reports you are going around the county asking about that Paige woman."

"Let's all get something to eat and take our posts around the quilt frame before we start interrogating Millie," Leah said in her unflappable way.

"*Danki*, Leah," I said as I moved my sewing basket to my seat.

"Oh! Cheese!" Raellen cried. "What a special treat! Do you have smoked gouda? It's my favorite."

It really didn't take much to make Raellen happy, which was something I appreciated about her.

We sat down at the quilt frame, and once everyone was settled, Ruth was ready to ask her questions. "Millie, you have to tell us what has been going on since our last meeting."

I briefly filled them in with the events of the last several days. I left off the fact that Gerome was Lois's ex-husband, but Ruth remembered the detail and made sure to tell the others.

"Lois must be a suspect then," Leah said.

"She was," I said. "But she couldn't have done it. Not that I would ever believe she could kill anyone. But I am her alibi. When the cable was cut, she was with me, and we were just about to walk into the chalet. There's no way she could be involved."

"How do you know the cable was cut at that very

moment?" Leah asked. "Perhaps the culprit cut most of the way through, so that it was weakened and would eventually break."

"That's possible," I said. "But that's not what we think happened, and neither does Deputy Little."

"Why not?" Raellen asked.

"Because the cable wasn't frayed. It was a clean cut. Lois said it looked like it was done with a bolt cutter."

"And I believe that is something Lois would know," Leah said, peering over her reading glasses. "I saw her pull a pair of bolt cutters from her purse once."

"She doesn't carry them any longer," I said. "They were too heavy. Either the bolt cutters or the brick had to go."

Leah nodded, as if this made perfect sense.

No one reacted to the news that Lois had a brick in her purse. I don't know if this said more about Lois or the quilting circle.

"Does the husband, Gerome, have an alibi? The husband or significant other is always suspect number one," Iris said as she threaded her needle.

"Not exactly. He arrived shortly after the cuckoo fell . . ." I trailed off.

"I'd take a closer look at him, then. Where did he come from?" Leah asked.

It was a good question. Now that I thought of it, Gerome had come from around the back of the clock tower. That meant he could have cut the cable and then run down the stairs. Then I reminded myself Lois had said Gerome was terrified of heights. Had he been motivated enough in wanting to kill his wife that he'd managed to overcome his fear? Also, Gerome had had plenty of opportunity to ask Paige to wait for him under the clock tower. He wouldn't have needed to call or send a phone message—Deputy Little had said they'd found neither on her phone. I had to admit it was possible he was the killer. Even if Lois didn't want to believe it.

However, another aspect of the case tickled my mind. There seemed to be a connection between the Smucker family and Delpont Furniture Warehouse, Paige's family business. How did they really fit together?

I held my breath for a moment and wondered if I should say what I was thinking. These were my friends, even Ruth. If I couldn't say something to them, then who could I say it to? I took a breath. "I can't help but wonder if Paige's death and John Michael Smucker's drug overdose death are somehow related."

The entire group stared at me. Raellen, who had been about to eat a grape, held the small piece of fruit suspended in the air in front of her mouth.

"That is absurd." Ruth was the first to speak. It came as no surprise to me, as she was often the first to share an opinion.

"Did they know each other?" Leah asked.

"According to Elijah Smucker, *nee*," I said. "But Paige's furniture store was asking to commission dressers from Smucker Dressers. She wanted those dressers to have secret compartments like the furniture and jewelry boxes she'd already commissioned from Elon's Furniture Warehouse and Swiss Carpentry, respectively. Elijah Smucker said he never met Paige; her brother was the one who contacted him. He turned the offer down."

"Why would she ask for secret compartments?" Raellen asked.

"I might know," Iris said.

We all looked at her, and her face flushed.

"When my husband was coming home from a job in Medina County last week, the van driver had to pull over to let a bunch of police cars pass. When they got back on the road, a little farther down, the police had pulled over a semitruck loaded with Amish-made furniture." She lowered her voice. "The police had pulled some of the furniture out, and were removing plastic bags from inside the pieces." She swallowed. "The *Englisch* told my husband and the other Amish workmen in the van that it was drugs, and a lot of drugs, too. Worth thousands of dollars."

Silence fell over the group.

"What kind of drugs?" Raellen asked, leaning forward.

Raellen was always the first one to want to hear all the gossip. She was a *gut* source of gossip, too, but you would not want to share any of your deep dark secrets with her. By the end of the day, they would be all over the district.

Iris shrugged. "I don't know."

"Did your husband say what the side of the truck said?" I asked. "Was it Delpont, perhaps?"

Iris shook her head. "He didn't say. I don't know whether he would remember now, even if I asked him. He was pretty upset about the whole incident. I believe most people think about their kids when they see something like that." She shot me a glance. "We worry our own children will make the wrong choices."

"That's awful," Raellen said. "And terrifying. I don't know what I would do if any of my children got into that sort of trouble." Raellen was a mother of nine, so she had reason to worry.

"With *gut* childrearing and *Gott's* protection, you have nothing to worry about," Ruth said with confidence.

I bit my lip, because I knew those things could help. Of course, they helped. However, they weren't always enough. You could do everything right when raising children, and they could still make poor choices that would impact the rest of their lives. I had seen it in my own family. And whether she would admit it or not, Ruth had seen it in hers, as well.

"Do you think the Amish making the furniture and boxes knew they were being used to move drugs?" Leah asked.

"Absolutely not," Ruth said. "That is completely against the Amish way. No upstanding Amish person would do such a thing."

Leah clicked her tongue. "No upstanding Amish person, true, but you are turning a blind eye, Ruth, because there are many Amish in Holmes County who are *not* upstanding. Our people are sinners just like the *Englischers*. We are not better or worse than they."

Ruth scowled at her. If anyone other than Leah had said that, Ruth would have told them off. However, Leah always had a practical, no-nonsense way of looking at the world.

"We don't even know if Paige was aware of what was going on, assuming they were pieces she had made for her store. Someone could have hidden the drugs in those pieces without her knowledge," I said. I wanted to give the murder victim the benefit of the doubt, since she couldn't defend herself.

"This case is bigger than just murder, Millie. It's about the drug problems happening in our villages and communities. I know we don't like to speak of such things," Leah said. "I don't like to speak of them, I can promise you that. But we have to put an end to it."

"But can you?" Iris asked with a sad face. "Can you ever really put an end to it?"

Leah looked at her. "I don't know. This is a fallen world, but we must try." Leah turned to me again. "If you find the killer, you might also find out who is making or bringing these drugs into the area. You might save countless lives."

I swallowed and stared at the unthreaded needle in my hand. That's as far as I had gotten on the quilting, just removing my needle from my pincushion. As if I didn't feel pressure enough to solve this case, I had been charged with protecting the youth of the county. I was an Amish matchmaker and quilter. I wasn't sure if I was up for such a challenge as this. But I had to try, as Leah said. I knew Lois would feel the same way when I told her everything I had learned at the quilting circle.

Chapter Twenty-seven

When I saw Lois the next day at the café, she was outraged. "Deputy Little has been holding out on us! You can't tell me he didn't know about this truck situation. He might have even known about it when Paige died." She put her hands on her hips. This day, she wore black jeans, a polar bear–printed sweater, and a shamrock apron. As Valentine's Day was over, she was already gearing up for the next holiday.

I glanced around the café. A man in the corner shook his newspaper in frustration.

In a quieter voice, which I hoped would give Lois the hint to lower her volume, I said, "That may be true, but we have to remember as an officer of the law, he's not allowed to tell us everything. He could get into real trouble with the sheriff if he did. And," I went on, "we still have no proof the drugs are connected to Paige."

"They sure sound like they are." She folded her arms and muttered to herself.

"What we need to do is track down Deputy Little and find out what is going on," I said. "I think at this point, he would even want us to be informed. He doesn't want us chasing after drug dealers. I don't want to be chasing them, either."

"*I* don't even want to do that. Those people are scary," she said, as if the killers we had caught in the past weren't equally scary. Maybe she was right, and they weren't.

"We also need to talk to the craftsmen on Paige's list again. Were their pieces on that truck? Did they know their furniture was used to hide drugs?" She removed her cell phone from her shamrock-covered apron. "Let me text Deputy Little now. Perhaps he can come to the café and fill us in."

I glanced around the room. The café was half full. I knew for sure that Deputy Little would not want to have this conversation with an audience.

Lois's phone pinged. "He says he can't come right now, but will catch up with us later today." She frowned. "He added that we should stay out of trouble. Fat chance. This case is bigger than ever."

The door to the café opened, and a short, stocky man came inside. He had on work boots and a thick coat. Lois smiled from ear to ear when she saw him. "Dexter! Just the man I wanted to see."

I wrinkled my forehead. I couldn't think of a time when Lois had ever spoken about a man named Dexter, and then it dawned on me. Dexter was the name of the building inspector who'd declared the bell tower safe just three months ago.

"That's quite the greeting," he said in a gravelly voice. He sat at the empty coffee bar.

I walked across the café and slipped onto another empty barstool two seats away from him.

"Don't I always greet you like that?" Lois asked as she grabbed a coffee mug from the rack behind her, set it in front of him, and filled it with coffee.

He looked up at her. "Nope. What is it that you want?"

"Why do you think I have to want something?" Lois asked. "Can't I just be happy you're here?"

"Nope," he said for the second time.

"Okay, fine," Lois said. "What can you tell us about the bell tower at the Munich Chalet?" She leaned across the counter, all ears.

He groaned. "Not you, too. The sheriff's department has been on my case about that place all day, too."

"And what did you tell them?" Lois cupped her chin in her hand.

He frowned at her. If Lois thought cute was going to win over building inspector Dexter, she was wrong. "You're not the police."

"No," Lois agreed, and then she held her coffee carafe up in the air. "However, I am the keeper of the coffee."

"You play dirty," he said. "Okay, fine, it's all public record, anyway. The bell tower was fine when I was there three months ago. I looked at everything. More importantly, I took digital pictures of everything—the stairs, the track, the walls, the cables, and the cuckoo. Those pictures have been turned over to the authorities at this point. There was nothing wrong with that bell tower when I was there. It was in perfect working order."

"Then what happened?" Lois asked.

"It's not my job to speculate."

"Come on," Lois said, waving the coffee carafe back and forth. The way she moved it was reminiscent of a clock pendulum.

"Nope." This third nope sounded final.

Lois continued to argue with Dexter, and I went back to my table.

After Dexter left, Iris walked through the door, followed by her son, Carter Jr. The teen had the same auburn hair as his mother. He removed his black felt hat when he came through the door, looking as if he wanted to be anywhere but at the café.

Iris shot a worried glance at her son and then gave me a wavering smile. "Millie, Carter Jr. and I are here. You said that you might have some ideas about how he could help at the counseling center."

I smiled at the young man. "I know Reverend Brook would like more young people involved in spreading the word about the center."

Carter Jr. nodded. "My *maam* told me this." He looked from his mother to me and back again. "I don't know how I can help. I wasn't even able to help my *freind*."

"Iris and I have work to do here at the café," Lois interjected. "Millie, why don't you walk Carter Jr. to the center and show him around."

"Would that be okay?" I asked.

The teen shrugged, and I supposed that was the closest I was going to get to a *ya*.

I bundled up in my bonnet, mittens, wool coat, and scarf. Carter Jr. put his black felt hat back on his head. The wide-brimmed hat didn't do much to protect his ears from the cold, and he wore only a denim jacket over his blue work shirt. He reminded me of the *Englisch* teenagers I would see walking home from school when I drove out of the village in the afternoon. Even in the winter, many of them refused to wear a hat or coat in the colder months. Thinking of them made me smile. *Englisch* teenagers and Amish teenagers weren't that much different from each other after all.

Carter Jr. shoved his hands in the pockets of his jacket. "Are you sure Reverend Brook would like my help?"

"I know he would," I said as we made our way down the sidewalk. "Before we reach the church, can I ask you about John Michael?"

He kicked a clump of gray snow on the sidewalk. "*Ya.*" His answer was barely audible, but I found it encouraging.

"You knew John Michael was using drugs."

"*Ya*, all of his friends did."

This surprised me. Usually, if an Amish person were doing something he knew would be frowned upon in the community, he kept it a secret.

"How did all his friends know?"

He sighed. "Because he tried to sell drugs to all of us. We all pushed him away when he did that. When we pulled back from him, I got the impression that he started using more. I don't know for sure, because by then, I avoided him as much as possible." His face fell. "I avoided him when I should have been reaching out to help him."

"John Michael was a dealer?" I asked.

"I don't know if you would call him that. He wasn't on the corner trying to sell to strangers. Only friends."

I wasn't sure why Carter Jr. thought that was better. I wasn't an expert on these things, but I believed that still made him a dealer.

My heart ached for Elijah Smucker. No wonder he was so torn up. I suspected by now, Deputy Little knew that John Michael was dealing drugs, and it would explain why the deputies had searched the Smucker home and workshop after John Michael's death. It wasn't because he overdosed; it was because John Michael had been committing a crime.

However, I was still confused as to how all this was interwoven with Paige Moorhead.

"Did he ever mention a wooden box with a secret compartment?" I asked.

He stared at me. "*Nee.* Why?"

I shook my head. He honestly looked dumbfounded by the question. "Did he ever talk about someone named Paige?" I asked.

"*Nee*," Carter Jr. said, looking even more confused.

I wrinkled my brow. We were at the church now, walking up the steps. I wouldn't have much time to ask more questions.

"John Michael was my friend, but if you want to know more about him, you should talk to his very close friends. They might know."

"Who is a very close friend to John Michael?"

"Hosea Flaud was his closest friend. If he doesn't know, I doubt anyone does."

Hosea?

Just as I was about to ask more about John Michael and Hosea, the front door of the church opened.

"I thought I heard voices out here," Reverend Brook said with a smile. "Lois called ahead and told me you were coming. Carter Jr., you are interested in helping at the center?"

"I want to do what I can. John Michael's death really shook me up. I don't want that to happen to anyone else."

"Then you came to the right place." The reverend smiled at me. "I can take it from here, Millie. Lois asked me to send you back because you have some sleuthing to do?" His voice rose an octave.

I shook my head. Leave it to Lois to spell out what we were doing like that.

Reverend Brook waved Carter Jr. into the building. "I would love your help. Come on back, and I can show you what we do."

The young Amish man looked back at me, and I gave him an encouraging smile. It seemed that's all he needed to follow Reverend Brook into the church.

Chapter Twenty-eight

An hour later, Lois and I sat in her car and watched large flakes of snow hit the windshield.

"February can't make up its mind as to what it wants to do," Lois said. "Snow, rain, snow, rain. Pick one."

"I much prefer the snow to rain," I said. The flakes were so large that I could actually see their intricate designs just before they melted against the glass.

"Me, too. Gray, cold rain is the most depressing weather. I couldn't live in a place where it rains all the time. We get enough here as it is."

On the way to Elon's Furniture Warehouse, Lois and I planned what we were going to say to Elon. We had to be subtle. We had to find out if there was a connection between the furniture orders Paige had made and the drugs the police discovered hidden in furniture on that truck. If they were connected, it could very well mean that drugs, or something related to the drugs, were the reason that Paige was killed.

When we pulled into the warehouse lot, we learned that all that planning was for nothing. Deputy Little was walking Elon out of the warehouse with his hands cuffed behind his back. He didn't wear a coat or a hat. He kept his head bowed down. Young men from his staff stared open-mouthed as Deputy Little handed Elon off to another officer.

That officer bent Elon's head and put him in the back of a departmental SUV. A few seconds later, the vehicle left the parking lot with lights flashing but no siren.

Deputy Little turned around to talk to the young men. They nodded to everything he said. I knew that they didn't want to face the same fate as their boss.

Lois whistled. "They caught the killer without us?"

"I don't know. I don't know that this arrest is for murder," I said.

"There's only one way to find out," Lois said as she got out of the car.

I followed her.

Deputy Little thanked the young men for listening to him and turned around. He pulled up short when he saw Lois and me walking toward him. With his hand, the deputy pushed his department stocking hat up into his hairline and rubbed his forehead.

Lois wiggled her fingers at him.

"How did the two of you know this was going down?" the deputy asked.

"We didn't," Lois said. "We didn't know any-thing was going down at all. We were just coming here to talk to Elon." She folded her arms. "We heard about that furniture truck full of drugs that was pulled over. When were you going to tell us about that?"

He gasped. "That's why you're here."

"It just kept coming up that furniture and drugs were connected. Since Paige was ordering furni-ture, we had to know if she was related to all of this too."

Deputy Little groaned. "I really wish the two of you would stay out of this."

"That's more likely to happen if we understand what's going on," I said. "Was that furniture truck the Delponts'?"

He sighed. "It was. This is what we know. Delpont Furniture would make an order of furni-ture with secret compartments. When the furni-ture was ready, the drugs were brought in and hidden in the pieces, and then they were loaded onto trucks headed to various cities. Cities as far away as Philadelphia."

"And you intercepted one of those trucks," I said.

Deputy Little nodded and didn't even bother to ask how I knew. "A state trooper did, actually. I wasn't on that case. The trooper pulled the driver over for a busted taillight. The driver acted shifty, and the trooper decided he had better search the semi. After backup arrived, they entered the cargo bay. During transit, one of the secret compartments had popped open, and the drugs were found. There was over twenty thousand dollars' worth, street value, of drugs on that truck."

"So Paige was involved in the drug scene here in Holmes County. Does that mean Elon's the killer?" Lois asked.

Deputy Little shook his head. "I don't think so, for two reasons. First, he has an alibi. He was home with his family at the time of the murder."

"Could his family be lying to protect him?" I asked.

"That is always possible, but the second reason is that Paige's death is the event that blew this case wide open. Without her killing, it might have taken us a lot longer to make the connection."

"What about Paige's brother?" I asked. "Does he know this was going on?"

"I don't know," the deputy said. "But I intend to find out. Unfortunately, I'm having trouble tracking him down. He's no longer at the hotel where he told us he was staying."

"Where did the drugs come from? If they were moving through Elon's store, what was the source?" Lois asked.

"Elon claims that he didn't know. He said Paige took care of that part of the business, but we will press him more down at the station to see if that is really the case. He might know and just be holding that info back to use as leverage later."

"Do Amish defendants know how to broker a deal with the attorney general?" Lois asked. "It's not something I would think they'd be aware of. I'm not sure I would even know to do it in that situation."

"You wouldn't think they'd be trafficking drugs,

either, but apparently, some of them do. Very few, I expect, but some. So it might stand to reason that Elon knows enough to keep his mouth shut for now. My guess is Paige or even Ronan coached him as to what to say and what not to say if he ever came in contact with law enforcement."

My head was spinning with all this information. The sheriff's department had found the middleman who was moving the drugs through the county, but the source, the people making or acquiring the drugs, was still unknown. Would the problem ever really go away without finding that source?

"What about the other businesses on Paige's list—Smucker Dressers and Swiss Carpentry? Were they involved in this, too?" I asked.

Deputy Little shook his head. "We haven't found any evidence of that. It seems to me that Paige was speaking to other craftsmen to cover her tracks. If she was only working with Elon, it would be more obvious that he was involved in the drug trafficking."

"I have one more question for you, Deputy," Lois said.

He sighed. "What's that?"

Lois frowned. "Was Gerome involved in the drugs?"

His face softened, and I liked Deputy Little even more for that show of compassion.

"Not as far as we can tell," he said. "But that doesn't mean he didn't suspect something or have an inkling as to what his new wife was up to."

Lois pursed her lips and nodded.

"Where do you go from here, Deputy?" I asked.

"We keep working on finding the source," he said.

"What about Paige's killer?" I pulled gloves out of my coat pocket and put them on. The snow was picking up again. Lois was right—February couldn't make up its mind about the weather.

"We have to find that person, too, but it's more important to get the drugs off the streets. The opiate and meth crisis is a major criminal and public health issue in rural Ohio. It's something that is becoming more prevalent and even more difficult to track to the sources. It's going to take most, if not all, of the department's resources to crack this case. The sheriff in particular is determined to get these drugs out of the county. He has bet his next election campaign on it."

I didn't disagree with Deputy Little that getting drugs out of Holmes County was important. Very important. But whatever Paige had done, she deserved justice too. Despite her mistakes, she had been a child of *Gott*.

Chapter Twenty-nine

When we were back in Lois's car, I laid my head back against the headrest. The movement knocked my bonnet over my ears, but I didn't care.

"I feel the same way," Lois said. "It's unbelievable."

"What do you want to do now?" I asked. "I don't even know if we should continue. This case is much bigger than we realized."

"We can't give up the case, if that's what you're getting at," she cried. "Paige's killer is still out there and still dangerous."

I straightened up. "I was hoping you would say that, because I don't want to give up, either."

"Good." Lois grinned. "Then, Swiss Carpentry next."

"Swiss Carpentry," I agreed.

When we arrived at the main street in Charm, which was lined with businesses, Lois found a spot to park near the quilt shop. Faith Dienner stood outside the shop, sweeping snow away from the front door.

I glanced at Lois. "Can you stay here for a little bit?" I asked.

"Matchmaker stuff?" she asked.

I nodded. "I just want to talk to her, and I doubt she will speak freely to me if you are with me."

"It's my hair, isn't it?" She patted the purple and red spikes on the top of her head. "It intimidates people."

Faith was so focused on the task at hand that she didn't hear my approach. I cleared my throat.

She held up her broom, as if she were ready to hit me with it. She gasped. "Oh, Millie, I am so sorry." She dropped her broom to her side. "I didn't scare you, did I?"

I stepped back. "Just a little."

Her face was beet red. "I'm so sorry and embarrassed."

"Why did you react that way? Were you expecting trouble?" I asked.

She shook her head.

"Were you expecting Hosea?"

Her face fell, and she went back to sweeping. "If my *grossmaami* asked you to come here and speak to me about Hosea and what a wonderful match he is for me, you are wasting your time."

"She didn't. Not today, at least. I just saw you sweeping on my way to another shop. I thought I would stop and see how you are."

"Because it's been put into your head that I need a match, or I'll have to leave the Amish life. I know what my *grossmaami* said to you."

"Are you planning to leave the Amish?" I asked, keeping any hint of judgment out of my voice.

"I don't want to leave the Amish way. I have never said that I would leave the Amish way, but my *grossmaami* believes if I'm not married by my twenty-first birthday that I will have to leave. In her mind, marriage is the be-all and end-all of a woman's life."

"Do you not want to get married?" I asked.

"I never said that, either. I just don't want to marry someone that I don't love. I'd rather not marry at all than have that happen. My *grossmaami* has already told me that this shop will be mine when she's gone. It does well. I will have more than enough money to care for myself. I'm not in a position that I have to get married. I think my *grossmaami* is just embarrassed that I don't have any prospects yet. She thinks I'm not doing the work to attract someone, so she put it into Hosea's head that we were a perfect match. We are not."

"Why do you think Hosea isn't right for you?"

"I just don't like him in that way. He's a nice enough young man, but he's not *my* young man."

It was a fair answer, and I liked a young woman who knew her own mind. Many *Englischers* believed that Amish women were repressed. Some may be, I would admit, but there are so many more who make their feelings, wants, and needs known to those around them. I was impressed that Faith already seemed to be able to do so at a young age. For an Amish woman, it was usually something that came with time and experience.

"He asked me about courting six months or so ago. I said I wasn't interested," she explained. "I thought that was enough to put an end to it. I didn't know at the time that my own *grossmaami* was behind his idea of marrying me."

"And you've told him you weren't interested since then?" I asked.

"*Ya*, at least four times, but it doesn't do any good. The worst of it is he started to leave presents at the quilt shop for me. I almost hate coming to work in the morning because there will be some gift from Hosea that I don't know what to do with. At first, I tried to give them back, but I think that encouraged him because I had to take them to his woodshop. In his mind, he thought I was visiting him. My *grossmaami* made it worse by telling him I was playing hard to get. I'm not. I don't want to be gotten." She scowled at her broom with the same fierceness that I imagined she directed at Hosea.

"What kind of gifts?" I asked.

"Everything you can think of," she said. "Candy, flowers, yarn, a battery-operated sewing machine. I gave it all back, yet the gifts kept coming. Then it got worse."

"It got worse than that?" I asked. "How?"

"He thought he needed other ways to impress me. He bought a brand-new courting buggy, thinking that I would go riding with him in it. I won't. I don't want a husband who will just buy things to solve problems."

I raised my brow. A new courting buggy would have cost Hosea several thousand dollars. It was a major investment for such a young man. Many young men don't buy one until they are sure that they are courting the right sweetheart, and even then, they often buy it used and fix it up.

"The buggy was just the start of it. He's become so much more intense about courting since . . ." She trailed off.

"Since when?" I asked.

"Since John Michael Smucker died. John Michael isn't a member of our district, but he and Hosea were friends. They were both carpenters," she said as if that explained the young men's friendship. "Hosea seems desperate now to get married. He told me that life is passing him by, and he needs to start a life of his own. He can. I don't care what he does, as long as I'm not involved."

This was the second young person to tell me Hosea and John Michael were close. It gave me even more reason to want to speak to Hosea. Maybe he would know something about John Michael's history with drugs and how he'd started using them. Or even where he got them from.

"I would say, Faith, that Hosea is not the right match for you. I will tell your *grossmaami* if necessary."

Her shoulders sagged with relief. "Will you? I love her very much, but these last few months have been hard since she made up her mind about Hosea and me. I just want things to go back to the way they used to be. We worked in the quilt shop together and seemed to laugh all day long. I was happy then. We were both happy then."

"Is she here now?" I asked.

"*Nee*, she went into Millersburg to pick up a new shipment of fabric. I don't expect her back for several hours." She leaned on her broom.

"Then I will speak to her as soon as I can," I promised.

"*Danki.*"

"Did you know John Michael well?" I asked.

She shook her head. "I only knew him from youth gatherings. He always seemed to be a nice young man. He was quiet. I thought . . . I thought that he was sad."

"Sad, how?" I asked.

"I'm not sure. It's just a feeling I got. He always seemed to be a little down in the mouth."

"How long did he seem like that?"

"As long as I knew him. Five or six years. We all started seeing each other when we entered *Rumspringa.*"

This was an interesting detail about John Michael. "Did you ever meet his family?"

"I've seen his father, Elijah, from time to time, but I never spoke to him. I know John Michael's mother passed away when he was twelve or thirteen. There was an accident."

"What happened?"

"I don't know, but Hosea probably would. Like I told you, the two of them were *gut* friends."

I planned to ask him. I planned to ask Hosea a lot of things very soon, I hoped.

"I should go back into the quilt shop," Faith said. "I have a lot of shelves to organize to make room for the fabric order my *grossmaami* is bringing back."

I nodded. "*Danki* for speaking to me."

"You're welcome," she said. "And you will speak to my *grossmaami*?"

"I will," I promised.

Chapter Thirty

As Lois and I walked to Swiss Carpentry, I filled her in on what Faith had said. She shook her head. "Poor Faith. I would hate being told who to love and marry. I don't always make the best decisions. Gerome being Exhibit A for that, but at least they are my decisions."

"I was concerned to hear that John Michael Smucker was sad."

"From her description, it sounds to me like John Michael was depressed." She brushed snow off her coat sleeve. "It could be why he was attracted to drugs. Maybe he was self-medicating."

If that were true, it must have been very challenging for John Michael. While the *Englisch* would go to a doctor or to therapy to get help for such a condition, it was different for the Amish. We were told to lean on *Gott*, and the Lord would bring us happiness. Our joy was to come from our faith. But there were Amish who might need extra help dealing with their internal struggles. Finding that counseling in our community was difficult and could even lead to disputes within a family or a district.

I honestly didn't know how I felt about it. I was Amish. I'd grown up and lived my whole adult life believing that if I leaned on *Gott* and my community, I could survive anything. That idea was tested when Kip died. During the months after his death, I felt a sadness that seemed to sink into the very marrow of my bones. Waking up in the morning was hard; doing anything was hard. My family said I was in a black mood. I was in deepest grief.

To get out of it, I needed to direct my attention elsewhere. I poured myself into my brother's family. My brother had lost his spouse, as well. I helped him raise his children, Edith and her brother. Those children, the greenhouse, and busyness saw me through. My faith did, too, but I needed those things to sustain my faith.

Faith had said John Michael's mother had died in an accident. He didn't have any siblings, which was unusual in the Amish world. Maybe he didn't have any place to redirect his grief.

Lois and I stepped into the woodshop, and again the smell of varnish and sawdust filled my nose.

A voice that sounded like Hosea's called from the back of the shop, saying he would be out in a second to help us. On the worktable were five new jewelry boxes that were waiting to be painted or stained. Each carving on the boxes' lids was more intricate than the last. One of the carvings was of a pig that looked a lot like Jethro. I wondered if that was a special order for Juliet Brook. It would not surprise me.

Hosea stepped into the room, holding several clean paintbrushes of varying sizes. When he saw Lois and me standing there, he froze. "What are you doing here again?"

"Is that the way to greet a couple of mature ladies?" Lois asked.

He blinked at her as if he couldn't make sense of her question. It wasn't uncommon for Amish people to taken aback by Lois's way of speaking.

"I'm sorry." He set the paintbrushes in a neat row on his workbench. "Was there something wrong with the jewelry box I sold you?"

"Not at all," Lois said. "I love it. I've already painted it, too. I went multicolor. It looks like it went to a rave."

Hosea looked pained, as if the thought of one his jewelry boxes painted multicolor was too much to bear.

I wasn't surprised that Lois had already painted the box, despite the many hours she spent at her work at the café and on our investigation. I was certain she didn't sleep all that much.

"If that's not why you're here, is it about Faith?" He looked to me with hope in his eyes.

I undid the ribbon of my bonnet and removed it from my head. It was very warm in the woodshop. I set it on the edge of the workbench. "I just spoke to Faith."

He stood up a little straighter, and hope filled his eyes. I hated to be the one to give him unwelcome news.

Before I could speak, Lois jumped in, "Faith

mentioned that you were good friends with John Michael Smucker."

Hosea's shoulders sank, as if he were a balloon that had just been deflated. "I was. John Michael was a very close friend of mine. I can't believe that he's gone."

Lois sat on a stool across from the workbench. There was a second stool next to hers, so I climbed on that. It was a bit high, so my perching on the bench was less than graceful. Lois lent me a hand.

"*Danki,*" I said to her, before turning back to Hosea. "Did you know about John Michael's struggles?"

He set the paintbrushes on the table in a neat row and selected a broad, flat brush. He dipped it into the can of stain. The sharp scent of the stain permeated the air. "John Michael had many struggles, but he was always a *gut* friend to me."

"But did you know that he was taking drugs?" Lois blurted out.

I folded my hands on my lap. Leave it to Lois to cut right to the heart of the matter.

He wiped the excess stain on the edge of the can. "I was the one who found him—his body, I mean."

I realized that I really didn't know the circumstances of John Michael's death. It was an overdose, *ya,* but I didn't know where he'd died, or until now, who'd found his body.

"I'm so sorry," I said.

He ran the paintbrush over the box. "It was awful. He was at home. I drove over in my new courting buggy. I wanted to show it to him. No one answered the door to the house, so I figured that

John Michael and his father were in their work-shop. His father wasn't there, but John Michael was dead on the floor. There were still drugs in his hand."

"What kind?" Lois asked. Her voice was soft now.

"Pills," he said. "But there was a pipe there, too. He'd smoked something. As you said, he had struggles." He made eye contact with us, and his look was so fierce, it took my breath away. "He had struggles, but I know he didn't want to die. He would not kill himself." He looked down at the jewelry box again. "He just went too far that one time to numb the pain."

"Could he have gotten the drugs from Paige Delpont Moorhead?" Lois asked.

"I know why you are asking that. I have heard the news about the truckload of furniture with drugs that was intended for Paige. I did not know that's what she was using the secret compartments for. If I had known, I would never have suggested that she talk to Elijah Smucker about making pieces for her stores."

"Elijah said he wasn't working with her," I said.

"I did not know that. I only gave her their name. I do know that she was working with Elon's Furniture Warehouse. He must have been a better fit for her. He must have been, since he went into the drug business with her. For Elijah's sake, I'm glad he wasn't working with her."

"You said that John Michael had struggles. What were they?" I asked.

At first, I thought he wasn't going to tell me. I could hardly blame him for keeping his friend's confidence.

"When we were twelve, John Michael's mother died. He never recovered from it." He looked me in the eye. "Because he killed her."

Lois and I sat across from Hosea with our mouths hanging open.

"What?" Lois asked. "How?"

Those were the same questions I had, but it was impossible at the moment for my mouth to even form the words.

"It was in a tractor accident. His father borrowed a tractor from an *Englischer* to clear some of the land on their property. When his father was away, John Michael decided to see if he could drive it. He lost control and hit his mother. She died at the hospital."

"She didn't see him coming?" Lois asked.

"She was hanging clothes on the line and had her back to John Michael and the tractor. By the time she realized what was happening, it was too late." He took a breath. "His father blamed him for his mother's death. It was John Michael's fault, and Elijah never let him forget it. He reminded him every day that he killed his own mother. It just ate away at him. He tried so many things to deal with it. He spoke to his bishop. He threw himself into the community. He threw himself into work. He tried alcohol. Finally, he tried drugs."

"So you knew he was using," Lois said.

He frowned at her. "I suspected. A lot of us did. I wasn't surprised that it was something like that based on his pattern of dealing with his mother's death. His *daed* never forgave him for what happened." Hosea dipped his paintbrush into the can of stain again.

"Are the Smuckers allowed to use a tractor in their district?" Lois asked.

It was a very *gut* question. Every district bishop determined the level of technology that his church members would be allowed to use. I thought that the Smuckers were Old Order Amish. A tractor was unlikely to have been approved.

Hosea shook his head. "His bishop said that tragedies happened when church rules were broken."

"His bishop sounds like a—"

"That's awful," I interrupted Lois before she could say something that would shock Hosea.

I felt my shoulders sag as I thought of the carefree twelve-year-old boy who'd climbed on that tractor on a whim. That child was gone long before John Michael died. He died that day and never forgave himself for what had happened. His father never forgave him either. Our faith preached forgiveness. Preaching about forgiveness and granting it were two very different acts. Clearly, it was a difficulty that Elijah Smucker wasn't able to overcome.

"After what happened to John Michael, I want to marry Faith more than ever. I know that there is no time to waste in this life. I know that I'm meant to be with her. I don't know why we should wait."

He ran the bristles of the brush across the top of the jewelry box, smoothly and expertly following the grain of the wood. It was something that he had done thousands of times before. Something that he could do in his sleep.

"It's more than waiting, Hosea," I said as gently

as I could. "Faith has not consented to be courted by you."

"But that's what you talked to her about, right? Netty told me that she was going to talk to you about convincing Faith that I am the best match for her. I *am* the best match for her. I know it deep in my heart."

I shifted on my stool and studied the young man. He was so sincere. He really did believe that he should marry Faith. Yet he'd admitted to us before that he didn't love her. Why was he so sure? And why the urgency?

The back door in the shop opened, and an Amish man with a salt-and-pepper beard came through it. He leaned heavily on a walnut cane.

"Hosea, did you finish staining those jewelry boxes? I want to make sure that they are dry before the order is picked up tomorrow." He blinked when he saw Lois and me, sitting on the pair of stools like a couple of schoolgirls. "Oh, I am sorry," he said kindly. "Are you ladies interested in a jewelry box? These are spoken for, but we have more in the back."

"I bought one the last time I was here," Lois said. "I love it. The craftsmanship is unbelievable."

He smiled. "I'm glad to hear it. That's my son's work. The boxes were his idea, too. Since we have started selling them, business has really picked up. He's a very talented young man."

"This is my father," Hosea said. "James."

I could see from where I was sitting that his leg was crooked. It was twisted in at a strange angle and appeared to be painful.

Lois hopped off her stool. "Here. You can have my seat."

He smiled. "That's very kind of you, but I'm used to leaning on this cane. It's very sturdy. I have been leaning on it for over a decade."

James smiled and brushed sawdust off the table and onto the floor. "You must excuse our mess. Without a mother in the home, Hosea and I do our best. It would be nice to have someone to help with the cooking and the cleaning, though."

I felt Lois bristle beside me, and I willed her not to say anything. I knew how she felt about that kind of sentiment over a woman's place being in the home. Hers wasn't the Amish way of thinking. That was for certain.

"You don't have any other children?" I asked.

"We were just blessed with Hosea. He was one when his mother passed. She wasn't well. I never remarried." He tapped his injured leg with his cane. "No one would want to marry a man with a crooked leg and my condition."

"What is your condition, if I may ask?" Lois said.

"You can ask. MS, I'm afraid. I was diagnosed when Hosea was just a boy. It's gotten worse over the years. My leg injury isn't from the disease, at least not directly. I lost my balance on a ladder, and down I went." He shook his head. "I'm a mess, but I have a loving son who cares for me day and night."

"I'm sorry to hear about your wife and everything you've been through," I said.

"*Danki*, but it was a long time ago." He smiled at his son. "I am lucky that I have this boy here. He would do anything for me, and I know that. Makes me proud to know I raised him right. Soon, too, he will be married. I hope to live to see my grandchildren. That's all I really want before I pass on."

Hosea picked up a chisel from the table and flipped it around in his fingers, as if he needed something to occupy himself.

Lois looked as if she were about to speak. Fearing that she might say Hosea wasn't about to be married, I put a hand on her arm. That was news Hosea needed to share with his father.

James smiled at us. "If you are not here to buy a jewelry box, what brought you by today? Window shopping? I know that's popular with *Englischers*."

"Millie and I are trying to find out what happened to Paige Moorhead."

"Oh." James slowly settled on a stool then and propped his cane against the worktable. "That is a sad story, and we were hoping to get more commissions from her. However, now that we've heard the rumors, perhaps it was best she never showed up for our meeting."

Lois and I perked up.

"Rumors?" I asked.

He nodded. "Just that the Delpont Furniture Warehouse was very demanding and cared more about quantity than quality. We are about quality in this shop. That's why it takes us so long to build every piece. Paige bought a number of our carved boxes, but mass production is better for other furniture stores."

"Which ones?" Lois asked.

"Elon's, for one. He approached us, too, about making pieces to sell wholesale for him, but I said no. If he wanted mass production, find something made in the *Englisch* factories. People buy Amish furniture and wooden pieces for the care and thought that is put into each piece."

"Did you know Elon was arrested this morning?" I asked.

James's mouth fell open. "*Nee.* Arrested why?"

"He was involved with moving drugs. The drugs were hidden in his furniture."

"Oh my heavens, that's shocking," James said.

However, I noted that Hosea didn't seem shocked at all. He grimaced, as if he were halfway expecting this news.

James shook his head and ever so slowly stood up. He wobbled when he went to grab his cane. Hosea jumped into action and steadied his father. "*Daed*, why don't you go lie down in the back. I can handle the shop for the day."

James smiled at his son. "I know you can. It was nice to see you ladies."

"I'm going to go get my father settled," Hosea said to Lois and me.

It was a clear hint that it was time for us to leave.

As we walked back to Lois's car, she said, "Don't you think it's interesting that both John Michael and Hosea just have their fathers for family? Neither had mothers in their lives. Hosea's father seems to be the more cheerful of the two, despite his injury."

I hadn't thought about it before, but it was a bit surprising. "I'm not sure it's fair to make that assumption. We only met Elijah Smucker after his son died of an overdose. It's impossible for us to say what he was like before then."

"You're right," she agreed. "I take that back. Besides, James Flaud apparently thinks a woman's job is to stay home and keep house. I'm not on board with that."

"I knew you weren't. I appreciate your holding your tongue when he made that statement. I know you wanted to say something."

"Oh, I very much did, but sometimes the case has to come before making my feelings known. I hold my tongue more often than not, Millie. Much more often than not."

That was hard to believe.

Chapter Thirty-one

The next morning, I took the goats for a walk to the phone shed I shared with Raellen Raber's family.

Phillip and Peter bounced around me as we made our way across the snow-covered fields between the two farms. There was nothing the goats loved better than to go on an adventure. In nice weather, I would have taken them for a bike ride. Meaning, I would ride my bicycle, and they would run alongside me. When I worked at my niece's greenhouse, I took the goats with me as much as Edith would allow. This turned out to be about once a week, as they wore out their welcome quickly by eating the plants and generally making a nuisance of themselves.

Raellen's husband wasn't a fan of the goats, either. He believed they corrupted his docile sheep and taught them to misbehave. He forbade me to bring the goats to the shed phone, but he wasn't my husband or bishop. I saw no reason to listen to him.

I wasn't saying his reasons for wanting to keep the goats away from his sheep were unfounded. However, there was a killer on the loose in the county, and I felt a lot safer making the half-mile trek across the fields to the shed phone with Phillip and Peter at my side. It wasn't that I thought the goats could protect me. On the contrary, they would much rather play with my attacker than fend him off, but I knew at least they would be a distraction and give me more time to escape.

It seemed my concerns about the walk were unwarranted. The goats and I didn't see anything out of the ordinary on the way to the Raber sheep farm. There was no sign of Raellen, her husband, or any of her nine children, either. But the sheep were out. They were just normal sheep, minding their own business. They weren't at all like the sheep at the Munich Chalet. Those sheep were shifty.

Before I went into the phone shed—which looked like an old outhouse from the outside, but thankfully, had never been used as one—I said to the goats, "I'm counting on the two of you to be *gut* while I make this call. Leave the sheep alone. If I see you near the sheep, no more walks to the Raber farm for you. I can't have Raellen's husband upset with me all the time."

They hung their heads, as if they understood what I'd said, or maybe they just understood my tone. They knew when I meant business.

I stepped into the phone shed. There was a snow shovel and a pair of snowshoes in the corner, and the phone sat on a small table by the only window. Next to the table was a chair. From my coat pocket, I removed the piece of paper with the phone number of Netty Dienner's quilt shop on it.

Netty answered on the very first ring.

"Good morning, Netty. It's Millie Fisher," I said into the phone.

"Oh hello, Millie. It's always so *gut* to hear from you." Her voice was pleasant but nervous too, as if she was unsure what I might be calling her about.

Amish don't chat on the phone to socialize. Conversations were held face-to-face, so there was less chance for miscommunication. That was what I wanted too, and why I was calling. It was time Netty and I had a conversation face-to-face on neutral territory.

"I wondered if you could meet me at the Sunbeam Café this morning, say around ten. I would love to talk to you."

"Oh, why? Is something wrong?"

"I wanted to talk to you about Hosea and Faith, where Faith cannot overhear."

"Oh! *Ya, ya,* I would like to talk to you about that. I suppose I can be gone for a few hours. Faith can mind the store."

The irony that Faith would be minding the store while her *grossmaami* and I would be discussing her future was not lost on me. However, my conversation with Netty was one Faith both needed and had asked me to have with her *grossmaami*.

"Let me check with Faith. I don't know why it wouldn't be all right, but sometimes she has deliveries I don't know about."

I heard her set the phone on the counter.

Less than a minute later, she was back. "It is fine. I will see you at the Sunbeam at ten. Would that work?"

I agreed that it would and ended the call with a smile. The conversation had gone much better than I'd anticipated.

I stepped out of the shed. Phillip and Peter were waiting for me with goofy looks on their faces. I knew what they were thinking. "The sheep are still off limits."

They hung their heads.

"Millie," Raellen called, stepping out of the nearby barn. She wore a dust-covered apron over her thick woolen coat. "It's so nice to see you!" She smiled from ear to ear.

I had never seen Raellen disappointed to see anyone. She always appeared to be cheerful.

"Oh, it's a *gut* day for you to take the goats for a walk. I won't tell my husband they were here." Raellen didn't have the same issues with the goats that her husband did.

"*Danki,*" I said with a smile. "Is your husband home?" I asked, looking about.

She shook her head. "I'm here all by myself. The older children are at school, and my mother took the youngest ones for the day. With everyone gone, I'm trying to catch up on some chores. Things I never have time to do in spring, summer, or fall because we are so busy keeping up the farm."

"It will be spring soon enough," I said.

She nodded. "I know. I love the warmer days, but I do enjoy the slow pace of winter. I also like having the farm to myself on days like today." Her eyes twinkled. "There are ten of them, including my husband, so it is nice to have a little peace and quiet. Would you like to come in for a cup of coffee? I just put on a fresh pot."

I smiled and thanked her. "I can't stay. I'm meeting someone in town."

"Oh?" She perked up. "Who?"

"Lois will be there," I said evasively.

She wrinkled her nose, and I knew it wasn't the answer she'd been hoping for. Raellen wanted more gossip to add to her warehouse of information. I needed to distract her.

"You know when Lois and I were at the Munich Chalet, we saw a flock of sheep there."

"Sheep? I didn't realize the Munich Chalet had sheep. Do you know the breed?"

I shook my head. "I don't, but I thought they were odd sheep, at that. They followed the deputy around the grounds."

"If sheep are watching you, they either think you have food or want to play. I wouldn't worry too much about the sheep at the chalet."

I smiled. "I'll remember that." I turned to go.

The goats were inching their way toward the sheep, so I knew it was time to leave. I didn't want the goats to be blamed for any of the sheep's bad habits.

"Oh, Millie, have you heard the news?" Raellen asked with a hint of excitement in her voice.

I turned back to her, keeping one eye on the goats. I thought they could sense me watching because they were no longer making their way toward the sheep pasture.

"News?" I had a feeling that Raellen was going

to tell me about the arrest of Elon Troyer. I knew
that Raellen would be thrilled to tell me that type
of news. It wasn't because she was malicious or
would be happy that an Amish man had been arrested. She just loved to be the first to share the
news, any news. "What's the news?"

"Uriah Schrock is coming back to Harvest," she
said triumphantly.

I stared at her. It was the very last thing that I'd
expected her to say. I stopped breathing for a second. When air entered my lungs again, I managed
to ask, "What did you say?" Perhaps I'd heard her
wrong.

"Uriah Schrock. He's coming back." She frowned.
"Honestly, I thought you would know, since the
two of you are old friends."

Old friends was one way to describe it.

"I—I didn't know."

Raellen cocked her head like one of her sheep
when it was inspecting a fresh blade of grass. "Are
you happy about this? You don't look too happy
about it."

"I—I—Who told you this?" I asked. Raellen didn't
always have her facts straight. She could be wrong.

"I heard it when I went to the market the other
day. Margot Rawlings was complaining to the clerk
there about how hard it is to find help for the
events on the square. Leon is doing an okay job,
but with the expansion of the events on the square
that are scheduled for the year, she didn't think he
could keep up. She said only Uriah was up to the
task."

I nodded. I didn't doubt it was true. Margot was

exacting about how she wanted things when it came to the square. She'd told me that Uriah had done so well because he'd been good at anticipating what she wanted for every event, from the tables to the number of chairs and the square decorations. I let out a sigh. Just because Margot wanted Uriah to come back to Harvest did not mean he would return. It was likely a false alarm. Just another piece of gossip Raellen could not help but share.

There was no question Raellen had an ear for gossip. She knew what people were talking about in the village and the county as a whole, but her information wasn't always right. Even though people were talking about something, that didn't mean what had been said was always accurate, or would come to be.

Part of me also thought Uriah would have surely written a letter to me if he had decided to come back to Harvest. He was my friend. Or I had believed we were friends, at least.

Just to be sure, I said, "So he's not coming back. Margot just wants him to."

Raellen sighed, as if I'd popped her balloon. "I guess so, but Margot did say that she had written him and offered him his old job back. He might return."

That was hard for me to believe. Uriah was a hard worker, and I didn't doubt for a second that he would be able to find work in Indiana, where his children and the rest of his family lived. He would have no reason to come back to Harvest. No reason at all.

Even so, I wanted to go home to process the possibility. I said goodbye to Raellen and whistled for the goats.

On the walk back to my little farm, the goats were quieter than normal. They reacted to my change of mood as if they weren't sure what I would do next. I wasn't sure either. I couldn't understand why even the possibility of Uriah Schrock returning to Harvest shook me so badly.

It was time I headed into town. I would have to take Bessie and my buggy into town, and the trip that took twenty minutes when Lois drove me would take at least forty-five minutes by buggy. I also wanted to get to the café before Netty to collect my thoughts about Faith and Hosea.

Focusing on Netty, I hoped to push thoughts of Uriah out of my mind. It was not to be. Still, the rumor that Uriah Schrock might be returning to Harvest unsettled me. When he'd left, I thought I had made peace with his decision. However, I wondered now if that were really true.

Chapter Thirty-two

"Darcy, fire up the blueberries!" Lois called toward the café's kitchen. "Millie's here."

I removed my bonnet. "Fire up the blueberries?" I arched my brow.

"I'm trying to bring diner talk into the business."

"But this isn't a diner."

She shrugged. "That's never stopped me before. Did you get hold of Netty?"

I nodded. "She will be here soon."

"Good. I saved the front table for the two of you. Take up your post. I'll bring out the blueberry pie." She wiggled her brow. "You do want pie, don't you?"

I did. I glanced at the table by the window. It wasn't lost on me that it was the closest table to the counter.

"Better for eavesdropping?" I asked.

"You bet. I want to know what's going on here. Be sure to speak English, so I can follow along." She pointed the coffeepot she was holding at me.

Darcy appeared in the kitchen door, holding a piece of blueberry pie. "Blueberries on deck, Gram!"

Lois grinned. "That's my girl. Did I raise her right or not?"

Darcy grinned back.

"Darcy, tell Millie all about our new man!" Lois buzzed with excitement.

Darcy blushed. "Grandma!"

"Oh, come on. The only customer who is in here right now is that old codger in the back. He couldn't hear the tornado sirens go off. Besides, Millie is like your second grandma. You can tell her."

Darcy brushed flour from her apron. "His name is Victor Pennington, and he works for the county."

"What does he do for the county?"

"I'm not sure. He works in the office."

"He's a paper pusher," Lois declared. "Which means he's a nice stable young man with a state pension. What more could you want?"

"Grandma." Darcy gave an all-suffering sigh.

"Hush, you. Your grandma is just speaking facts." Lois set her coffeepot on the table. "Millie, you will have to see the two together to give your Amish sixth-sense stamp of approval."

"That's not what I call my matchmaking gift."

"Well, whatever you call it, Darcy needs it!"

Darcy waved her arms back and forth, as if she were directing traffic. "I don't want the two of you meeting him just yet. We just started dating. I don't want you . . ."

Lois narrowed her eyes. "You don't want us to what? Ruin it, embarrass you, scare him off?"

"I don't want any of that," Darcy said.

Lois put her hands on her hips. "I am your grandmother. I have every right to meet every man who loves my granddaughter."

"Grandma, who said anything about love? We've been on four dates. That's it."

"I see that gleam in your eye. I know it. You're my granddaughter too. We fall hard and fast for men. I just hope you got a good one. That's why I want Millie to check him out before you fall in too deep. Believe you me, you do not want to find yourself in a situation like the one I have with Gerome Moorhead. Besides, one of those dates was Valentine's Day. That means something." Lois folded her arms like it was an open-and-shut case.

Darcy groaned.

I decided it was time to step in. "Lois, weren't you just telling me that young people have to make up their own minds?" I arched my brow.

"I, well, yes, but . . ."

I tilted my head to one side.

"Oh, Millie, how am I going to meet the mystery man if you are on Darcy's side? You are supposed to be on my team."

"I can be on both of your teams," I said.

Lois grunted.

"If I show you a picture of him, will that satisfy you until I'm ready to introduce him?" Darcy asked.

Lois clapped her hands. "Yes. Gimme."

Darcy removed her phone from her apron pocket, tapped the screen, and held it out to Lois and me. Inside the outline of the heart was a picture of a pleasant-looking man with a wide smile.

"You met him on a dating app?" Lois cried. "I've been waiting to try that. Can you set up a profile for me?"

"Dating app?" I asked.

"It's a place to meet someone online. It's really cool because you can weed through the guys and avoid going on a lot of uncomfortable dates. It's called Like to Love Dating," Darcy explained. "I can set up a profile for you, Grandma. I'm sure you'd get lots of hearts."

"Hearts?" I asked.

"When a guy is interested, he sends you a heart. Victor sent me five before I got up the nerve to send him one back." She blushed.

"Ohhhh!" Lois cooed. "I'd be great at collecting hearts. Let's do it now." Lois wrapped her arm around Darcy's shoulders. "It's quiet upfront now. Millie can handle anything that might come up. Right, Millie? Let's go in the back and get me all set up. I need some hearts!"

After Lois and Darcy went back into their kitchen to play with the app or whatever it was, I sipped my coffee and eyed the piece of blueberry pie Darcy had brought to the table. I refused to take a bite of it until Netty arrived. Also, to be honest, I didn't know if I could eat it, feeling so nervous over my conversation with Netty. I didn't know how this would go. I prayed Netty would be receptive to what I had to say.

Through the front window, I watched as a buggy parked next to the square. The quilt shop owner stepped out of the buggy and tethered her horse to the hitching post.

The bell above the door rang as Netty stepped into the café. She removed her gloves and then her bonnet. I started to stand up. She waved me back into my chair. "Please, Millie, don't get up." She hung her bonnet and coat on the pegs near the door and then took the seat across from me.

"Would you like anything to eat?" I asked. "I'm having blueberry pie."

"That looks scrumptious. Do they have cherry pie?"

"Cherry pie coming up!" Lois cried through the open kitchen door. "Millie, I already have two hearts."

Netty's eyes went wide. "Two hearts."

"*Englischers*," I said with a shrug.

She nodded as if this answer made perfect sense. "I'm just so happy you called me to meet with you about Faith. Have you spoken with her?" There was hope in her voice.

I hated to be the one taking that hope away, but she needed to know the truth.

Lois slid a piece of cherry pie and coffee in front of Netty. "On the house."

Netty thanked her, and Lois stood there for a long moment.

"Lois, don't you have some other customers to take care of?" I hinted.

"Nope," she said.

"I'm very sure you do," I said. "Or don't you need to look at that app?"

"Oh, fine." She walked away, but only as far as the café counter.

"App?" Netty asked.

I shrugged. "I really don't know what it means."

Netty picked up her fork and poked at her pie, but she didn't take a bite. "I would love to hear what you have to say about Hosea and Faith. They are a perfect match, aren't they? I have known it since they were young. I've been telling both of them for years."

I set my fork beside my plate. "It was your idea for Hosea to begin courting Faith."

She nodded and added cream to her coffee. "It just makes so much sense, don't you think? Our businesses are so close to each other. Faith will inherit the quilt shop when I'm gone. Hosea will inherit the woodworking shop when his father passes. It's a *gut* match."

"It may make sense, but it's not how Faith feels."

She set her coffee cup back on the table. "It's not how she feels now, but feelings change in the passage of life. She just needs time."

"That can happen, I agree, but Faith does not love Hosea, nor does she want to marry him. She has told both you and Hosea this many times. I believe they are not a *gut* match, and you should let the girl be." I paused. "Usually, I do not try to get involved in familial matters. I'm telling you this now because the situation has the potential to harm your family. If you push Faith too far, she might leave the Amish way. She doesn't want to do that."

"But when Hosea told me he wanted to find a wife, I knew Faith was the perfect fit."

Clearly, she wasn't listening to me, and I imagined she spoke to Faith in much the same way. She was so fixated on her idea, she wasn't seeing any other option.

"However," I said for what felt like the hundredth time, "it's not what Faith wants. She is your grand-daughter. Shouldn't your loyalty be to her?"

"Not when she is wrong," Netty said stubbornly. "She can't leave the community." Tears gathered in Netty's eyes. "She is baptized. If she leaves now, she will be shunned. I won't be able to see her again."

And there was the heart of Netty's concern. She didn't want to lose her granddaughter. I knew she was going about it the wrong way, but I did have compassion for her. Every Amish mother, grand-mother, and aunt worried about the young people in her family. Would they make the choice to stay in the community or to leave? Netty wanted Faith to stay. Netty was just squeezing a little too tight, trying to control Faith's choices. However, Faith was the one who had to choose. That was the tenet of our faith.

"She doesn't want to leave the Amish," I said as clearly as I could. "She just doesn't want to marry Hosea."

Netty blinked as if she were coming out of some kind of trance. "I—I didn't know she felt that way. All this time, I thought she was reluctant to marry him because she wanted to leave the Amish way. So many young women have left recently. Look at Charlotte Weaver."

"Charlotte was never baptized as Faith was." I wrapped my hands around my coffee mug. "She had been struggling with being Amish for years. Her parents were hard on her. Her situation is different."

She shook her head. "The idea of leaving can rub off on other young people. I want Faith to take over the quilt shop. I want her to be Amish."

"And she can do both of those things whether she marries or not," I argued. "I do not think she is asking too much to wait and marry for love. She'd rather not marry than marry a man she doesn't love. She wants to work at the quilt shop and stay Amish. That was never in question for her."

"Why didn't she tell me this herself?" There was hurt in her voice.

"I believe she tried," I said as gently as I could.

Netty folded her arms and bowed her head. "I have made a mess of everything, haven't I?"

"You can fix it. Go home now and speak to Faith."

She nodded. "I will."

Lois appeared at her elbow, holding two takeout boxes. "You want that pie to go? You didn't even touch it. I have another piece here for Faith, too. You all have a nice chat over some pie and tea." Lois didn't wait for Netty to answer but packed up the piece of cherry pie from the table.

Tears came to Netty's eyes. "That's very kind of you. I think I will do that." She put on her coat and bonnet and accepted the takeout boxes from Lois. "*Danki*, Millie. I am glad we had this chat."

"Me too," I said with a smile.

After Netty left, Lois fell into her empty chair. "I'm glad that's settled. Family dynamics can be so exhausting. Now, we can get back to the case of who killed Paige Moorhead."

"We can," I agreed. "But who do we talk to at this point? We have spoken to everyone involved several times, and never seem to get very far."

"We haven't spoken to everyone," Lois said, picking up Netty's unused fork and stealing a bite of my pie.

"Oh?" I asked.

"Ronan Delpont. We haven't talked to him. If anyone knows what Paige was up to when she died, it would be him. She was in the business with her brother."

"Deputy Little wouldn't like that."

"He doesn't like any part of our investigations, does he?" Taking another bite of pie, she asked, "Has that ever stopped us before?"

"Not really," I admitted. "But how do we find—"

Juliet Brook stormed into the café in a cloud of new snow and indignation. "I have never come across someone so rude in my life!" She held Jethro, her polka-dotted pig, close to her chest.

She squeezed the little pig so tightly, it looked like his eyes would pop right out of his head.

Lois jumped from her seat and rescued the little pig. "Let me take Jethro, and you sit down and collect yourself."

"Thank you, Lois," Juliet said, removing her scarf and fluffing her hair. "I need a little kindness after what I've just been through."

"What happened?" I asked.

"Well, Jethro and I were on a walk, you see. Since he's going to be a movie star, we really have to think about keeping him fit. He's on a special diet now too. No more table scraps."

Jethro sighed in Lois's arms. The table scrap rule seemed to come as a real blow to the little pig. When Lois set Jethro on the floor, he shuffled over to the counter and slid under a stool, as if he was exhausted by the whole ordeal. Or he was exhausted by his mistress. It was hard to say.

"And while we were on our walk," Juliet continued, "we were crossing the street, coming from the market. This black sports car sped out of nowhere and almost hit us. If I hadn't been holding Jethro, he surely would have been run over. The man parked the car and yelled as if it were our fault he almost hit us. Before I could say anything, he stomped into the market. It really shook me up."

"Who was this man?" Lois wanted to know. "If I run into him, I want to be able to tell him off."

"Would you?" Juliet asked. "As the pastor's wife, I'm not in the position to tell people off. I have to be kind, but sometimes . . ."

"I don't have any qualms about that," Lois said.

"He was *Englisch.* A tall, blond man, and he was wearing a jacket that said Delpont on it. I have never seen him around here before."

Lois and I shared a look. Her physical description could have fit any number of men, but it did sound a lot like Ronan Delpont, and the jacket was a dead giveaway. It was the only possible lead we had on his whereabouts, so we had to follow it up.

"Do you think he's still at the market?" Lois asked.

"I don't know." Juliet shook her head.

Lois hurried into the kitchen without saying anything else. But I knew what she was doing, telling Darcy yet again that she and I had to leave to solve a murder. It was amazing Darcy took this behavior from her grandmother in stride. However, I supposed a person had to if Lois was their grandmother.

"I'm sorry this happened, Juliet," I said.

"Thank you." She smiled at me. "I feel better just talking about it. I am very protective of Jethro, you know."

We knew. The whole village knew.

Lois reappeared and grabbed our coats and my bonnet from the pegs on the wall. "Millie and I will go find this man for you, Juliet, and tell him what's what."

"Oh, that's very kind of you."

"In the meantime, Darcy is getting you a bowl of chicken noodle soup to soothe you."

"For Jethro, too? He can have chicken soup."

Looked like that table scrap rule was about to be broken . . .

"For Jethro, too," Lois agreed.

Chapter Thirty-three

I had to quicken my pace to keep up with Lois on the slippery sidewalk. "Lois, please slow down. You're going to fall in the snow, and we don't have time for a broken hip."

"There is never a good time for a broken hip," Lois said, but she did slow down just a little. "We have to be quick if we're going to have any chance of catching Ronan before he leaves the market. I can't believe our luck that he's in town. He might be the missing piece of this case."

"We don't know for sure it was even Ronan that Juliet saw," I said.

She eyed me. "Who else would be wearing a Delpont jacket around here?"

She had a point there.

The market came into view. The store was the largest business in the downtown area of Harvest. Situated just a block over from the central square, it sold essential and mostly bulk foods. It catered to the Amish in the community and was as simple as a store could be. If an *Englischer* or even an Amish person wanted a name-brand product, this was not the place to find it. At the market, the portions were large, and the prices were cheap.

A black sports car was parked right out front.

Lois yipped. "He's still here. That's perfect." She started to march toward the market door.

I grabbed her arm. "Wait. Maybe we should call Deputy Little. That's what he would want us to do."

"There's no time for that! Besides, we don't know if Ronan drove the car. We have to check first. Then I'll call the deputy."

This seemed like a very bad idea to me. But since I didn't have a phone of my own, I couldn't make the call.

Lois grabbed a shopping cart from under the overhang near the market door. "Our cover," she explained.

This was a terrible idea.

We stepped into the market, and the owner waved at us from behind the counter. "It's nice to see the two of you. Can I help you with something?"

"No, we're just looking," Lois said, and then grabbed a bag of beans from a nearby shelf before dropping them into her cart. I had never seen her buy beans in her life. It was part of her cover, I supposed.

Lois added onions to her cart. "Did a tall English man with blond hair come in here?" she asked as casually as she could. However, the question didn't come out casual at all.

"A blond man?" the merchant asked.

"Yes, I think he was driving the black car parked just outside."

He wrinkled his nose. "I saw him." He lowered his voice. "He's not the friendliest. Must be a tourist."

Lois nodded agreement.

"He's in the back of the store, I think. Near the paper products."

"Thanks!" Lois said and steered her cart in that direction.

I tugged on her sleeve. "Let's just verify it's Ronan and call the deputy."

"That's what I'm doing," she whispered back.

At the very back of the store, near the storage room, a tall blond man stood looking at his phone.

"It's Ronan," Lois whispered triumphantly.

"Okay, it's time the call the deputy."

"Sure. In one second."

If I'd had the ability to find her phone in her massive purse, I would have taken it from her at that moment and made the call myself.

"I always like the paper towels with the little pictures on them," Lois said to Ronan. "Don't you? It just brings some cheer to cleaning."

He stared at her.

"Oh, are you Paige Moorhead's brother?" Lois said.

He said nothing.

"I guess you don't remember, but we met briefly at Swiss Carpentry over the weekend. I'm Lois, and this is my best friend, Millie. People think it's odd that we are best friends because, well, look at us. We couldn't be more different. But I can assure you, you won't find a tighter pair. We were there when your sister died." She lowered her voice. "We are so sorry for your loss."

"You're friends with Gerome." He wrinkled his nose as if he smelled something bad. "That troll."

"I know Gerome can be a bit of heel, but calling him a troll is a little much. What are you still doing in the county? More business?"

He tried to step around Lois, but she positioned her shopping cart to block the aisle. There was only a dead end behind him. He had no means of escape.

"What are you doing?" he asked.

Lois smiled up at him. "I find it so interesting that Paige and you were requesting custom orders of Amish furniture with hidden compartments. Did you hear about that big drug bust? Drugs found in all those 'secret' compartments. Guess the secret's out, huh?"

He pushed her cart. "Get out of my way."

"Lois." I pulled on her purse. "Step out of the man's path."

There was no question Lois was brave. Or in this case, too brave for her own good. Ronan was twice her size. He could easily push her aside if he wanted to. She could really get hurt. I should have insisted she call the deputy before we came into the market.

To my surprise, Lois did move.

After Ronan had passed us, he turned for a moment. "I'm just trying to find out what happened to my sister. Why can't you people understand that?"

"Who is 'you people'?" Lois asked after he was gone.

It took some convincing, but I finally talked Lois into calling Deputy Little, and half hour later, Lois and I were sipping tea at the Sunbeam Café, while Deputy Little rubbed his head as if he had a headache. "This case is complicated enough without the two of you going around upsetting suspects."

"Oh, is Ronan a suspect in the murder?" Lois asked. Her eyes sparkled with interest.

He scowled at her. "Everyone is a suspect in my book until the case is over. Some are just more suspicious than others."

Lois placed a hand to her chest, and her bright nail polish gleamed in the café's light. "You can still think I'm a suspect, Deputy. Millie is my alibi. You would be hard-pressed to find a more upstanding person than my friend Millie."

He sighed. "You are not a main suspect."

"Who is?" I asked.

He shook his head, as if he knew the question was a trap of some sort and he wasn't falling for it. The deputy blew out a breath. "In the meantime, just please stay away from Ronan. I don't know exactly how he's involved in all this. It's safer if the two of you stay away from him."

"We will," Lois and I promised in unison. I noticed that Lois had her fingers crossed under the table.

Chapter Thirty-four

I was about to head home from the Sunbeam Café late that afternoon when an unexpected visitor walked through the door. Lois was wiping down the empty tables when the bell above the door rang.

When she looked up from her task, she frowned. "Gerome, I didn't expect to see you here again."

He cleared his throat. "I never expected to be back. I didn't have the warmest welcome the first time."

She winced. "That was my fault. I never did get to apologize for how I behaved. That's why Millie and I were at the Munich Chalet Saturday morning. I wanted to say sorry."

He nodded. "Consider it forgiven." He looked around the room.

"Would you like a cup of coffee?" Lois asked. "Can I talk you into a piece of my granddaughter's world-famous pie?" She lowered her voice. "Her pie is better than Amish pie, but don't let any Amish lady hear you say that, besides Millie, of course."

I smiled. But behind the smile, I was wondering what he was doing there.

"I'll take some coffee. No pie for me, thanks."

Lois picked up her rag from the table and went behind the counter to get the coffee and a mug.

Gerome looked around the room as if he didn't know where to sit.

"Why don't you sit with me, Gerome?" I said.

He scrunched up his nose as if he wasn't comfortable with that idea but could not think of a reason to say no. When he was seated, Lois put a mug of coffee in front of him. "Cream, no sugar."

He looked up at her. "You remembered my coffee order."

"I remember all coffee orders I serve more than once, whether I want to or not."

He nodded and looked down at the table.

Lois crossed her arms. "Why are you here, Gerome?"

He looked from Lois to me and back again. "You said that you were going to find the person who killed my wife."

"We said that we would try," I corrected. It was a very important distinction.

He cleared his throat. "Well, yes. I just came by to see if you'd learned anything new."

I glanced at Lois. We had learned many new things about the case since we'd spoken to Gerome last, but we didn't know how they all fit together.

"Not really," Lois said. "We are piecing it together like one of Millie's quilts, and like a quilt, it's taking time."

Gerome scrunched up his face. "Time is not something I have. Her family . . . well, you saw when Ronan was talking to me at the chalet the other day. Her family is becoming impatient to know what happened and to have her body moved back to Cleveland. I believe they expect me to be able to do both of those things."

"They can't expect you to solve the murder," Lois said. "You're not law enforcement or super sleuths like us."

I shook my head. Apparently, *super sleuths* was a new title that Lois had just dreamed up. I wondered what she would come up with next.

He frowned. "That's the situation I am in, so I really need you to wrap this up."

Lois cocked her head. "If I may ask, Gerome, why did you marry Paige?"

He stared at her. "What?"

"I'm curious why you married her. Because from what I see, you have demonstrated very little love or affection for her. Maybe some when she was alive, and you called her that pet name. What was it? Oh, right, Honeybee—but since then, you just seem to be more inconvenienced by her murder than anything else."

He gaped at her. "How dare you say such a thing? I loved my wife."

"Could it be that you were already bored and ready to move on? The same as you were with me?"

He jumped out of his chair so quickly that it toppled to the floor. He didn't even bother to try to stand it up. "I loved Paige. But—"

"But what?" Lois wanted to know.

"But it's none of your business."

"If you want us to find her killer, it *is* our business. The more we know about Paige and her life, the easier it will be to find the person who might have done this," I said.

"Do you want the truth?"

Lois and I nodded.

"I don't know. I don't know anything about my wife. Other than that she came from a family that made millions selling chairs and desks. Who makes that much money on such a thing these days, when people can buy furniture online and have it delivered for free? Somehow, her family did, and I'm learning—" He stopped abruptly.

"What are you learning?" I asked. I was relieved that I'd beat Lois to ask the question, because it was very likely her tone at the moment would be sharp. He wasn't accepting of that. Clearly.

"The Delponts aren't who they seem, and everyone has been lying to me since the beginning. That includes my wife." His voice cracked.

The café door flew open, and Ruth Yoder stormed through it in a puff of snow and outrage. "Is that him?" She pointed at Gerome. "Is that Rocksino-Guy?"

"Yes." Lois blinked at her as if she couldn't believe what she was seeing.

Ruth walked right up to Gerome, who was still standing in front of his overturned dining chair. "How dare you come into our county and make trouble like this, especially after the horrible way you treated our Lois."

I gaped at Lois. She mouthed to me, *Our Lois?*

My eyes felt as if they were the size of saucers.

Ruth shook a finger in his face. "You owe her an apology for what you did to her."

Gerome shook from head to toe. "What?"

"Apologize to her!"

"Ummm, Lois, I'm sorry." His voice quavered.

I couldn't say I blamed him for being afraid. Ruth always looked a little scary, more so if you didn't know her, but standing there in her bonnet and long cape, with her face a mask of outrage, she was downright terrifying.

Lois smiled. "Thank you. I accept your apology."

Ruth pointed at the door. "Get out of here," Ruth said. "You are not welcome."

Gerome opened and closed his mouth.

"Out!" Ruth cried.

He yelped and then ran out the door as if he were a cat whose tail had been stepped on.

Chapter Thirty-five

Once a week, I had dinner at Edith's house. It was something that I always looked forward to. When I arrived, the excitement of her three children and numerous cats always put a smile on my face.

Bessie turned at the sign that led to the greenhouse parking lot. The sign read, EDY'S GREENHOUSE. CLOSED FOR THE SEASON.

I knew that even though the greenhouse was closed, Edith was tirelessly working on the plants for next year. The greenhouse would be full of seedlings by now. The seedlings would be nurtured to grow into plants that could be sold to Edith's many customers starting in early May.

I was so proud of all that my niece had accomplished. She had inherited the greenhouse from her father and made it on her own while surviving a rocky marriage and raising her three children as a single mother. Single mothers in the Amish world

were at times looked down upon, but after another rocky romance, my Edith was no longer willing to settle. I believed that she'd finally come to
the conclusion that no father for her children was
better than a bad father.

Bessie parked the buggy—because she really was
better driving it than I was—by the greenhouse be-
neath her favorite shade tree. Even in the winter, it
was her preferred spot to wait when I was at Edith's.

The screen door to the greenhouse flew open,
and four-year-old Ginny and ten-year-old Micah
came flying out. They were ready to wrap me up in
a hug even before my feet hit the ground.

"Wait, wait," I said. "Let me get down to give you
a proper hug. You two are as bad as my goats."

This announcement made Ginny giggle, and
her long blond braid flew into the air as she
wrapped her little arms around my skirts. Warmth
filled my heart as I hugged her back.

"*Aenti* Millie," the little girl said excitedly. "One
of our cats is pregnant again. More kittens."

"Oh my! I do love kittens, but I can't take any
home this time. Peaches would not like it. He likes
being the cat about the house."

"I want to keep them all," the little girl cried. "I
love cats."

She was a child after my own heart. Peaches had
joined my farm a little over a year ago, and I could
not imagine the place now without him. He also
helped me keep the goats in line, which was a
bonus.

The door to the greenhouse opened again, and
Jacob, the eldest of Edith's children, came out. He
walked at a much more sedate pace. Jacob was

eleven, only one year older than Micah, but by the way he carried himself, you would have thought he was approaching middle age.

When Edith's husband died, Jacob, just seven at the time, took over the role of man of the house, and he wore that mantle as if the weight of the world was on top of it.

"Good evening, *Aenti* Millie," he said formally.

"Hello, Jacob. Is your mother in the greenhouse?"

He gave a solemn nod.

Ginny ran back into the greenhouse, and Micah followed. I walked in at a much slower pace with Jacob. I wrapped my arm around his shoulders. "You are doing a *gut* job, my boy, taking care of everything here."

I felt him relax. Reassurance was something that Jacob craved.

As I expected, Edith was in the greenhouse, watering the seedlings. She had a propane-powered heater in the room to keep the plants warm. She walked down the line of tiny tomato plants and sprinkled them with water, taking care not to get any on the leaves.

"Oh *Aenti* Millie, I thought you were here by how the children ran out."

Two cats walked around her feet. One was noticeably rounder than the other. It would not be long before those kittens arrived.

"I'm done watering," Edith said. "Let's go inside and get washed up for dinner. The roast should be ready to pull out of the oven."

Micah pumped his fist in the air in excitement. "I love roast."

Jacob gave him a sideways glance. "You love food. It doesn't matter what it is."

"Is there something wrong with that?" his younger brother wanted to know.

Jacob shook his head and left the greenhouse.

Edith pressed her lips together, as if she wanted to say something to Micah but thought better of it. "You two go wash up." She shooed the younger two out of the greenhouse.

"Is Jacob all right?" I asked.

"He's eleven going on forty. Sometimes it's difficult just being Jacob."

I furrowed my brow. When we got into the kitchen, Edith pulled the beef roast out of the oven. It smelled delicious. The side of meat was surrounded by baby onions, carrots, potatoes, and turnips. While she let the roast rest, I tucked a tray of dinner rolls into the oven to be warmed.

We moved around the kitchen like two people who had cooked together countless times before, and that was true. My brother lost his wife around the same time that my Kip died. As a widower, he needed help with his young twins: Edith and her brother. I sold my home and went to live with them. I spent the next ten years raising the twins as my own. Edith and I always had been close. It was not the case between her brother and me. I tried to put sad memories out of my head and focus on the new ones I was making with Edith and her three children that evening.

Edith started on the mashed potatoes. *Ya*, there were roasted potatoes with the meat, but mashed potatoes were always welcome at a family dinner.

"What have you been up to, *Aenti* Millie?" Edith

asked as she moved the masher up and down in a rhythmic manner.

"Lois and I are on another case."

Her masher froze in place. "*Aenti* Millie."

I was in the process of arranging pickles and deviled eggs on a tray. I couldn't say that Edith didn't feed me well when I was there. "What?" I asked in the most innocent voice I could muster.

She sighed and began mashing again. "What's the case?"

I told her.

"I heard about that," Edith said in a worried voice. "*Aenti* Millie, you and Lois aren't getting in trouble again, are you? You're not in any danger, are you?"

"We are very careful."

She squinted at me as if she didn't find that encouraging in the least. "In a way, I suppose I'm relieved that you are investigating this murder."

I removed the hot rolls from the oven and carefully placed them in a tea towel–lined basket. "You are?"

"I was afraid you were going to say that you were somehow involved with that truck full of drugs the deputies found."

"How do you know about that?" I asked.

"An *Englisch* customer came by to place his spring vegetable orders. He likes me to save the strongest seedlings for him. He told me about it and said it happened not too far from his home. He said that he could see the whole thing from his house. Scary stuff."

"Why would you think Lois and I might be looking into that?"

She laughed. "I don't know. I get these ideas in my head, and I worry about you. I love Lois like a second *aenti*, but I am afraid that she gets you into trouble from time to time. I also know that she loves furniture, so that had me concerned." She let out a breath. "It makes me feel so much better to know that you have nothing to do with that issue. Focus on the fallen cuckoo."

I ducked my head. "We are," I promised.

"What's a fallen cuckoo?" Micah asked as he peeked into the kitchen from the dining room.

"Hush, you," Edith told her middle child. "You are supposed to be setting the table, not listening to the adults."

He grabbed a fistful of silverware from the cutlery drawer and ran out of the room.

Edith brushed a delicate hand across her forehead. "I swear that one child is more trouble than the other two combined."

"I seem to remember you had a bit of a mischievous streak when you were Micah's age."

"Maybe when I was Micah's age," she said. "I grew out of it. Micah has been like this since the day he was born. I don't think that bodes well for his ever changing."

"Micah will be just fine. He gets his nose for trouble from his *aenti*, and look at me. I'm just fine, aren't I?" I picked up the roll basket and carried it into the dining room before she could answer.

Sometimes it was better not knowing what Edith thought of Lois and my antics.

Chapter Thirty-six

In the winter, night came early to Holmes County, and by six-thirty that evening, the sun had put itself to bed for the night. However, only a couple months ago, the sun was all but gone at four-thirty in the afternoon. Spring was coming. I reminded myself of that as Bessie and I made our way home from Edith's after dinner.

I hardly had to do anything at all to direct the horse home. She knew the way from Edith's as well as she did from the Sunbeam Café. They were, after all, the places I went the most on a daily basis.

It was after eight when Bessie turned onto my long driveway. I was eager to get her and the goats settled in the barn. Winter nights were so much darker than any other nights of the year. I very much wanted to scurry into the house and snuggle under a blanket with Peaches and sip a cup of hot tea.

It had been a trying week, and I had to admit that Lois and I weren't really any closer to finding the person who'd killed Paige. In the course of our investigation, we had been distracted by other incidents and crimes, namely, John Michael Smucker's death and the drug dealing.

I climbed out of the buggy with the aid of the new battery-operated lantern Lois had given me after I dropped the last one. In the light of the lantern, Phillip and Peter danced in the snow. It was nice to have such an enthusiastic welcoming committee.

"Okay, okay, settle down. Settle. Come on now," I said. "It's time for bed. You will have plenty of time to play in the snow tomorrow."

Apparently, they didn't like that idea, because they took off and ran away from me, out of the lantern's beam of light. I grumbled to myself. Somedays, I agreed with Ruth Yoder. Those goats were trouble.

To bring the goats back on the straight and narrow, I used the only tool I possessed to get their attention. The whistle Kip had taught me all those years ago. I put two fingers in my mouth and blew hard. The sharp sound pierced through the night air.

The goats didn't come. I whistled again. Still nothing.

Muttering to myself, I held my lantern high and looked around for them. I could just make out the shadow of a goat running around the side of the barn. I groaned. Those goats were going to be grounded tomorrow for not listening to my whistle, meaning no apples or carrots, their favorite treats. I knew they were spoiled. Ruth Yoder told me so any time she saw them.

Holding the lantern out in front of me, I followed the hoofprints in the snow, all the way to the other side of the barn. There I found Phillip and Peter, standing on either side of Hosea Flaud.

I gasped and placed a hand to my chest. My heart thundered so loudly against my rib cage, I felt the beat of it deep into my palm. "Hosea, you should really learn to knock on my door. Creeping around my farm is not the way to convince me to help you."

He gripped his glove-covered hands together. "I know. I was just working up the nerve to knock on the door when your goats found me." He shivered.

"How long have you been standing out here in the cold?" I asked.

"I don't know. An hour. Two maybe?"

"Oh my, you must be frozen clean through. Can you do me the favor of unhitching my horse and bedding her down while I get these rascals to bed? Then we can get out from the cold and talk."

He nodded and seemed eager to have an assignment.

With Hosea's help, it took no time at all to put the buggy and Bessie in the barn for the night. However, the goats weren't having it. They ran around the barn, refusing to enter. "All right, you two," I said finally, with my hands on my hips. "You can stay out as long as Hosea is here, but then you must go to bed."

They leaped into the air as if it were the very

best news they had ever heard. I suppose for goats, it was.

As I pulled the barn door closed, I said, "*Danki*, it's *gut* to have a strong young man to help me on a cold night like this. It would have taken me twice as long to do that without your help."

He nodded and pulled at the sleeves of his barn coat as if he didn't know what to do with his hands.

"Let's go inside and get you warmed up."

He followed me to the back door, which I unlocked with my key.

In the kitchen, Peaches met us at the door, arched his back, and hissed.

"Peaches, is that any way to greet a guest?" I asked.

The little peach-colored cat flicked his tail and sauntered away, as if he didn't care to grace that question with a response.

I shook my head. "I will have to apologize for my cat. Lois says he's what the *Englisch* call a diva. I have to be honest. I don't know entirely what she means when she says things like that."

Hosea paced back and forth in front of the kitchen island. "Why don't you sit down while I make us some tea?" I suggested.

He perched on one of the stools in front of the kitchen island.

I set the kettle on the stovetop to boil the water and then removed tea and teacups from the cupboard. While we waited for the water to be ready, I asked, "Why are you here, Hosea? This is the second time you have come to my home in the dark. I'm very glad that this time you didn't run away."

"I'm sorry about that," he said, and removed his gloves. He shoved them into the pockets of his coat, which he still had on.

I snapped my fingers. "That reminds me." I opened a drawer in the island and pulled out the wood chisel that I'd found outside on the ground on Valentine's Day night. Sliding it across the island to him, I said, "I believe this is yours."

He picked up the chisel and rolled it back and forth in his fingers. "This is my father's chisel. It's all beat up and slightly bent, but it was his favorite one. He gave it to me when I started to take over the shop, because he was too weak to work anymore. Woodworking is hard labor."

"I know that," I said. "My late husband was a woodworker, too."

"This chisel represents a lot of responsibility. Sometimes I don't think I can handle it all."

"Your father seems to think you can. When Lois and I were at the shop, he was singing your praises."

"He doesn't know . . ." Hosea trailed off.

"He doesn't know what?" I asked.

Hosea shook his head.

"Why are you here, Hosea? For the chisel? I could have dropped it off at your shop anytime."

"I just had to talk to you," he continued.

"About Faith, then?" I asked, because it was the only topic he could possibly wish to discuss.

He nodded.

The kettle whistled. I thought it was an opportune interruption. He could gather his thoughts as I got the tea things together. At the same time, I thought of a saying that had been a favorite of my mother's: "Be like the teakettle; when it's up to its neck in hot water, it sings."

Across from me, Hosea seemed to be neck-deep in hot water, but he wasn't singing. He was barely speaking. Perhaps I could help with that, or maybe the tea would soothe him enough so he would finally say whatever it was he'd come here to tell me.

I loved loose-leaf tea. I scooped peppermint tea into two metal tea balls, set them in mugs, and poured steaming hot water over them. Hosea accepted the tea and wrapped his hands around the mug.

Taking my tea, I sat on the opposite side of the island from him and waited.

A long stretch of silence passed between us. Such a silence would have driven Lois to talk. She hated long bouts of quiet.

He cleared his throat. "Netty told me you spoke with her today. She said you believe Faith isn't the right match for me. Is that true?"

"It is." I studied him.

His face fell. "How could you say that to her? I need to marry Faith."

"For your father?" I asked.

He stared at me. "How did you know that?"

"I realized you might want to marry Faith so she can care for your father. He mentioned that you did not have a mother in the home to care for him. But would that be fair to Faith?"

"It is the job of the woman of the house to care for those in her family."

"But Faith is not in your family," I said gently.

"She could have been, if she had just listened. If

she'd married me at the start, none of this would have happened." He wrapped his hands so tightly around the chisel, his knuckles turned bright white.

"What wouldn't have happened?" I asked.

"I—I wouldn't be in this position with my father." He looked as if he wanted to say something else, but instead stared into his tea. "I came here to ask you to reconsider and talk to Faith again. She will listen to you."

I shook my head. "I think you believe I have more leverage over her than I really do. As a matchmaker, all I do is make observations which tell me who is a *gut* fit and who is not. Based on how Faith feels and on how you feel, the two of you are not a *gut* fit."

He opened his mouth to argue when a set of headlights swept across my front windows. I hadn't yet pulled the curtains closed for the night. I usually did so once the goats were in bed. When they were out and about, I liked to have the curtains open to keep an eye on them.

"That's strange," I said. The only *Englischer* who would come to my home at night would be Lois. I went to the window but saw it wasn't Lois's car in front of my house. It was a black sports car. I swallowed and hurried to lock the front door. So as not to alarm Hosea, I quietly walked to the back door of the house and locked that, too.

I needn't have worried, however, as Hosea was staring forlornly into his tea. At least he'd put the chisel down. I was happy for that.

Someone banged on the front door. Hosea jerked back into the present. "What's going on?"

"I think Ronan Delpont is on my doorstep, and he's not happy," I whispered.

All the color drained from Hosea's face. "He's here for me."

"You? Why?"

"Open the door!" Ronan shouted. "I know that Amish boy is in there! Open it!"

"I should go," Hosea said, standing up. "I can't let anyone else be hurt because of me."

"Who else was hurt?" I asked as I pulled a set of curtains closed.

"Come out here, you coward!" Ronan cried. "You ruined everything. You and my sister ruined it all."

I glanced at Hosea. "What does he mean?"

Hosea's eyes darted around the room. "I have to go out there. I shouldn't have brought you into this, Millie. I'm so sorry."

"What have you brought me into?" I asked quietly.

There came a loud bang, as if Ronan had kicked the door. It was followed by a scream. A moment later, the car engine started, and the headlights disappeared down the driveway.

Hosea and I stared at each other.

A *tap-tap* sounded on the front door. I walked over and peered out the window. Phillip and Peter stood on the front stoop.

I opened the door. Peter had a coat sleeve in his mouth.

"You two saved the day by chasing that man away. He probably thought he was under attack by wild beasts." I scratched Phillip under the chin.

Peter grinned, and the piece of fabric fell to the ground. He was quite proud.

Hosea zipped up his coat. "I'm so sorry about this, Millie. I should never have come here. I put you in danger. I have to leave."

A cold wind came through the open door.

"Are you going home? Won't Ronan look for you there? You should stay here. I have a spare room."

"Don't worry about me." He made his way to the door. "I wouldn't be able to sleep if I stayed here. I would be too worried that I'd be putting you in harm's way. I don't want to do that. I don't want to do that to anyone ever again."

"What did Ronan mean when he said you'd ruined it for him?" I asked. "Were you caught up in the drug trafficking?" It was a question I had been pushing around in my head for several days.

"I have to go." He went out the door, and the goats let him pass.

In the moonlight, I watched him run across the frozen fields toward the Raber sheep farm. Maybe he would find safety among the sheep.

Chapter Thirty-seven

After locking up the goats, I tossed and turned in bed until midnight, when I could not take it any longer. I was too frightened to be alone in my home. With every creak of the house settling and every crack of a frozen branch in the wind, I jumped. I got up and dressed and weighed my options. Since I didn't have a phone to call for help, I really only had two. Hitch up Bessie and drive to either Edith's or Lois's home, or walk across the frozen field to call for help from the shed phone I shared with the Rabers. Neither of those options were *gut*.

In the end, I decided walking to the Rabers was the safest choice. My reasoning was that Ronan was out driving in his black sports car. I would be more likely to encounter him on the road than walking across a field.

In the middle of the night, the temperature had plummeted into the twenties. I put on my thickest skirt, two pairs of stockings, a heavy sweater, my barn coat, Kip's stocking cap, and my bonnet over that. I had so many clothes on, I could barely lower my arms. Then, I found a canvas bag, lined it with a bath towel, and picked up Peaches. I put the cat inside the bag. I wasn't going to leave my animals behind. I wouldn't be able to rest knowing they were at my farm alone with Ronan possibly lurking about.

To my surprise, Peaches didn't fight me when he was in the bag. I thought it must have been because he could sense my tension. I grabbed my lantern, locked the house, and hurried to the barn.

I could hear the goats crying inside. They knew I was coming. I opened the barn door, and they ran out. Peaches stuck his head out of the bag and hissed, as if to tell the goats to calm down. They paid him no mind.

I knew the goats would be up for an adventure. Bessie the horse was another story. I put on her bridle and tugged on it to get her to walk out of the stall. Bessie shook her head.

"Come on, girl. We're just going for a little walk over to the Rabers' farm."

I wasn't sure that a half-mile tromp through the snowy field could be considered a little walk, but I needed to say something to talk the horse into it.

"You can sleep in their warm barn. Think of all the cozy sheep who will be there to keep you warm." I scratched her nose.

Finally, she let me lead her out of the barn.

I had to wonder what kind of picture the five of us made in the moonlight as we walked across the fields. It must have been an odd sight to see a woman with a cat in a bag, followed by a horse and two goats, walking outside this close to midnight.

I constantly looked around as we went, but the farther we walked, the more I began to relax. I knew the goats would warn me if there was trouble.

I gave a sigh of relief when the Rabers' large sheep barn and sprawling farmhouse came into view. Even better, I could see a candle glowing in the kitchen window. Someone was still awake.

I tethered Bessie to a hitching post by the driveway and told the goats to behave themselves, then walked up to the kitchen door and knocked.

The door opened almost immediately.

Roman Raber, Raellen's husband, stood in front of me in worn trousers and a wrinkled work shirt. "Millie! What are you doing here?"

As if she sensed something was happening, Raellen's head seemed to pop up out of nowhere behind her husband's shoulder. "Oh my word, Millie Fisher, what are you doing here?"

"Can I come in?" I asked.

"*Ya*," Raellen cried. "Let her in." She wore a night dress and robe, and her feet were bare.

When I was safely in the house, Raellen gave me a hug. Peaches hissed in protest.

Raellen hopped away. "You brought your cat!"

I opened the bag, and Peaches's head popped out. He looked around the kitchen and then sniffed the air. I couldn't blame him. Raellen was an exceptional cook and baker. Her kitchen always smelled heavenly, no matter what time of day.

"And my goats and horse." I gave Roman a weak

smile. I knew how he felt about the goats. "I need help."

"Oh, you poor thing!" Raellen exclaimed, and guided me to a kitchen chair. "You sit down right here and tell us all about it."

Raellen was always willing to listen, and even though she was a gossip, I knew her heart was in the right place. I gave them a brief version of the night's events. "I have to call Deputy Little. Maybe he can find Ronan, Hosea, or both."

"*Nee*, you stay in here. Roman can call Deputy Little. You're about frozen through. Let me make you some hot cocoa, and I have some strudel that I made for dessert tonight. It will be just the ticket to warm you up. I would guess that Peaches would like a saucer of warm cream, too."

The cat wriggled next to me, as if he liked the sound of that.

"I'll go make that call and tend to the horse and goats. Don't you worry about them, Millie," Roman said.

"*Danki*," I said. "I know the goats aren't your favorite, Roman."

"That's all right," Roman said gruffly. "The sheep are in the barn for the night, so they can't influence them. I'll put Bessie and the goats in the horse barn."

Just before he went out the door, I said, "Can you call Lois, too? Her number is in the Rolodex by the phone."

He nodded and went out the door.

Three small faces peered around the kitchen wall. Raellen spotted them as soon as I did. "Now off to the bed with all of you. Millie is just here for a visit with your *maam* and *daed*."

The children scattered.

Raellen smiled. "I can't blame them. I was that curious as a child."

She was that curious now.

Raellen was right—the hot cocoa and strudel were just what I needed, and Peaches loved the warm cream. After he finished his saucer, he rubbed his furry self against Raellen's legs. If I wasn't careful, he might want to move to the Rabers' for *gut*.

A half hour after he made the calls, Roman let Deputy Little into the house. "Millie," the deputy began. "I'm glad to see that you are all right."

"*Danki*, Deputy. My animals and I have had a bit of an adventure this night."

He nodded. "I can see that." You'd never guess it was the middle of the night from looking at the deputy. His hair was freshly combed. His uniform was pristine, and his eyes were alert. I knew that I must have been a sight, as I was starting to grow very sleepy.

He removed a notebook from his coat pocket. "Tell me what happened."

I had just finished my story when there was a sharp knock on the kitchen door. Roman opened it, and Lois flew into the room. "Millie!" she cried.

I stood up. "I'm right here. I'm fine."

She ran over to me, grabbed my arms, and looked me up and down. "We're getting you a phone! I don't care what your bishop says." Tears gathered in her eyes. "I don't know what I would do if something happened to you." She wrapped me in her arms and gave me a massive hug.

I hugged her back, and tears pricked my eyes, too. I didn't know until Lois was there how scared I had actually been. To feel that vulnerable was one of the worst things I had experienced. I wasn't going to argue with her about the phone.

"As for those goats," Lois said, "they are heroes, and they are welcome to my house any time."

I pulled back from her hug. "I'm glad to hear you say that." I blinked at her. It was the first time since we were little girls that I had seen Lois devoid of an ounce of makeup. Her hair was sticking up in all directions. She wore pajamas under her hastily thrown-on coat, and she didn't have on a single piece of jewelry. She must have been really worried about me.

Lois hugged me again. "Don't scare me again like that. Promise?"

My face was pressed into her shoulder, so I don't know if she could even hear me speak. However, I said a muffled, "I promise" into the fabric of her coat.

Chapter Thirty-eight

The next morning, I sat at the table by the window in the Sunbeam Café. The sun shone bright. It was almost hard to believe the ordeal I had gone through the night before. After Lois arrived at the Rabers', and Deputy Little had finished questioning me, Lois insisted that I go home with her.

Raellen and Roman agreed to care for my animals until I felt safe to go back home. I prayed that was soon. I offered to take Peaches with me at the very least, but the cat knew when he had a *gut* thing. He opted to stay where the warm cream was. I can't say that I blamed him.

Even tucked safe and sound in Lois's guest room for the night, I had trouble sleeping. Every time I closed my eyes, I saw Hosea's terrified face. What had the young Amish man gotten himself into?

I knew by the time I finally fell asleep that Deputy Little had certainly woken up James Flaud and questioned him on the whereabouts of his son.

I sipped my black coffee and looked out the window.

Lois came over to the table.

"Wow, you are really shaken up, aren't you?"

"I'm too worried about Hosea to eat. You should have seen his face, Lois. He was terrified. Absolutely terrified." I stared down into the black pool of my coffee as if the view would erase the memory of Hosea's frightened face.

Before Lois could respond, Deputy Little entered the café and sat in the chair across from me. "How are you?" His question was gentle.

"I'm fine. Worried for Hosea more than anything. Have you found him?"

He shook his head. "Not yet. We are looking. We're having trouble finding Ronan, too. I'm guessing that Ronan is a long way from here by now. Hopefully, Hosea will be much easier to locate."

"I think Ronan killed his sister," Lois blurted out as she circled back to my table.

Deputy Little pressed his lips together. "We don't know that. He's a suspect, but we don't know that he is the culprit."

"If he's not up to some sort of crime, why did he scare Millie so much last night?"

Deputy Little steepled his fingers together. "I wish that I told you sooner. If I had, you might not have had such a scary night." He shook his head.

"Tell us what, Deputy?" Lois asked as she pulled

up a chair and sat down between Deputy Little and me.

"After combing through all the evidence we found and following up leads in relation to that drug bust on the truck, we believe Paige Moorhead and her brother Ronan Delpont were the masterminds behind the drug transport. The driver of the truck, after taking a plea deal, confirmed what we already suspect. A warrant for Ronan's arrest was issued shortly thereafter, but somehow, he must have got wind of it. From his drug network is my best guess. He disappeared."

"Did you make this connection before or after Lois and I spoke to Ronan at the market?" I asked.

"It was just about that time," he said and rubbed his brow. "I should have told you then or at least made it more clear how dangerous Ronan actually was. I didn't, and look what happened."

"Deputy," I said, "it is very likely that Ronan would still have come to my house last night looking for Hosea. You could not have stopped that. Fortunately, I knew enough not to open the door, and the goats took care of running him off."

"I love those goats," Lois said with a happy sigh.

"What does Hosea have to do with this?" I asked.

"That's the piece we don't know. When you said that Ronan came to your house looking for Hosea, honestly, that surprised me. I suspect he's involved with the drugs we found somehow, but the only way to really know how he is connected is to find him." He rubbed the back of his neck. "We aren't having much luck doing that at the moment."

"Could Ronan have murdered his sister?" Lois asked.

"It's possible, if he thought she was going to mess with the business. And when I say business, I mean the drug side of things," the deputy admitted. "However, in my experience, dropping a cuckoo clock on a person isn't usually the way drug dealers remove someone they see as a threat."

"Maybe he did so to frame someone else," Lois offered.

"Maybe," Deputy Little said, not sounding sure at all. "In any case, I want the two of you to stay out of this. Please. Millie, if those goats of yours hadn't jumped into action last night, it could have ended very badly for you."

He was right. I owed the goats a lot. Extra apples and carrots all around.

"Millie, you should really think about getting a phone closer to your home for times like this," the deputy said. "I can talk to the bishop if you need me to. You are pretty vulnerable out there alone. I mean, it's impressive to hear about your nighttime trek to the Rabers with all those animals in tow, but at the same time, you could have tripped, fallen, and been seriously hurt."

I knew everything he said was true. I had made it to the Rabers' farm with *Gott*'s protection. There was no other explanation for it.

"Don't you worry, Deputy Little. I have already put in a call to the bishop about getting Millie a phone. I'm on it."

Deputy Little nodded, as if that were all he needed to hear. Everyone in the village knew that if Lois decided to do something, she did it. The bishop didn't stand much of a chance fighting her on installing a phone closer to my home.

The deputy's cell phone rang. He looked at the screen and got up from his seat, taking the call outside.

"I hate it when he won't take important calls in front of us," Lois complained, looking forlornly out the window.

We watched Deputy Little pace back and forth in front of the café.

"Seems big," Lois said.

A moment later, he stepped back into the café. "I have to go. I'm begging the two of you to stay here. Please."

I nodded, but Lois simply smiled.

After the deputy left, Lois made the rounds of the café to deliver meals and make sure all of her customers had what they needed. I stared out the window and worried about Hosea. Was Deputy Little right in thinking that Hosea might be involved in the drugs that Paige and Ronan transported in that furniture?

Lois came back to my table. "Why the long face?"

I looked up at her. "Hosea."

She nodded. "I thought it might be, and I have something that will distract you." She got her coat.

"Where are you going now?" I asked.

"To the chalet." She stuck an arm through one sleeve of her coat, and then the other. "Gerome is leaving Holmes County today. His wife's body was released. It's being transported to Cleveland for the funeral."

"And you want to say goodbye to him?" I asked dubiously.

"I guess I just want closure," she said. "To put a

final period on that time in my life. I need it to end, so that I can really enjoy this dating app Darcy set me up on. Do you know when I woke up this morning, I had eight new hearts? Eight. It seems I'm quite popular." She grinned. "You're coming with me, aren't you?"

"*Ya*," I said, as if there was any other option.

There wasn't.

Chapter Thirty-nine

When we arrived at the Munich Chalet, I was happy to see the doors that'd been hanging precariously from the top of the clock had been removed. At least there wouldn't be any more accidents involving the clock tower.

"Those sheep," Lois said as we walked toward the room where Gerome had been staying for the last week.

I looked behind us, and sure enough, the odd flock of sheep were following. I told her what Raellen had said about sheep, "They either think we have food or want to be our friends."

Lois eyed the sheep again. "I'm thinking of those two; it's food, because I don't like how they are looking at me. I might be their next snack. I have more meat on my bones than you do, so they would certainly pick me off first."

"Sheep are vegetarian."

"That's what they want you to think." She tugged at her beret.

As expected, the sheep followed us almost the entire way to Gerome's room, but stopped on the hill, leaving them with a clear vantage point of everything going on. I had heard of guard dogs before, but this was the first flock of guard sheep to my knowledge.

Lois knocked on the Hillside room door. No one answered.

After knocking a second time, she tried the handle, only to find it unlocked. She pushed the door open and started to take a step inside.

I grabbed the sleeve of her coat. "Lois, you can't just go in there."

"Why not?" she asked. "It's unlocked, and he's about to check out. He might already be gone." She pointed at the luggage sitting in the corner of the room. "Oh wait, look, he's already packed and ready to go."

I groaned and stepped into the room, too.

It was dimly lit, as there was only one window, and none of the lights were on. Lois flicked a switch, illuminating the room from overhead. Lois was right; Gerome was all packed up and ready to leave.

On the side table sat a box that looked familiar to me. I walked over to it. "Come look at this!"

Lois turned around.

I pointed at the jewelry box.

"That looks like one of the boxes Hosea made," she said.

"I don't think it just looks like one. It *is* one," I

replied. "All the way down to the carving on the top of it. Hosea's work is very distinctive. I would be shocked if anyone else could carve the way he does."

"Why would Gerome have that?" Lois asked.

I shook my head. "A gift for someone back home? Maybe during the time that he was in Holmes County, he visited Swiss Carpentry and bought one." I tapped the daisy in the middle of the jewelry box, just as I had seen Hosea do in his shop. I half expected to see drugs when the secret compartment popped open. To my surprise, there didn't seem to be anything valuable hidden within. Just a small slip of paper with writing on it.

"Please meet me at eight a.m. under the cuckoo clock. I need to talk to you. –H," I read aloud.

There was only one *H* name I knew that was connected to Paige or Gerome.

"Hosea?" she gasped. "Could it be? Hosea arranged for Paige to meet him at the clock tower? He set her up to be killed?"

When we'd stepped into the Hillside room, we'd left the door standing open. We didn't notice Gerome enter with his camera in hand until he was only a step away from us. "What are the two of you doing in here?"

"We were just stopping by to see you off, and we found this." She pointed at the jewelry box.

"What about it? It belonged to Paige. She bought it while we were down here."

"And the police didn't take it?" Lois asked.

"Why would they? It's just an empty box."

And I realized that at the time of Paige's death,

the police had had no reason to suspect Hosea. They would have just seen the box as a souvenir from Amish Country.

"It's an empty box Hosea Flaud made," Lois said.

"Who?" Gerome asked.

"Did you know the box has a secret compartment?" I asked.

I pressed the daisy again, and the compartment opened.

"That's amazing!" He stared at the box. "I didn't know that."

"This was inside of it." I showed him the note, but I didn't hand it over. I knew Deputy Little would want it.

"We need to call the deputy," Lois said.

"Who is 'H'?" Gerome asked, clearly confused.

"You don't know?" Lois asked.

He scowled at her. "If I knew, would I be asking you?"

Lois put her hands on her hips and studied him. "What are you still doing here, Gerome? The authorities released your wife's body last night. You could have been gone hours ago."

"I could have, but I still don't know who killed my wife." His voice caught. "I deserve to know that."

He did. That was true.

"What have you been doing to find out who killed your wife?"

"I've been looking through my pictures, searching for any evidence that would give me a hint as to what happened that morning. Let me show you." He opened a briefcase and handed a manila folder to Lois.

It seemed to me he wasn't giving us any choice but to look at his pictures. Was he trying to delay Lois's call to the deputy about the jewelry box?

Lois flipped through the photos. They were all trees and light. For me, it was difficult to tell one from the other. Lois must have had a better eye, because she complimented him on a few of the pictures.

"You said before that there wasn't anywhere to develop these prints," Lois said. "How did you get these?"

"I eventually found a place in New Philadelphia that could do it."

Lois came to the very last one, and was about the close the folder and hand it back to Gerome, when something caught my eye.

"Can I see that one again?" I asked.

In the lower right-hand corner of the picture was a shadow. At first, it looked like the root of a tree, but I realized it was a boot, an Amish boot.

"When were these pictures taken?" I took a closer look at the photo. Since it was in black and white, the shadows stood out starkly.

Gerome took the folder from Lois's hands. "I took them the first morning we were here."

"The morning Paige died," I said. "I thought you were supposed to give that film to the police."

"I thought I did, but I must have given them the wrong roll. The rolls became mixed up in my bag. I'm pretty certain that Deputy Little has a roll of wedding pictures. Honestly, I'm surprised he's not said anything to me about it. I thought he would by now."

"Why haven't *you* said anything to him?" Lois asked.

"Well, that's not my job."

Lois gave him a look.

He cleared his throat. "And I didn't want to get in trouble for handing over the wrong roll of film. It was an accident, but how do I know that the small-town police around here are going to realize that?"

Lois shook her head and removed her phone from her giant bag. She didn't have to say it; I knew she was calling Deputy Little.

Chapter Forty

The deputy handed the jewelry box and the photographs over to one of his officers to be taken in for evidence. "What am I going to have to do to make sure the two of you stay out of this case? Because it's clear to me that you are not listening to a word I say on that matter."

"Without us, you would never have found the note," Lois said. "Or gotten those prints from Gerome."

He shook his head.

"Do you think Gerome was telling the truth?" I asked. "Could he really have given you the wrong roll by accident?"

"It's possible," Deputy Little said. "I can't say that I believe it one hundred percent, but it is possible."

Gerome had been taken down to the station for questioning, while Deputy Little and his officers thoroughly searched his room again. They didn't come up with anything new. Both Ronan and Hosea were still missing, and it was looking more than ever as if Hosea was involved in Paige's death.

"Deputy, do you think the 'H' that signed that note was really Hosea? What would he gain by killing Paige?"

"I don't know the answer to either of those questions. But can the two of you agree to drop all of this now?"

We didn't agree, but Lois and I did leave the chalet at the insistence of Deputy Little.

"Let's make one stop before we go back to the village."

"Where to?" she asked.

"Swiss Carpentry, Hosea's business."

She grinned. "You got it."

As Lois parked her car on the main road in Charm, I saw through the window of the quilt shop that Faith and Netty were laughing together as they restocked the store. At least there was one happy ending for someone I had helped over the last week.

Even though it was the middle of the day, the CLOSED sign was on the front door of the wood-shop. However, I had learned a thing or two from Lois in these investigations. I tried the handle, and the door swung in.

"That's my girl," Lois said approvingly. "Although I am a little down that I'm not getting another real-life chance to test out picking the lock. The best lock pickers practice a lot."

"I'm sorry. We're closed," a frail voice said from the back of the workshop.

When we had seen James a few days ago, he had

been happy and smiling. He was neither of those things now.

"Oh, you were the ladies who spoke with my son." There was the slightest hint of a smile on his face.

"*Ya,*" I said. "Do you know where Hosea is now? We're looking for him."

His head drooped, and he painfully lowered himself onto one of the stools behind the workbench. "You are not the only ones. The sheriff's department is looking for him too. They think that he killed that *Englisch* woman, the one hiding drugs."

"And what do you think?"

He didn't meet our eyes. "I think my son has suddenly started making a lot of money and was able to pay my medical bills. At first, he told me it was from the jewelry boxes he was making, but it was so much, that was very difficult to believe."

"In addition to paying your bills, he bought himself a buggy too. Faith mentioned the new courting buggy."

James nodded. "He did it for Faith, but I don't think she ever agreed to ride in it."

"Do you know where the money came from?"

"He told me it was from selling the jewelry boxes to Paige. He claimed she couldn't keep them in her store because they sold so quickly. But now I wonder."

"You wonder if he knew what she was really using them for—to hide drugs," I said.

He nodded and looked at his hands. "The worst part is he did it for me. He wanted to take care of me because of my disease. It breaks my heart he would resort to something so terrible for me. I still really can't believe it, but with the deputies coming in and out of my shop all day looking for clues as to where my son might be, I realize it's possible. I never would have thought that before today."

"He loves you," I said.

"But at what cost?" James asked. "If my health costs him his freedom, it will not lead to *gut* health for me. Knowing that my son might go to prison over this makes me feel worse than ever."

Lois and I left the woodshop shortly after that. While walking back to her car, I thought of how distraught Hosea must be over everything, from John Michael's death to Paige's murder to his father's disappointment. It made me think of one final place to look, the place where it all started.

"Deputy Little is not going to like that we're back here," Lois said as she parked in front of the chalet for a second time that day.

"He won't," I agreed. "But I just have to see if my theory is right. If I'm wrong, then we will go home and let the police handle it."

"Sure we will," Lois said dubiously. "So where do you think he is?"

I pointed at the clock tower. "Up there."

"Why would he go there?" she asked.

"Assuming he is the 'H' who sent Paige that note and maybe even gave her that box with the note inside it, he just might want to go back to the scene of the crime. Lois, when I saw him, he was distraught. This is the only place I can think he might have gone. I'm afraid for him."

As I told Lois my theory, a shadow passed over the opening in the tower.

"I think you might be right," Lois said.

We went to the back of the tower. Much to Lois's disappointment, it wasn't locked this time, and the doorknob turned easily. Silently, we stepped inside the building.

Lois pointed at the stairs, and I nodded. "I'll go first," I whispered. "You call the deputies just in case I'm right. We saw a shadow. Someone is up here."

She silently agreed.

The stairs were hard to climb, just as they'd been the first time. Sweat gathered on my forehead. I couldn't tell if it was from the exertion or from anxiety at what I might find at the top. Every painful step seemed to take twice as long.

When I finally made it over the last step, I saw Hosea.

He stood on the edge of the cuckoo's open door, looking down. His back was to me.

I held onto the railing. Lois was calling the police. They would be here soon. But would it be soon enough?

"Hosea," I said in a soft voice.

"Leave me alone," he said. He sounded like a broken man.

"What are you doing by the edge there?" I asked. "Why don't you step back?"

He turned his head to glare at me. "What do you think I'm doing? I just have to end it. I've made a mess of everything."

"What did you make a mess of?" I asked, trying to keep my voice as calm as possible. However, I would be surprised if he didn't hear my heart thundering inside my chest.

"Everything." He spun around and glared at me. "Didn't you hear me?"

"You can fix it," I said.

"*Nee*, I can't. I can't." He turned back to the opening and leaned forward again.

My stomach twisted uneasily.

"Hosea, you don't want to do this. What about your father?"

"I did all of this for my father. I knew I couldn't care for him on my own. I couldn't be at home all the time because I needed to work at the shop to keep making money for his care." There was anguish in his voice. "That's why I needed a wife, to care for him when I couldn't. Faith was supposed to marry me. She just wouldn't do it. I tried to give her everything so she would."

I had been right about the reason Hosea had been so desperate to marry Faith. It had never been for love.

He had other options for help, of course. If he'd shared his problems with his district, the community would have stepped up. However, asking for help would have wounded his pride and revealed to the whole district that he couldn't take care of his father himself. His dignity would not let him speak up.

However, I still didn't know what had happened to John Michael and Paige. I now very much believed John Michael was also tied up in all of this, but I didn't know how.

"John Michael was your friend," I said gently.

"He was my best friend." He blew out a breath. "When I told him about Paige's plan, I never thought he would start using drugs. I thought he would just get involved for the money like I did."

"But he did use them," I said softly.

Tears came into his eyes, and he nodded. "By the time I found out, he was in too deep. He couldn't pull himself out. When he died—" He licked his lips. "When he died, I knew I was in too deep, as well. I wasn't using narcotics, but money was my drug. I had to get out before it was too late. I told Paige I was done and wanted out. I promised I wouldn't say anything to anyone about her business."

"But she wouldn't let you out," I guessed.

"Worse than that, she said she would tell the bishop and—and my father. I couldn't let that happen! My father is sick. News like this would destroy him."

"So you sent her a note asking her to meet you here." I paused. "To kill her."

Despite the cold, sweat trickled down the sides of his face. "*Nee, nee.* I never planned to kill her. I just wanted to scare her and show her what could happen to her if she didn't let me out. She was going to ruin me. My *daed* has been through so much. He would have been disgraced. I couldn't add so much to his troubles."

His father had been disgraced anyway. James already knew every law enforcement officer in the county was looking for Hosea.

"I didn't know the cuckoo would hit her. It was a one in a million chance. I never for a moment thought she would die. I just thought she would be scared."

"Just step back from the edge, and we can sort this all out," I said as calmly as I could.

"Sort what out?" he wanted to know. "What do I have ahead of me now? Spending the rest of my days in prison? What kind of life would that be?"

"Every life is important, no matter what mistakes might have been made. Your life is important. If you can't step back for yourself, think of your father. As long as you're living, you have time."

"Time for what?" he asked.

"Time to make amends for what you did. You will never bring Paige back. You will never bring John Michael back, either, but you're alive right now. They aren't. Change your life and become someone your father can be proud of."

His face seemed to close off again. "He can never be proud of me now. Because of me, he will always be the father of the son who was an Amish drug dealer. I knew what Paige and Ronan were doing. I knew people were getting addicted and even dying, and still, I let it happen. The money was too good to walk away from."

"You did it out of love for your father."

He nodded.

"Your father loves you. No matter what you have done, he loves you. He knows you love him, too." Tears gathered in my eyes. "Hosea, your father wants you to come home."

"But I made a terrible mistake. I made so many mistakes. I just couldn't get out of it. Every decision I've made since I agreed to work with Paige was worse than the last." He started to cry.

"Then, start again. There have been too many losses already because of what the Delpont family has done to this county. Don't let them turn you into another victim. Don't let those mistakes be the defining moments of your life."

I stepped as close to him as I dared and held out my hand.

"Please give me your hand," I said in Pennsylvania Dutch.

He stared at my outstretched arm, and I willed my hand not to shake. I was close enough to him now that he could grab me and fling me out the window like a paper doll. I was much smaller than he. It would take little effort to throw me over the side. But it was a risk I had to take to save this young man's life.

"Hosea, look at me," I said, barely above a whisper.

He lifted his gaze from my hand to meet my eyes.

"Give me your hand."

He put his hand in mine.

Epilogue

The bitter cold of February gave way to the slushy and unpredictable days of March. Spring was on the way. There was a hint of change in the air. It was something the village of Harvest needed after recent events.

Nothing could be done to bring John Michael Smucker or Paige Moorhead back, but there was hope to be found in the new drug counseling center set to open in June. Hopefully, the counselors would spread a message of caution for others in both the *Englisch* and Amish communities. However, I knew it would be a battle that would go on in our fallen world. I could only pray drugs would harm as few people and families as possible.

Paige's brother, Ronan, had been caught by the highway patrol at the Kentucky border. It had been clear he'd intended to leave the state, as the Delpont furniture empire's involvement in running a major drug ring in Ohio and neighboring states had made national headlines. Deputy Little had been commended for his work on the case.

Gerome Moorhead had left the county shortly after Hosea Flaud had been taken into custody. It was yet to be determined if Gerome would face charges of tampering with evidence related to the film he'd never given the police. I supposed it would come down to whether the sheriff's department could prove that it wasn't an accident, as Gerome had claimed it was.

The person I thought of most often when I looked back on this case was Hosea. Deputy Little had told me that by sharing information about how the Delpont network operated, he would get a lighter sentence. But if convicted of murder, he would likely spend the rest of his life in prison. He claimed that he hadn't intended to kill Paige, only scare her. Deputy Little said the sheriff's department and prosecutor were taking Hosea's claim into consideration. I believed him, and I knew his father did. Whatever his sentence, I prayed he accepted the love of *Gott* and then took the chance to begin again.

I was grateful to hear through the Amish grapevine that the Flauds' district had taken James—Hosea's father and another innocent victim—into their care.

The drug counseling center in the church would soon open with Reverend Brook at the helm. He'd hired Iris's son Carter Jr. to share the message of the center with the Amish youth in the county. Iris had been nervous about how Bishop Yoder would react to her son's involvement, but the bishop was supportive as long as Carter Jr. worked on a volunteer basis and not for pay. If Carter Jr. was a volunteer, Bishop Yoder saw it as a form of ministry to the community. Carter Jr. was happy to comply and also honor the memory of his friend John Michael Smucker in the process.

Through the front window of the Sunbeam Café, I watched as Margot Rawlings struggled to wrap a bright green garland around the gazebo. It seemed she was getting the square ready for the St. Patrick's Day parade she had planned for the weekend. Her helper, Leon, was on the other side of the square, hanging giant shamrocks from the bare trees. It didn't appear to be going well for either of them. Margot really did need more help out on the square.

"Yes!" I heard Lois cry from behind the counter.

I glanced in her direction. "What is it now?"

She was staring at her phone, of course. Lois had become obsessed with her phone ever since Darcy had put that dating app, whatchamacallit, on the little device.

"I have a date! Saturday night with a very nice-looking man." She grinned from ear to ear.

"What's his name?" I asked.

"R45G."

I wrinkled my brow. "R45G? What kind of name is that?"

"It's just his name on the app, like a code name. I'll learn his real name on the date."

That didn't sound like the best idea to me, but I certainly knew nothing about online dating. "Just be careful," I said.

"Always," she said, without looking up from her phone.

I rolled my eyes. It was a habit I'd learned from Lois, and I couldn't think of a more appropriate time to use it. I finished off the rest of my blueberry pancakes and stood.

"Where are you off to?" Lois asked, finally setting her phone down.

"I'm going to help Margot. That garland is getting the best of her. Even through the window, I can tell she is getting angrier by the second."

She peered out the window. "It certainly is. She has big ideas, but she's not a craftswoman. What is she doing with all that tape? Why doesn't Leon run over and help her?"

I stepped toward the door. "He's probably scared to."

"Good point. Before you go—" Lois touched my arm. "Are you all right? I've noticed you staring off into space a lot lately."

I sighed. "Just thinking about Hosea, I suppose."

"You saved Hosea's life, Millie," Lois said. "I truly believe that. He would have jumped from the clock tower if you hadn't been there."

"I'd like to believe that's not true. I don't want to think he would have made that choice in the end."

"You ensured he didn't."

I nodded.

Outside, Margot threw the garland on the ground.

"Yikes," Lois exclaimed. "You had better get out there and help her. She's liable to hurt herself."

I laughed, put on my bonnet, and went out the

door. I dodged the raindrops as I hurried to the gazebo. "Margot, do you need help?" I asked.

"Bless you, yes. This garland hates me." She pulled on her curls.

I studied the mangled garland on the gazebo floor. It was going to take some time to unravel it. Margot had really taken out her frustration on the string of tinsel.

I had started to pick it up when a voice behind me asked, "Do you ladies need any help?"

A stone lodged in my throat. I turned around to find Uriah Schrock standing on the gazebo steps.

Please read on for an excerpt from the next Amish Candy Shop mystery by Amanda Flower.

BLUEBERRY BLUNDER
An Amish Candy Shop Mystery

Amanda Flower
USA Today **Bestselling Author**

A sweet tooth for the blues . . .

Bailey King, star of TV's *Bailey's Amish Sweets,* is building her dream candy factory in Harvest, Ohio. But no sooner is the frame of the new building up than she finds the dead body of a surly contractor who has a long list of enemies—including people in the Amish community. To add to the drama, Bailey is being filmed by a crew for her upcoming show . . .

When Bailey's TV producer pitched a reality show about building the factory, Bailey was shocked that the network picked it up. She's not shocked that many of the Amish working on the jobsite refuse to be on camera. However, local community organizer Margot Rawlings is ecstatic—because the filming coincides with Harvest's First Annual Blueberry Bash. Margot believes the media attention will make Harvest the most popular destination in Holmes County. But now, the county may become known for all the wrong reasons . . .

Bailey will have to sift through a crowd of angry villagers and thousands of blueberries to solve the murder, save her new venture, and protect her Amish friends. At the same time, she and her longtime boyfriend, Aiden Brody, are making big decisions about their future together—a future that may be in jeopardy if Bailey is the next pick on a killer's list . . .

Chapter One

My heart was racing faster than the little pig that zoomed around the factory like his curled tail was on fire.

"Jethro! Jethro!" I shouted the polka-dotted black and white pig's name, but it was no use. He flew by me in a squealing blur. The sound of his squeals could break glass and grated on my very last nerve.

The blunt nails of Jethro's hooves clicked on the concrete slab like a tap dancer on Broadway, and the sound echoed through the hollow shell of Swissmen Candyworks. My candy factory that I had thought was such a wonderful idea months ago had now turned into a bit of a nightmare. When construction began in winter, I'd been excited and optimistic about the future of the candy-making business I shared with my grandmother Clara King. Six months later, we were knee-deep into construction and I was beaten down by never ending bills and the minutia of delays.

At the moment, I had little more than the foundation and frame to show for my efforts to build the factory and open in record time. The project should have been much farther along at this point. I had been told it would be all but done by the end of June. How wrong that was. The plan was for the factory to open at the end of August, which would position it perfectly to work out all the kinks in production and service before the busy holiday season, but since it was deep into summer and I still didn't have all the interior walls up, it wasn't looking good.

Jethro buzzed around the cavernous space, and then around and around the multi-level scaffolding in the middle of the room like it was a Maypole. The top platform was easily ten feet long and six feet wide. The Amish framers had used the scaffolding to raise the rafters over the building, and even though I'd been told it would be removed a week ago, there it sat. It wasn't hurting anything by being there, I supposed, but it was just one more thing to deal with. I wondered if at this point, the workers installing the insulation could use it. At least I would be spending money on moving the project forward. Any forward motion at this point would be more than welcome.

"Jethro, stop!" I said for what felt like the tenth time.

"This is great! This is great! Are you getting this?" Devon Cruz asked her cameraman as she brushed her frizzy dark hair out of her face and adjusted her glasses.

The cameraman, who just went by the name of Z, grunted in reply as he adjusted his large video camera on his shoulder. By the way he moved, it was apparent that he was used to the weight. It didn't hurt that he was six three either. I supposed the grunt meant that he was in fact "getting it."

I winced. This wasn't the professional candy entrepreneur that I wanted to present on the show. "Are you sure this is good for the reality show? I'm not sure it gives off the image that we are looking for."

"Of course it is. Stuff like this is perfect for when the storyline slows down. Who doesn't want to watch an adorable pig on the screen?" She glanced around the room. "I have to record something. Nothing else is happening here."

She didn't even bother to hide the criticism in her voice.

As if I didn't have enough stress with the build, I had to deal with the small film crew too. Devon and Z were there to capture the construction of the building for a new reality show on Gourmet Television that I very much regretted agreeing to.

I had worked with Gourmet Television and executive producer Linc Baggins, who did in fact live up to his name and look like a hobbit, for several years on my popular cooking show *Bailey's Amish Sweets*.

The show was inspired by recipes from the Amish candy shop in Harvest, Swissmen Sweets, which I shared with my grandmother. She and my grandfather opened the shop decades ago and lived in an apartment over the shop for the majority of their lives. When my grandfather passed a few years back, I left my big city job as chocolatier at world-famous JP Chocolates in New York City behind and moved to Ohio to help my grandmother.

I'd never thought for a moment when I'd left New York, that the big city would come to Holmes County looking for me, but it had. A few months after my move, I was approached by a Linc to film a candy making show, and the rest was history.

When he had asked to make a show about the new factory, I'd been hesitant, but I hadn't felt like I could say "no." This factory—which would take our family business to a global market—would never have been possible without *Bailey's Amish Sweets* because of the money and exposure I got from it. Against my better judgment, I'd agreed, thinking at least I knew what it was like to work with Linc, but he wasn't the one who knocked on my door the first day of filming. It'd been Devon, an eager young producer with neon yellow hair, baggy jeans, and hungry for her big break.

I had nothing against a person wanting to fulfill their dreams; I was certainly a dreamer myself. I wouldn't have been standing in an empty building at the moment if I wasn't a dreamer, but Devon was a tad more aggressive than I would have liked. She wanted to be with me every waking moment to catch every last second of my life. I suspected if it had been an option, she'd record me sleeping at night.

Now that I thought about it, I wondered if I was like her and more aggressive, perhaps I would have better luck in convincing the contractors to do their jobs.

"Don't worry. The running pig is B-roll," Devon said. "It's always good to have filler when on a shoot. Lots of it ends up on the cutting room floor, but it's better to have too much than too little. When is Wade supposed to show up?"

In my case, all I felt was dread. Wade Farmer was my general contractor on the candy factory build. I had booked him because of his excellent work of construction across the county, his glowing reputation, and to be honest his low quote for the job, but at this point, I was wondering who had been lying. When the project started, Wade had been on point. He answered my thousands of questions and seemed enthusiastic over the idea of building a factory from the ground up. It was true he could be a little rough around the edges at times, but it was something that I expected from an English contractor who had almost solely Amish employees. The Amish could be direct and blunt when it came to work. This was especially true with Amish men, so it was no surprise to me that Wade took up that manner of speaking to his men and his clients. Overall, we had a good working relationship until about three months into the project and everything started to slow down. He claimed that it had been materials delays and issues with employee retention. He told me that if I advanced him more money that he'd be able to continue the work. He claimed that the men he hired wanted higher wages and the price of materials skyrocketed.

I hadn't been a business owner for years without the ability to sense when something was off. I told him no and that we were going to stick to our original payment agreement. I would allow his next draw when the insulation was put in.

Apparently, it had been the last straw with him because work had come to a screeching halt four months in. During April and May there'd been no movement on the building. Devon and Z had arrived the first week of June with the belief they would be documenting the end of the construction project, only to find we hadn't even made the halfway point yet.

To my credit, I'd warned Linc, the executive producer, that the building wasn't as far along as I'd hoped it would be by June. However, he said he was sending Devon and Z anyway to "capture the drama" or my nervous breakdown, whatever came first.

I touched the dark circles under my eyes. I hadn't slept a wink the night before as I worried over what I would say at this meeting with Wade. I had also worried over the fact he might not even show up, which was the problem in the first place. With so many other things going on with the candy shop, my cooking show, and just in my personal life, I let the candy factory project get out of hand. I ignored the delays and assumed Wade would take care of it. He didn't, and when I finally got around to asking him about it, he avoided my calls, text messages, and countless emails.

I was now at the end of my completely frayed rope, and at this point it felt like he'd left me very few choices as to how I could deal with him.

"He'll be here soon," I said, forcing myself to sound positive even though I wasn't feeling that way in the slightest. Wade was already forty minutes late.

Jethro circled the scaffolding for what seemed like the fiftieth time.

Devon grinned at him. "Have you thought of taking the pig on call?"

"On call?" I asked as Jethro zoomed by.

"Yes, on an audition in New York. He really has the potential of getting a lot of parts, especially in press and media commercials. You should try it. There's a lot of personality in that little oinker."

She had no idea.

"He's not my pig," I said, praying she wouldn't mention this idea to the pig's real owner, Juliet Brook, the pastor's wife and my boyfriend Aiden's mother.

Juliet was already trying to make Jethro a star, and I saw nothing wrong with that. My problem was that Juliet would most likely expect me to take him to auditions. But I couldn't add it to my to-do list between my candy shop, building the factory, *Bailey's Amish Sweets*, and now this reality show I regretted.

"What is going on in here?" a man bellowed.

My heart sank. I hated how I cringed every time I heard Wade's gravelly voice. That alone should've told me it was time to cut my losses and find a new general contractor.

Jethro stopped running and flopped over onto the concrete floor like he'd been shot. Perhaps the little pig thought Wade was a grizzly bear, and playing dead was the best option for survival. I couldn't say I blamed him. Wade *did* resemble a grizzly with a full salt and pepper beard, angry growl, and fierce glare.

I scooped up the pig before he recovered and ran around the building again. The last thing I wanted was Jethro misbehaving in front of Wade. The little pig wasn't wearing a hardhat. It was against protocol.

Wade stepped into the factory from what would be the loading area. At this point, there was a concrete ramp there and little else. He was followed by a young blond Amish man, Naz Schlabach. Naz was lanky and seemed to be all arms and legs. He was Wade's constant shadow on the job, so I wasn't surprised he was there. He held a clipboard and pencil in his hands. Naz smiled at me; Wade did not.

Wade scowled at Devon and Z. He then turned to me. "You think so highly of yourself that you actually believe someone will watch the construction of this building." He glared at Z. "Get that camera off of me."

Z stumbled back a couple of feet, but Devon put her hand on his shoulder to steady him. "Keep recording. He agreed to be part of this project, and he can't change his mind now."

She was right. Wade had signed the release form to be included in filming. He'd done it of his own volition. My guess was because his contracting business would receive free publicity. However, not all press was good. Z had caught on camera dozens of times how rudely Wade had spoken to me and how slow progress had been. I believed anyone who saw the show would think twice before hiring Wade Farmer.

Wade turned his angry expression onto me. "Why did you drag me out here this morning? I'm a busy man, and have several projects I'm working on. I can't run to an owner's side to coddle them every time they are bellyaching."

As he spoke, I knew this wasn't going to end well, but I decided to give him one more chance. I took a breath. "I'd like an update as to what is going on with the building. There's been no progress in weeks, and the target completion date is August twenty-seventh."

"Construction takes time. Ask anyone. There are always delays. Things go wrong. I could speed up the process if you were willing to put more money into it, but since you're not." He shrugged as if it were my fault.

Naz made a note on his clipboard. I had no idea what he could have been writing. Perhaps, "Client is being a pain."

"We agreed on the estimate and the fund draw schedule. We have a contract. I shouldn't have to put more money into it like you say outside of that agreement."

He removed his ball cap and used it to wave away my concern. "When was the last time you built anything? This is my area of expertise. If you won't listen to what has to be done, the delays are on you."

I shifted Jethro under my arm and hoped I looked intimidating, even though I was holding a small pig like a football. "I understand delays, but there's been no movement for two months. This project has to be ready for the grand opening in August. We agreed to that. It's also in the contract."

"I agreed to try, but I can't make materials appear out of thin air. There are delays on all building materials now. Your loading dock door for example is on a three month back order. There's nothing I can do about it."

"I understand delays, but there must be a way to work around them. Cancel the order and get the garage door from another supplier."

He slapped his cap back on his head. "You don't tell me how to do business. I don't tell you how to make your little candies."

I squeezed Jethro tight.

"Anyway, you should never have scheduled the grand opening until we passed all the rough inspections."

"And when is that going to happen?" I asked.

"I don't know. We have delays," he shot back.

I was no longer trying to be nice. It was time to be firm. "You told me on more than one occasion that an eight-month timetable was plenty of time. In fact, you said this project would be done in six months, not the eight I required."

He shrugged as if it was none of his concern. "Things change. You have to be flexible. Not everyone is going to be able to move at the pace you need. Money makes business run better. You're holding back on that, and now you can see what's happened."

"What materials are we missing? If I knew what they were, I could help you look for other sources."

Naz opened his mouth as if he was about to answer my question, but after glancing at Wade, he snapped his mouth closed.

"You don't work in construction. You can't help with that."

"Making calls, asking if a company has something for sale is not the same as driving a nail home. I do it all the time for my own business."

"This conversation is insulting," he spat. "I don't have to put up with that. When I say there are material shortages, you need to believe there are. I'm the general contractor."

"I need evidence. Can I see some evidence of that?"

"Excuse me?" His face morphed to bright red.

"If it's really true your suppliers are having these terrible delays, you must have an email, a letter, or something from them telling you so. I'd like to see them."

He opened and closed his mouth as if he could not believe I would have the audacity to question him or to ask for evidence like that. I couldn't believe I was the only client who had ever asked, especially if something was missing.

"I'm sure other things can be done while you wait for materials. What about the electrician? Can he begin to work on the wiring?" I asked.

"When a building is under construction it has to be done in a certain order. I don't expect you to understand. It's why you hired me. If you knew what to do, you could have built this place yourself."

"Burn," I heard Devon whisper.

I shot her a look. Weren't reality television producers supposed to be quiet and just capture the events unfolding in front of them?

I let out a breath. This conversation was going

nowhere and I knew there was only one thing left to do. "I'm sorry, Wade, but this just isn't going to work. I have a firm deadline for the project, and I need to get this done. If you can't make it, I have to find someone else who can. I'm going to have to let you go."

His eyes went wide. "You can't do that."

"I can. I've already called my bank and asked them to put a pause on anymore draws to you until they receive my permission. I'm about to call now and tell them to remove your name altogether."

"You can't do that!" He shouted it this time. "We have a contract."

"We do, and it includes a termination clause. The lack of progress is grounds to end the contract. I'm going to have to ask you to leave." I sounded calm and in control, but on the inside I was shaking. Wade was unpredictable, and despite how hard he was to work with, I felt a little bit guilty over firing him. I really hadn't wanted it to come to this. I'd given him every chance I could, but I was out of options. I had to get this building up and running by the end of August.

Devon whispered something to Z, and the cameraman zoomed in on Wade's reaction, which was something to behold. His face flushed from bright red to purple to red again.

I took a couple steps back from him. Had I been alone with him I might have been frightened. This was one time I was happy Devon and Z were present with their microphone and camera. If Wade tried anything, it would be on tape.

"This is so good," Devon whispered behind me.

"Thank you for what you have done so far on the job, but I need to go in a different direction," I said with finality.

He opened and closed his mouth as if he couldn't believe this was happening. Finally, his voice returned. He shook his fist at me. "I will sue you for breach of contract!"

Naz wrote so furiously now on his clipboard, his pencil tip might break at any second.

I straightened my spine. "You can try, but I already had an attorney look over the contract, and he said I'm within my rights to let you go. I have plenty of documentation proving there's been no action on the jobsite in weeks. If anything, I can sue you . . ."

He glared at me. Car headlights illuminated the docking area, and a moment later we heard a car door slam shut. Margot Rawlings ran into the factory. Her short curly brown hair on the top of her head bounced as she moved, and she was wearing her summer uniform of jeans and a solid colored T-shirt. In the winter she switched out the T-shirt for a sweatshirt.

"Bailey! Bailey!" She said in a frazzled voice. "We have a blueberry emergency. A blueberry 911."

Of course we did.